Small Bomb at Dimperley

www.penguin.co.uk

SMALL BOMB AT DIMPERLEY

LISSA EVANS

doubleday

TRANSWORLD PUBLISHERS
Penguin Random House, One Embassy Gardens,
8 Viaduct Gardens, London SW11 7BW
www.penguin.co.uk

Transworld is part of the Penguin Random House group of companies
whose addresses can be found at global.penguinrandomhouse.com

First published in Great Britain in 2024 by Doubleday
an imprint of Transworld Publishers

A CIP catalogue record for this book
is available from the British Library.

ISBN 9780857528292

Typeset in 12/15 pt Bembo Book MT Pro by Jouve (UK), Milton Keynes
Printed and bound in Great Britain by Clays Ltd, Elcograf S.p.A.

The authorized representative in the EEA is Penguin Random House Ireland,
Morrison Chambers, 32 Nassau Street, Dublin D02 YH68.

Penguin Random House is committed to a sustainable
future for our business, our readers and our planet. This book
is made from Forest Stewardship Council® certified paper.

Small Bomb at Dimperley

1

From Prosser's *Companion to Buckinghamshire* (published 1908):

Dimperley Manor may be described as lacking in architectural harmony, though its mongrel elements are nonetheless pleasing to the eye. At its heart is an early-Tudor fortified house of roseate brick with stone battlement-copings and half-timbered projecting bays.

The building originally sported six turrets, but a third of it was pulled down in the 1700s, the moat partially filled in, the courtyards roofed over and a neo-Palladian Dower Wing, originally somewhat severe in aspect (until the addition of a lavish High Victorian Gothic facade), added to the west side and linked to the Tudor building by a tunnel. The latter is purportedly the setting for N. J. Larby's famously gruesome ghost story, 'What was Down There', written after the author had visited the Manor in 1890.

A later and perhaps more architecturally successful addition was the Indian-style two-storey East Wing, built in sandstone in the 1820s, topped with a large copper Mughal dome and extending on one side into a long, curved Orangery, ending in an octagonal library. A hedge of topiary elephants enhances the theme.

Dimperley Manor's extensive gardens contain numerous mid-century follies, including a gated Hermit's Hollow and a sixty-foot free-standing tower decorated with a trio of carved wyvern. The house stands in a fold of the Chilterns south-east of Aylesbury and is home to the Vere-Thissett family, who were granted the land in 1404 after rendering an unspecified service to the King. The family holds the hereditary office of 'High Woodsman' with the requirement that the senior male must attend each coronation in order to present a beech log (no shorter than three ells), nine bundles of brushwood and a bushel of hazel-nuts to the new monarch. It was only at the Coronation of Queen Victoria that this tradition was left out of the ceremony. Henry Vere-Thissett – High Woodsman at the time – was created a Baronet by way of compensation. His grand-son Sir Grevell Vere-Thissett was an amateur taxidermist of some distinction.

Pollux usually did his business at the foot of the Wyvern Tower, although he sometimes preferred to wait until he reached the Obelisk, a basalt spike erected by the first Baronet in memory of his favourite wife. In the old days (and before Castor had succumbed to distemper), the dogs would have been followed at a distance by the odd-man with a shovel, but since there was no longer an odd-man – nor a boot-boy, nor a stable-lad, nor even an under-gardener – it was nowadays necessary for Irene, Lady Vere-Thissett (accompanied on the morning walk, as always, by her middle son, Cedric), to carry with her a small velvet drawstring bag; it contained sawdust, which she would sprinkle on the offending pile, clearly marking it for later disposal. It was the kind of inconvenience that, until recently, she had chosen to view as part of the war effort, but since the war was now over, it had become yet another painful reminder of irrevocable change.

On this particular August morning, the early warmth promising a day of great heat, the sky the colour of the Celeste ceiling in the Orangery, Pollux deviated from his usual route and left a second deposit on the Great Lawn, and it was some moments before Irene could spot its location amidst the shockingly long grass, blistered with dandelion clocks.

'Epple says the petrol mower's broken a blade,' her daughter-in-law had reported last week, 'and he can't use a scythe because of his lumbago. And he says it would be easier to mow if the washing-line posts came up, but he'd need the crowbar for that and it's currently being used to prop up the roof of the Shell Grotto.' Why there need be talk of a servants' Trade Union when they had Barbara to act as their champion seemed a mystery.

The washing-line posts in question were of concrete and had been sunk into the greensward when Dimperley Manor had been requisitioned as a maternity home in 1940; for nearly five years, a quadruple row of sepia-stained napkins and sheets had been visible from every South-facing window, including those of the Dower Wing, to which the family had been confined for the duration. Also visible had been the monthly disembarkation of a slowly moving herd of swollen young women from a motor-coach that had brought them from Aylesbury Station. Traffic in the opposite direction had been more erratic, since not all the women had returned to the slums of London but had instead been found billets with their new offspring in the Buckinghamshire countryside. And even though it was now several months since the last (but one) had left, evidence of their stay was still ubiquitous — every polished surface scarred by cigarette burns and the pale rings of enamel tea-mugs, blotches of dubious origin disfiguring the carpets, grooves worn into oak floorboards by cheap canteen furniture, the scents of beeswax and wood-smoke displaced by the lingering smell of disinfectant, the Morning Room mosaic of Phoebus 'Mid the Laurels — once washed daily with milk to keep its shine — now dulled, its surface pocked with tiny holes where an idle fingernail had prised out random pieces. Collapsible cots filled the dovecote, while in the ice house lay piles of mattresses, the striped ticking already sooty with damp-mould. Irene was not a fanciful woman, and yet, re-entering the hall after the last uninvited guest had departed, she had felt as if the house had been kidnapped, maltreated and then returned, trembling, to the family's care.

'Ceddy!' she called, as Pollux squatted yet again, this time at the base of the statue of Minerva. 'Did you give him one of your Liquorice Allsorts yesterday? After I had expressly told you not to?'

There was no answer, and she turned to see that her son had paused beside the moat.

'No, come away from there.' She could never bear to see him so close to those horrid green waters.

He pointed at something, and she retraced her steps to find him gazing at a naked, headless doll that was floating a yard or two from the bank. 'Oh, that must belong to the Baxter child. No, leave it alone,' she added, as Ceddy knelt down. 'Epple can use a rake, and you shall come and watch. I said *no*,' she repeated, as he ran a palm back and forth across the surface of the water, as though assessing its finish. 'Come along.' He tutted loudly and gave a couple of heavy sighs but stood up again, although not before she'd noticed, for the first time, a few fine pale threads visible along the dark hair of his parting. It was unsurprising, perhaps; her husband had begun to go grey at much the same age, and Ceddy was the image of him. 'Good boy,' she said, as they turned away from the moat.

Pollux, reliant on smell rather than sight these days, nosed along his usual route, past the entrance to the maze, the yew hedges once clipped every fortnight but now heavily whiskered, and towards the high walls of the kitchen garden. The mention of the Baxter child led Irene to glance automatically in the direction of the library at the end of the Orangery, where Alaric, her late husband's brother, would already be at work on his book (a history of the Vere-Thissetts), aided, no doubt, by the houri from Hackney, tippety-tapping on her typewriter. 'I'm sure Barbara could learn to assist you when Mrs Baxter goes back to London,' Irene had said, only last week, and Alaric had reared back, like an ageing hunter faced with a brick wall. 'No, no, no, that wouldn't be the same at all.'

'Wouldn't it? Barbara can type, I believe, after a fashion.'

'It's far more than simply typing, far more – there's the filing and the . . . the . . . the . . .'

There had been a pause; no further task beyond 'sitting opposite me in an unnecessarily tight blouse' seemed to have sprung to Alaric's mind. 'Besides,' he'd continued, eventually, 'Mrs Baxter's husband's still in Malta so there's absolutely no urgency about her return. No urgency. She's assured me of that.'

'Has she?'

'It may be months, and in any case, Barbara will have her girls back, won't she? She'll be fearfully busy. No, I need to forge onward. I've very nearly reached the nineteenth century.'

At the spinney on the far side of the kitchen garden, after Pollux had stopped for a fourth time and Irene had tipped out the last of the sawdust, she turned in the direction of the house. 'No, we no longer go there, do we?' she said to Ceddy, who was lingering beside the stile that led out of the trees and into Brook Field, which had once been part of the Dimperley estate. It had been a favourite route, the path skirting a hazel coppice and then winding gradually upward through sheep-cropped pastures to the brow of Farrow Hill, the view from which was celebrated in a local rhyme ('If up on Farrow Hill you be, two counties and eight spires you'll see'), although these days the first object to catch the eye was the hideous biscuit factory just outside Aylesbury, constructed of brick the colour of horse-liver and counting amongst its employees most of the village girls whose mothers and aunts had at one time been happy to fill the servants' hall at Dimperley.

Iniquitous death duties had forced the sale of Brook Field in 1935, and to walk across it now was to risk an encounter with the new owner, a farmer named Jeffries who habitually spoke to Irene with a familiarity which suggested they'd first met when queueing at a whelk stall and who had actually clapped her on the back last year when she'd been presenting the trophy for best heifer at the county fair.

It was all part of a gradual descent into careless informality that had begun well before the war – she could almost have drawn a graph charting the slow decrease in the depth of curtseys she'd received over the years, the most recent of which (accompanying the presentation of a posy at the VE Day Supper) had been a mere twitch of the knees, more suggestive of a small child urgently in need of a lavatory than a mark of respect. And now, of course, since the appalling, inexplicable events of July, when the populace had flung aside Mr Churchill and filled Parliament with baying reds, there was no knowing how far or how quickly the descent would continue, how soon before the tumbrils came clattering through the lodge gates, five centuries of noble service to the common weal swept aside by savagery and persecution.

'Good morning, Lady Vere-Thissett, good morning, Mr Cedric,' said Epple, limping from behind the Chinese Pavilion with a wheelbarrow containing a spade and a pile of earth-encrusted beetroot. 'Been meaning to ask you something, Lady Vere-Thissett, if I might,' he added, lowering the barrow and removing the pipe from his mouth.

Irene inclined her head.

'My nephew just come out of the navy and he's looking around for a bit of work and he says he could help me out a few hours a week, temporary, and I wanted to ask if he could start on Monday, only he needs to know what he might get paid given that the grocer says he could start there too, only he likes an outdoor life, does Fred, he's not a gardener but he's handy, so that's what I wanted to ask you, Lady Vere-Thissett, or maybe . . .' His mouth carried on moving but no further sound emerged – had he finished, wondered Irene? – and then something wet and brown began slowly to emerge from between his lips, like a stocking from a mangle, and he lifted a hand and extracted a long shred of tobacco and looked at it with apparent pride before continuing, '. . . or maybe I should speak to Lady Barbara about it?'

'Yes, I think that would be more appropriate,' said Irene. Ceddy was tutting again, impatiently this time, and she called the dog and moved away at a smart pace before Epple could request anything else – her assistance in tarring the potting-shed roof, perhaps, or helping to lift the seed-potatoes – and she found herself remembering McHugh, the unsmiling Scottish steward who had run the estate in her husband's time. On the first of every month, he had been ushered into the Baronet's study, where he had silently placed his black-bound ledger on the desk, open to the relevant weeks. The Baronet had glanced through, making an occasional comment, and then McHugh had bowed and taken the ledger away for another month. Wages, rents, purchases, produce, maintenance, transport – all had been under his aegis; the business of the estate had been conducted with invisible efficiency, the engine purring onward; as owner, one had not been expected to take an active part in its maintenance. Did the passengers of a Rolls-Royce need to know how to change the . . . whatever it was that apparently had to be changed on a regular basis? No, they did not.

McHugh had died, suddenly and inconveniently (one might almost say inconsiderately), actually during the Baronet's funeral, which meant that her eldest son, Felix, inheriting his father's title, had had to face a multitude of hideous financial decisions entirely unguided, although his natural abilities had, as ever, carried him through.

'Pollux, come here,' she called, as the Jack Russell veered off towards the Shell Grotto. 'Come here, *now.*' Reluctantly, Pollux veered back again.

Ahead of her, Ceddy had already disappeared into the stable block, and Irene followed him through the arch, across the carriage-yard and into the cool interior, dimly lit at intervals by high, semi-circular windows, their glass uncleaned for at least half a decade and now barely transparent. There were sixteen stalls, fifteen of them either empty or packed with dismantled bedsteads awaiting collection. A thin film of straw dust coated the dark metal.

At the loose-box at the far end, Ceddy was standing with Smokey, her neck resting on his shoulder, lips pushing at his closed fist.

'Horse,' he said, opening his fingers to reveal a damp ball of yesterday's braised cabbage.

'Are you in there?' Her daughter-in-law's voice, projecting from the entrance, was unnecessarily loud. 'Lady Vere-Thissett?'

'Yes, I'm here. What is it?'

'We've had a . . .' Her footsteps hurried towards them.
'Oh, hello, Ceddy.'

'It's a horse.'

'We've had a telegram.' Barbara's voice was high and
uncontrolled, the slip of paper she was holding very bright
in the gloom.

'You opened it?'

'Well, it was addressed to me.'

'But did it say—'

'Oh, please don't start this again. Please, not now. It *didn't*
say "Irene, Lady Vere-Thissett" *or* "Dowager Lady Vere-
Thissett", it said "Lady Vere-Thissett", which means that, *as*
Lady Vere-Thissett, I was perfectly entitled to open it, and
in any case . . .' Her voice disappeared momentarily; Irene
could hear her trying to swallow, her throat clicking. Behind
them, Smokey shifted, hooves scraping the flagstones.

'It's a horse,' said Ceddy.

'. . . in any case, what it says—' Barbara held out the telegram, the paper wavering in her grip '—it's . . . well, it's . . .
oh God, I'll have to tell the girls as soon as they arrive, I'll
have to . . . I'm afraid it's . . . well, it's what we've known all
along, haven't we? . . . It says that Felix is . . . that he . . .'

Irene took the paper and held it at arm's length. The
print was small, and since she never wore her spectacles
outside the house she could read only odd words. But
amongst them were 'CONFIRMED' and 'DEATH'.

Beside her, Barbara gave a little gasp. 'So I suppose that
we're *both* Dowager Lady Vere-Thissett now, aren't we?'
and then, incredibly, she giggled – a watery bleat that made
Irene, and not for the first time, want to slap her.

Irene turned, with an effort, to her second son; he was resting one cheek on Smokey's flank, his lovely profile so much like that of Felix. This should, of course, have been the moment when Ceddy was looped by the silken cord of inheritance that would bind him to his grandfather, the fourth Baronet, his father, the fifth, his older brother, the sixth . . .

'Horse,' said Ceddy, who had stopped using most other words after an attack of brain fever when he was ten and who could, therefore, never be the seventh Baronet.

'I shall have to place a telephone call,' said Irene and, leaving Felix's widow behind, she walked briskly to the house. There was work ahead; the silken cord would need to be fashioned into a lasso.

2

Just before Dusty Miller hit Valentine with a sledge-hammer, they'd all been talking about their demob plans. The exact date of discharge was based on age and on how long one had been in the services, so Offord, who was over thirty and who'd joined right at the start, was off home in a couple of weeks, whereas Valentine, at twenty-three, was still months away.

He had kept his own wishes small but fervent ('*Hot* water to shave with, no more tin cups, and I'd like to spend at least six hours a day slouching and keeping my hands in my pockets'); Offord had launched into a bitter diatribe about his ex-sweetheart, who'd married a Canadian called Jean-Yves ('It's a bloody girl's name, for a start, in fact it's *two* bloody girls' names'); Crockett had stunned them by saying that he was thinking of signing up for another five years; and then Miller had taken the floor and, though he was usually the sharpest talker of the lot, with a gift for officer impressions that had kept him firmly in the ranks, Valentine had gradually stopped listening because Miller had clearly been making his plans for some time and the account had begun with him stepping off the train at Northampton and continued minute by minute from there on ('Two pints of mild at The Engineer, might make it three depending if

Ruby's at the bar, then I'll call for my cousin Frank and we'll have a whisky at The Admiral Rodney, maybe a double, and then another pint of mild at The Bald Stag . . .').

Beyond the spinney beside which they were supposed to be re-erecting a fence, a tractor was intermittently visible as it chugged up and down a field of red clay. A cloud of lapwings was banking and wheeling behind the plough; Valentine had heard them mewing when he'd woken up that morning, the plaintive sound audible between the occasional gaps in the snoring. That was another one for the list of wishes, he thought: a bed in a room on his own.

Miller was still talking, and his audience had relaxed into various idle postures, Offord cleaning under his fingernails with a matchstick and Crockett tipping his head back as though resting on an invisible pillow; as Corporal, Valentine was nominally in charge of the work party, but since they'd been given the entire morning to complete the task, it was difficult to muster any sense of urgency.

The fence had been knocked over the previous day by a group of Hereford bullocks who'd wandered into the woods and then ambled across the trampled wire and up the field towards the camp. When they'd peered between the flaps of the mess tent, nostrils dilating wetly at the smell of burned potatoes, Private Liston (always a card) had let out a girlish scream and someone had shouted, 'Nazis!', and the subsequent round-up had been the most entertaining thing that had happened in Camp 14J for weeks, with Sergeant Fisk organizing twin flanks into a pincer move, his eyes narrowed like those of John Wayne in *Santa Fe Stampede*.

They'd been shown that film by a mobile unit the month

before, and it had been preceded by a series of informational shorts about their imminent return to civvy street. *'Of course, all soldiers complain about army grub, but one complaint you can never make is that there isn't enough. So when you get back home, try and remember that the piece of cheese on the table may have to serve the family for a week, and that an egg is a treat, not to be expected daily.'* There'd been footage of bombed streets: *'Danger and suffering haven't been reserved for those serving overseas'*; and tired-looking women in headscarves: *'She's been at her factory job since six a.m., and then had to queue for the family rations on the way home. So if she isn't looking her best when you arrive on the doorstep, I'm sure you'll understand.'* The atmosphere afterwards had been rather glum.

'I suppose we'd better get on with it,' said Valentine, positioning one of the posts.

'No hurry, is there?' asked Miller, who'd just reached the snug at The Travellers' Rest. 'If we finish this, they'll only think up something else. They should send us all home tomorrow if they don't have nothing for us to do.'

'Or back to Germany,' said Offord. 'My cousin's stationed in Hanover and he says there's more beer than you can drink. It's piss, he says, but there's no end of it, and the girls are smashing.' He curled one hand around an imaginary pint glass and reached for a female buttock with the other.

'Sarge is coming,' said Offord. They all turned to see Fisk, still fifty yards away but walking purposefully in their direction, and suddenly they were all at work again, Valentine holding the post, Miller the hammer, the others scampering over to the next section of fence.

'. . . so after that I'll go to my mum's,' said Miller, taking advantage of the sudden silence, 'and when I get to her house, I'll do my special knock so she knows it's me, it goes dup dup dup, *whack* – I use the flat of me hand for the last one. Dup dup dup' – he swung the sledgehammer – '*WHACK*.'

'Thissett!'

Valentine straightened up. 'Yes, Sergeant?'

'The CO wants you.'

'Me?'

'No, someone else. I've come all this way for my health.'

'But Sarge, he doesn't know me from Adam.' Lieutenant Colonel Ripon was the pale, unpopular, non-speaking type of CO, whose gaze glided over the khaki ranks like someone checking the wax finish on a Bentley.

'Is Toff in trouble?' asked Crockett.

Fisk ignored him, continuing to eye Valentine with an odd, unfamiliar expression that seemed partway between disbelief and derision.

'The CO asked for you by name,' he said. 'AND YOU OTHERS GET ON WITH YOUR WORK,' he continued, effortlessly raising his voice. 'He asked for you by your *full* name, Valentine *Vere*-Thissett. *And* your full title,' he added, pointedly, just as Miller swung the sledgehammer again, and Valentine, who'd been moving forward, swayed back as if slapped, his hand shifting its grip on the post.

They ended up needing two stretchers, after Miller, who'd been through Dunkirk, Monte Cassino and Normandy, fainted dead away when he realized that the tip of Valentine's index finger had lodged inside the neck of his shirt.

3

From *Woodsman to the King: The Vere-Thissetts of Bucking-hamshire*, by Alaric Vere-Thissett:

No record remains of the circumstances by which William Thyssett of Dimperley received his honorary title, but perhaps the reader may forgive a little phantasy, as we turn the eye of imagination toward a verdant copse 'twixt the parishes of Whatton and Addenham, on a May evening in 1404.

Through the sylvan twilight, plangent with birdsong, passes a line of finely caparisoned horses, one of which seats his noble highness, King Henry IV, as tall as his father, John of Gaunt, but narrow of shoulder, his disfiguring skin condition barely visible in the leafy shadows. Behind the riders, in a covered litter carried between two milk-white steeds, lies the Queen, dark-eyed Joanna of Navarre, who is with child. But hark! The first horseman of the procession calls back, alarmed; the way is blocked by a fallen tree; the litter cannot pass, and night is swiftly a-falling. It is still half a league to their destination, the Manor of Nottley Saye, and who knows what footpads and cut-throats may be lurking in the gathering darkness?

It is the King whose keen ear first discerns a steady step approaching through the brushwood and it is he who rises in

16

the stirrups and espies a sturdy fellow with an axe, and sum-
mons him hither, to deal with the fallen tree.

The fellow makes no great hurry, and is admonished by
one of the King's men. 'Dost thou not recognize thy King?'

'Every man is a king in his own wood,' says the fellow,
and then sets about the fallen log with a will, soon clearing the
path.

'Shall I reward yon sturdy yeoman?' asks one of the King's
companions, loosing his purse, but the King shakes his head.

'What is thy name?' he asks the yeoman.

'William Thyssett, sire.'

'And this is thy wood?'

'Yes, sire. The land all around is Royal land, but this
wood, though no more than two chains across, is mine own.'

At that, the King smiles. 'From henceforth, William
Thyssett, it shall be two leagues across, and you shall be my
Royal Woodsman.'

The string of horses departs, the milk-white stallions disappear into the mists of the past, my little tale is done. Mere
fancy, perhaps, and yet something of the sort must have happened, for, beside his royal duties, William Thyssett appears
quite suddenly in the records as a land-owner of note, and the
construction of what was to become Dimperley Manor began
in 1405. It is true, also, that the unfailing vigour of the Vere-
Thissett line, which has continued unbroken from father to
son since William's time (the interesting story of how 'Thyssett' became 'Vere-Thissett', I shall save for a later chapter),
seems, to this distant scion, far more likely to have sprung from
healthy peasant stock than from the feeble stem of aristocracy;
from the same origin, surely, came our motto: 'Probitate et

labore' ('By honesty and toil'). Planted deeply in the rich soil of Buckinghamshire, we continue to flourish . . .

After ten days, Valentine's hand still hurt like hell. Waiting at Marylebone for the delayed 11.23 to Aylesbury, he found himself walking up and down the platform, trying to outpace the pain; the missing ends of the three injured fingers felt as if each were being gripped by a pair of red-hot iron tongs, an image which he realized was straight from the Judgement painting in Addenham Church. As a child, he had spent at least an hour every Sunday morning staring at the most interesting section, which featured sinners being dragged into the abyss by a moustachioed devil who looked exactly like the man who came to Dimperley Manor four times a year to re-hang the pendulums.

It was far more painful than the shrapnel injury he'd received in Sicily, which had left him with a large scar on his right thigh in the shape of a letter V. 'What you need to do,' Miller had advised, 'is find some doll called Verna and then drop your trousers and say, "Baby, I've been looking for you my whole life!"'

The thigh wound had resulted in surgery and three weeks of pampering on board a convalescent ship, whereas on this occasion the MO had stared gloomily at the damaged hand for a few seconds before shaking his head.

'Well, that's a heck of a mess, Corporal.'

'Yes, sir.'

'Not very much we can do about it. Are you right-handed?'

'Yes, sir.'

'Pity. And what's your job in civilian life?'

Valentine was spared an answer by the simultaneous application of an iodine swab to the affected fingers, and by the time he'd recovered his voice, the doctor had been called away and an orderly was wrapping his hand with layer upon layer of gauze and cotton wool.

The CO had come to see him in sick bay, and Valentine had felt an absolute fool, trying to salute with a bandage the size of a coconut on his hand. 'No, no, please don't stand up,' the CO had said, and the other three men in the room, members of L platoon felled by an under-cooked chicken, had watched boggle-eyed as Ripon had drawn up a chair and sat beside the bed.

'I've spoken on the telephone to your' – the CO had paused, as if the word 'mother' might be somehow indelicate – 'to Lady Vere-Thissett about the accident. She was very sympathetic.'

This was laughably unlikely, but Valentine had managed a nod.

'They're looking after you in here?'

'Yes, sir.'

'Jolly good, jolly good.' The CO continued nodding for a while, his eyes fixed on Valentine, and it was disconcerting to be pinned by the same flat blue gaze that had so often swept past him. 'I was awfully sorry to hear about your brother. I was lucky enough to meet him once, you know – we were at the same shooting party in Romania and he offered me a ride home.'

'In the Vega Gull, sir?'

'That's the fellow. A touch bumpy; we had to land three

or four times for him to make repairs, once bang in the middle of a village square – nearly hit a horse and cart. Caused quite a sensation with the locals!' The last few words were splintered by a chuckle. 'So he was in Singapore?'

'Yes, sir. With the RAF. He's been missing, believed killed, since '42.'

'Oh, I see. So perhaps not quite the shock that it might have been.'

'No, sir.' Though, speaking for himself, he felt as if Miller's sledgehammer had walloped his head as well as his hand because, all along, he'd been absolutely certain that Felix was still alive and in a prison camp and would come roaring home again at the end of the war, another scrape survived. And now that he was definitely dead, the ramifications were so appalling that Valentine kept trying to shove the thought aside, and it kept returning unbidden, like a loyal but filthy dog.

The CO was leaning towards him in order to speak more quietly; Valentine caught a whiff of good coffee. 'Obviously, er . . . Corporal, you understand that I had no idea that you were in the regiment. No-one informed me as to who you were, otherwise I might have been able to . . . to . . .'

'That's all right, sir,' said Valentine. 'No-one knew, so they couldn't have.'

Ripon appeared to chew on this statement for a moment or two. 'So you've been with the Gloucesters since . . .'

'Nineteen forty, sir.'

'You joined straight from school?'

'Yes, sir.'

'Which school?'

'You probably won't have heard of it, sir. Umberton.'

'No. No, it doesn't . . . er . . . Does it have an OTC?'

'No, sir.'

'I see.' Ripon nodded a few more times and Valentine felt a slight twinge of pleasure at the man's obvious bafflement; he looked like a bird-spotter faced with an unidentifiable Atlantic blow-in. There were, of course, other public-school boys in the ranks: over the years, Valentine had come across numerous soldiers nicknamed 'Toff', like himself, or 'Duke' or 'Swank' or 'Lardy' (short for 'La-di-dah'), but most were sooner or later moved onward and upward via an officer training course, or – if emphatically lacking in brains or physical prowess – shifted sideways into staff jobs, where their accent might oil the jerky wheels of inter-service communication.

Ripon took a final stab. 'Your family's from Buckinghamshire, isn't it? You didn't think of joining the Yeomanry?'

'No, sir,' said Valentine.

There was a further pause, and then the CO rose to his feet. 'Well, jolly good luck, Vere-Thissett. I'm sure you'll be more than capable of assuming your brother's . . . er . . .'

Mantle? wondered Valentine. *Debts? Wife?*

'. . . role,' said Ripon, making it sound as if Valentine were lined up to play the murderer in the Aylesbury Players production of *Death in the Saddle*.

After he'd left, there was an awkward silence in the room. 'Friends in high places,' muttered one of the others.

'I honestly wouldn't call him a friend,' said Valentine.

21

'You say that, but I can't remember the last time a Lieutenant Colonel told me my brother gave him a lift home from Romania. Mind you, he'd have had to climb in the back of the cart with the milk bottles.'

The next day, Valentine had received an envelope containing his early discharge papers, and the week after he'd been driven to the dispersal centre in Winchester, where he'd been issued with a sheaf of coupons, a railway pass, an identity card, a ration book, a trilby, a raincoat and a stiff brown serge suit sporting a wide purple stripe which made him look as if the sling he was still wearing was the result of a razor fight between rival spivs. Pacing along the station platform under the blacked-out glass roof, holding a cardboard box containing his effects, he might as well have been wearing a luminous sandwich board that read 'DEMOBBED'.

He wondered what Miller would have said about the suit; he'd had a note from him in sick bay, helpfully written in the large capitals that Valentine found easiest to read: *THEY'VE GOT ME ON REPORT SO CAN'T COME TO SEE YOU. SORRY ABOUT YOUR FINGERS, IT'S LUCKY YOU DON'T HAVE TO ASSEMBLE ANY MORE BREN GUNS, OLD COCK, OR SHOULD THAT BE SIR OLD COCK? KEPT THAT QUIET, DIDN'T YOU, YOU SLY BASTARD?!?! IF YOU'RE EVER IN NORTHAMPTON ASK FOR ME IN THE JOLLY SMOKERS OR THE ENGINEER. OR THE EAGLE. OR THE FREEMASON'S ARMS OR . . . YOU GET THE PICTURE. MUD IN YOUR EYE, DUSTY.*

'Once they've healed, you'll have to find a few new ways of doing things,' the MO had said when he examined

Valentine's injuries before signing him off. 'You'll find writing tricky. You might try the rubber thimbles that cashiers use for counting paper money – they'll protect the stumps and give you a better grip. Do you shoot?'

'Sometimes. Rabbits, mainly.'

'Might be a while before you bag a bunny again.'

The Bren gun reference in the note had been chastening; until last week he could have assembled one in his sleep and had once actually equalled the battalion speed record. He wondered which other hard-won army skills would now be beyond him: spud bashing, obviously; shuffling and dealing cards; dominoes; blancoing . . . And then, for the first time, he thought of the notebook he always carried with him, the pages filled with hurried sketches, and he flexed his fingers involuntarily. The twang of pain made him stumble, and a naval Lieutenant, standing on the platform with a folded *Times*, glanced up, and then peered at him more closely.

'Thickie! Thickie Thissett! It *is* you, isn't it?'

The chap was his own age and had a circular mole on his right cheek and a chin so square that it looked like the bottom half of a cigar-box.

'Byng Minor,' said Valentine, his voice dead. He glanced along the track, hoping to see the train.

'Byng Solo now, I'm afraid. Byng Major bought it at Arnhem.'

'Sorry. I lost my older brother too.'

'Didn't know you had one.'

'He was at Marlborough. And then the RAF.'

'Bloody glamour boys,' said Byng Minor, automatically.

23

'No offence. So, what happened?' He nodded at Valentine's sling.

'Accident, a couple of weeks ago.'

'Earning you an early ticket – well done that man! Another five months before I'm back in the office – it's my uncle's insurance company, nice little business. What about you?'

'No plans yet,' said Valentine. It was possible, he thought, that this was the longest conversation he'd ever had with Byng Minor, who, if he hadn't actually coined the nickname 'Thickie', had been one of its most vigorous users. They'd been in the same dorm for four years and might even have had a fight at some point; he vaguely remembered giving that right-angled jaw a deserved biff or two.

'Oi, Corporal Thissett!' shouted someone, and Valentine looked across the rails at the opposite platform, where a couple of privates were sitting on their packs. It was Leyton and Fleck, inseparables from B company, off on leave, presumably. 'Nice suit!' called Leyton, without apparent irony. Valentine gave them a wave, just as the Aylesbury train slid into view.

'Corporal?' repeated Byng Minor, lifting an eyebrow.

'Yes.'

'You never took a commission?'

Valentine didn't answer, and it was a second or two before Byng Minor's expression of puzzlement rearranged itself into one of humorous understanding. 'Ah, the old exam requirement,' he said. 'Written work was never your forte, was it?', and within that smirk was encompassed the whole of Valentine's God-awful years at Umberton

24

('recommended for boys who need extra encouragement with their studies'), that treadmill of tedium and humiliation, enlivened only by daily violence. He wondered, suddenly, why on earth he was still standing here, talking to someone he'd fervently hoped never to see again.

Doors were opening along the length of the train. Of course, there were other skills he'd acquired in the army, ones that didn't involve dexterity; Valentine leaned towards Byng Minor, as if to impart a confidence. 'Fuck off and leave me alone, you soft fucking prick,' he said, conversationally. 'Or you'll have to ring your fucking uncle to check if he'll insure you against having a newspaper rammed up your fucking arse.' Satisfied by the reaction – Byng Minor looked as if he'd been run through with a halberd – Valentine hoisted his cardboard box and stepped out briskly into the crowd.

4

There was at least one stuffed animal in almost every room of Dimperley Manor. The octagonal library that Alaric used as a study had two: a duckling dressed in a bonnet and holding a miniature parasol, conserved in a glass dome on a table between his desk and Zena's, and a three-pawed badger on the windowsill that leaked sawdust and maggots from both ears.

'I've told you not to touch that,' said Zena. 'It's full of germs.'

'All right, Mummy.'

Her daughter continued to stroke the badger's head for a full four seconds before cheerfully returning to her farm set, and Zena, who'd spent her own childhood arguing – endlessly, fruitlessly – against one inflexible rule after another, felt her usual surge of admiration; at the age of three, Allison managed to do more or less what she wanted, avoiding trouble by a technique of finely judged delayed obedience – it was an inborn skill, apparently, like having perfect pitch.

'Have you ever seen the attics here, Mrs Baxter?' asked Alaric, looking up from the magnifying glass he'd been using to study a barely legible steward's inventory from the early 1800s.

'No, I haven't,' said Zena. 'I'd like to, though.'

'Would you? The reason I'm mentioning them is that the bulk of the third Baronet's taxidermy collection is, I believe, still up there, including some of the larger items.'

'How much larger?'

'Er, well' – Alaric pondered for a moment, his profile silhouetted against the view of the Great Lawn in the window beside him, the upper half sternly handsome and the lower apparently modelled from blancmange – 'there was definitely a bear at one stage, and a stag, a whole stag, not just the head, and a brace of wild boar. And there was something else, with tusks – oh, what was it? Not an elephant, obviously. Ha ha *haaa*!'

Zena glanced swiftly at her daughter, who had recently perfected an impression of Alaric's laugh – a rising triple syllable – but Allison was concentrating on forcing her dairy herd into an old cocoa-tin.

'My brother had them removed when Felix was first toddling. In fact, I think Irene might have had a dream or a premonition of danger, rather like the Sleeping Beauty and the spindle in . . . oh, what was the story?' He tapped his fingers on the desk, features corrugated in thought.

'Sleeping Beauty?'

'Yes, that was it. She thought that something might fall on my nephew and kill him. Though of course that wasn't what happened in the end.'

'No.'

There was a rather sombre silence. The confirmation of Felix's death was less than a fortnight behind them, and it had soon become obvious to Zena that its implications reached far beyond the tragic yet commonplace loss of an eldest son. 'Death duties,' Alaric had said, on the day of the telegram, each word as freighted with doom as when, staring fixedly at the headline in *The Times* on July the twenty-seventh, he had first spoken the words 'Labour Government'.

'They'll try to take everything from us,' he'd added, on both occasions. 'And I wouldn't put it past these Bolsheviks to remove the title as well.' He had glanced, as he spoke, at the two silver frames on his desk, one containing a photograph of his nephews as children – Felix and Cedric, mini-gentlemen in matching Norfolk jackets, standing beside a pony on which sat their pudding-faced baby brother, glumly petticoated – and the other a pencil sketch of the first Baronet, copied from a portrait in oils. The original had spent the war with all the other paintings, linen-wrapped in the luggage room, safe from the sticky hands of strangers. Only last week, Alaric had supervised their re-hanging, and Zena had, for the first time, seen the full array of family portraits, from the earliest, a murky panel purporting to be William Thyssett himself and clearly painted by someone who couldn't do hands, all the way through to a full-length oil of Felix, dressed in a flying suit and leaning against a propellor, projecting the relaxed certainty of the truly handsome.

Zena had been staring at it for some moments before she'd realized that his widow was standing just behind her. 'Sorry,' she'd said, stepping aside. 'He was very . . .'

'Yes, wasn't he?' Lady Barbara had said brightly, her eyes full of tears. She'd looked, as ever, as if an air-raid siren had gone off just as she was getting dressed – everything trailing or askew, her necklace caught on her collar, an undoubtedly expensive brooch carelessly pinned on so that it drooped forward, exposing the hallmark. You wouldn't think there was a mirror in the house, thought Zena, though it didn't detract from the woman's prettiness, a girlish, curly-topped, saucer-eyed variety which sat a bit oddly on someone who was in their mid-thirties. Zena, ten years younger but knowing herself to be unexceptional in appearance apart from a slight overbite and a large bust (both of which, it had to be admitted, had had their fans), had always embraced smartness – or at least *neatness*, which was as near to smartness as you could get if you'd been alternating the same three blouses since 1941.

'I've got it!' exclaimed Alaric, who'd been frowning at the stuffed badger for some time. 'It was a *walrus*. The fellow with tusks, I mean. I even found it mentioned in Grevell's correspondence. Do you have the file? It was the letters he sent from Alaska, I think.'

Zena rose from her desk and went over to one of the bookcases that lined five of the eight walls from floor to ceiling. She ran a finger along a row of box files and pulled out the fourth. The first item inside it was a paper folder on which was written 'Alaska'.

'It's here, Mr V-T,' she said, placing it in front of him.

'Mrs Baxter, Mrs Baxter,' he said, shaking his head with wonder. 'In Ancient Rome you would have been Goddess of Efficiency.'

'Thank you,' said Zena, who had long since ceased bothering to be modest about what was actually a very basic filing system. And anyway, she *was* efficient; it was efficiency that had propelled her to the top of the class at Homerton Commercial College and elevated her with such speed from her first job in the typing pool at Dawson's Industrial and Military Glass to the post of personal secretary, and then Assistant to the Head of Ordering and Delivery; by comparison, sorting out Alaric's papers had been a simple matter, even though when she'd first viewed the library it had looked as if someone had left the windows open during a tornado. More than three years had passed since then and yet he continued to regard the use of clearly written labels and sequentially numbered shelves as near-miraculous, and Zena had eventually concluded it was because there'd never been any need for him to grasp – or even to *notice* – the principles of organization; all his life, unwanted items had been whisked away and then, when the need arose, instantly restored, like conjurers' doves. When, recently, the light-bulb in the library had blown, Alaric's initial irritation had turned to bewilderment: where was the new bulb? Why was it not being replaced? Why was he even having to *think* about such a matter? The chain of invisible events which would, in the past, have speedily linked the ringing of the servants' bell to the insertion of a new bulb had rusted away. There were no longer any bells and the only remaining servant was Miss Hersey, who still called herself Lady Irene's lady's maid, although (as far as Zena could see) she was now required to do almost everything except shovel coal, but even she hadn't been able to produce a bulb when none were being manufactured. 'Couldn't you just take one from another room that isn't used very much?' Zena had suggested (goodness knows, there were a few dozen of those in Dimperley). You would have thought, from Alaric's expression of dawning amazement, that she'd casually invented a space rocket.

She sat down again and resumed her typed transcription of yesterday's notes, part of a stunningly boring chapter on the agricultural reforms instituted by Selby Vere-Thissett in the 1790s and containing so many repetitions of the words 'crop rotation' that it required intense concentration on her part not to accidentally skip four lines or repeat the one she'd just typed. Not that anyone sane would ever read it, obviously, but she had her professional pride.

Alaric, after checking that the child was absorbed in her task of colouring in the white areas of a wooden Friesian cow with a blue crayon, permitted his eyes to linger for a while on her mother. He allowed himself to do this a maximum of three times a day, and for no more than thirty seconds at a time, and it quite definitely had nothing whatsoever to do with lust – he liked to define it to himself as the sort of gaze with which Constable would have viewed the Suffolk countryside: an artistic appreciation of the harmony of light and form – bright, billowing clouds, smoothly rounded hillocks, tall trees straining in the wind . . . The third hand of the watch moved relentlessly towards the half-minute mark as he watched her busy fingers dancing across the keys.

He'd noticed her from the moment she'd stepped from the motor-coach. He had been taking a stroll after a frustrating morning during which he'd been totally unable to find where he'd put the important letter from the Sheriff of Ivinghoe to Wrexholm Vere-Thissett, the contents of which were so vital to Chapter Five, and had happened to see the latest London passengers disembarking in front of the stable block. Zena Baxter had been as ripe and as rounded as all the other expectant mothers, but while the rest had been yawning and chattering, she'd been looking up at the house with what seemed a critical eye, though her judgemental expression, he realized later, was partly due to her habit of drawing her upper lip down over her slightly protruding teeth. She was certainly not a classic beauty and yet, over the weeks that followed, she'd continued to draw his attention – her habit of provoking yelps of laughter from the other women with comments that he never managed to overhear, her curiosity about her new surroundings. 'What's this object for?' he'd overheard her asking Epple of the wide brick box in the kitchen garden, the space beneath it still scattered with charcoal ends. 'Growing pineapples,' Epple had said, forbiddingly, and Alaric had seen the girl's face twitch. She'd had the baby by then – a swaddled bundle – and her figure had returned to a shape that might still be termed voluptuous.

A week or two later he'd spotted her using a pencil to correct the spelling on a directive about sheet-hanging pinned up by the local warden ('SHEETS MUST BE TAKEN IN ON MOONLIT NIGHTS AS THEY MAY ACT AS A BEECON FOR BOMBERS').

'I was a secretary,' she'd said, seeing him watching her. 'I can't stand spelling mistakes.' She spoke quite nicely, with barely a trace of a London accent. Not long after that, he'd asked her to glance through the opening chapter of

Woodsman to the King, which he'd typed himself on a Remington borrowed from the post-mistress, and she had immediately spotted three missing commas and the use of the word 'histororical' in the first paragraph.

She had agreed a salary, arranged accommodation in the village, from where she cycled daily, and, almost from the first, his writing had begun to flow like the rill through the Stumpery, enabling him to complete what he estimated to be almost two thirds of the book, while the baby had expanded into a plump toddler with the same judgemental expression as her mother. But always, on the horizon, there lurked the spectre of Zena's husband, returning to claim his bride at the end of the war. It was like hearing the dragging footsteps of approaching death.

The husband's name was Christopher, he was a Lance Corporal in the RAMC, he was stationed in Malta, and in civilian life he was a librarian. Alaric knew little more than this and was disinclined to ask, since every fresh fact was like dripping vinegar on to a graze, and yet the absence of firm information meant that he found himself involuntarily speculating about the man: was he a weedy type, with boils and horn-rimmed spectacles, whom Zena had married out of pity? Was he a brute who demanded silence in his home as well as his workplace? Did his wife's hazel eyes cloud with despair at his approaching footsteps or light softly with happiness? Did the sound of the key in the front door presage a contented evening of library-book perusal in adjacent armchairs (she was, he knew, a keen reader) or something rather more . . . energetic?

'All finished,' said Zena, laying three typewritten pages

on his desk, the diamond on her engagement ring flashing cruelly in the sunlight. 'Could I take Allison out for her morning walk now?'

'Of course, of course.' He patted the little pile of paper. 'Do you think I explained Selby's reforms in sufficient detail?'

'Yes.'

A hand appeared above Alaric's desk-top and walked a black-and-blue cow along the edge, accompanied by clip-clop noises.

'Perhaps when you return you might double-check my reading of the 1802 household inventory – your eyesight is so much sharper than mine.'

Zena nodded resignedly, knowing that she'd be spending the rest of the day squinting at hand-writing that looked like sepia embroidery and that every time she looked up, Alaric would pretend that he hadn't been moonily watching her. Admiration could be very wearing.

They left the library by the door that led to the Orangery and stepped into the garden through the first of the twelve sets of French windows.

'Sunhat,' said Zena. Allison took it from her and swung it around for a while, as if it were a hand-bell. 'On your head, please. Where would you like to go?' She loved asking her daughter this, loved being able to offer a choice – the easy largesse of it, like pulling aside the cloth on a baker's basket – loved watching the small features bunch in concentration as she considered her options.

'Dead doggies,' said Allison, who enjoyed running in circles around the gravestones in the pets' cemetery.

'And we'll look out for your doll, shall we? You might have dropped her there.'

They set off beside the long hedge. When Zena had first arrived at Dimperley, the topiary shapes had still looked vaguely like elephants, but no-one had clipped them for years, and now they were merely a series of grotesque bulges, looming over the gravel path.

'One,' said Allison, who liked to begin the walk by counting them, 'two, fee, pour, pive, pix, pate.'

'Seven comes before eight. And try to say the numbers properly.'

'Pine, pen, plebba plebba plebba.'

'You're just being daft now, aren't you?'

'Yes, ha ha *haaa*!' The impression of Alaric was so good that Zena involuntarily glanced back towards the library and saw Lady Barbara approaching at speed across the Great Lawn.

'Have you seen the girls?' she called out, long before she'd reached Zena. 'My daughters? Have you seen them, Mrs Baxter?'

'You mean today? No, I haven't. Sorry.'

Lady Barbara looked as if she were about to gallop past and then came to a sudden halt a yard or two away, as if someone had grabbed her reins. 'They're not *lost*,' she said, defensively. 'But I'm taking them into Tring to meet their new headmistress and they seem to have disappeared. I'm wondering if they've gone for a walk and forgotten the time.'

'Shall I look out for them, then?' asked Zena.

'If you would. Thank you.' Lady Barbara broke into a

trot again, taking the path through the rose garden and then halting with an exclamation as she stepped on something in the gravel. There was a large ladder running down the back of her nylons.

'Silly lady,' said Allison.

'No, you mustn't say that,' said Zena, privately agreeing. 'Go on, then – do you remember the way?' Allison set off, confidently, skirting the maze and taking the path that led past the Hermit's Hollow, which had been another favourite destination, until they'd found a tramp sleeping in it.

As the path started to climb towards the woods, Zena kept an eye out for the girls; she'd glimpsed them on the day of their arrival, the week before: two long-legged creatures wearing dresses in beautiful sweet-pea colours and matching jackets and hats, their suitcases powder-blue, everything fresh and bright, like a Deanna Durbin picture. Lady Barbara had travelled to Liverpool to collect them from the ship, and she had been weeping as she'd clambered out of the taxi on their return. Her daughters had stared blankly up at the house; they had been in America for five years. Zena was still staggered by this; why would anyone send their children away for *five years*? It wasn't as if the Manor had been in much danger, although you wouldn't know that from the number of times the inhabitants mentioned what they called 'The Dimperley Bomb', which had landed half a mile from the house in November 1941, resulting in a slight dent in a clover field.

'I can still hear that dreadful noise,' Miss Hersey had said, shuddering, only last week, and apparently Lady Irene continued to have nightmares about the near-miss, though, frankly, it seemed more likely to Zena that the bomb had thrown itself out of the aeroplane early rather than risk meeting her.

There had been almost no interest in Zena's own experience of the Blitz, since everyone here was bored of Londoners 'going on and on about bombs as if they owned them', as Mrs Procter, her landlady, had put it. She'd said it quite pleasantly, and Zena hadn't bothered to take offence, although it was quite galling to be forced to admire a piece of shrapnel that had somehow landed in Addenham churchyard and which was kept in a velvet-lined box as if it were a saint's jawbone, when she herself had been dug out of the basement shelter of Hackney Young Women's Hostel five hours after the building had suffered a direct hit, not to mention spending two nights a week fire-watching at Dawson's, standing on the rooftop in a tin helmet under a roaring sky.

Ahead of her, on the steepest bit of the path, Allison had stopped and turned, lips pursed, her hands on her hips.

'Are you out of puff?'

'Ermiling the view.'

'Oh, you're admiring the view? That's what I always do, isn't it?' Zena turned too and received the usual jolt, the one she'd first felt as the motor-coach from Aylesbury Station, laden with expectant mothers, had swung into the drive and she'd seen the preposterous house, like six chapters from a history book glued together: pillars at one end, an onion dome at the other, turrets and sundials in the middle, the green hyphen of the moat split by a bridge that must have carried knights on horseback, curricles and barouches, and all around it an upward sweep of grass and woodland and a scattering of follies like dropped bracelet charms. And the oddest thing was that she'd instantly *recognized* the place, though it had taken her a few days to work out why – had she seen it at the pictures? Or in a magazine? She'd kept walking around the outside, glancing up at the gables and the rippled glass of the windows, trying to startle herself into remembering – and then, all at once, the answer had jumped at her, complete and precise. She had been nine years old. 'Wait here,' the lady from the Welfare Board had said, patting a window seat in the Hackney Council office before disappearing behind a door; the walls of the room had been painted yellow at the top and maroon at the bottom, like a trifle. After a long time, the lady had returned and had given Zena a biscuit on a plate, and a book, before leaving again. The book had been called *The Enchanted Castle* and the illustration on the paper cover had shown two children looking up at the battlements, corkscrew chimneys and crooked windows of a huge old manor-house. And time had collapsed like an opera hat, so that she was both staring up at the walls of Dimperley and sitting in the custard-coloured room in a skirt too short for her and shoes that hurt, with a daub of camomile lotion on her chin to cover the crusts from impetigo and a book on her lap that had made her forget all these things. She'd read nearly half by the time the lady had come to collect her. She'd even been allowed to keep it, though it had eventually disappeared in the course of one move or another.

The house had been nicknamed 'Dumperly' by the other women who'd arrived in the coach with her. 'Who'd want to live there? Falling to bits. Middle of nowhere. Draughty. Spiders. Splinters. Rude statues. How can you clean something this size? *And* it's haunted.' Though the underground corridor where the ghost of a weeping servant was supposed to lurk was kept permanently locked, presumably to stop any of the London contingent wandering through to the Dower Wing and contaminating The Family. Zena, feeling strangely proprietorial, had both agreed with and flinched at every criticism; from the moment she'd arrived, she'd dreaded leaving.

'Come on,' commanded her daughter, who had never yet lived anywhere else, who had freckles and no scabs, who ate an egg for breakfast every morning, and who could run as far and as fast as she wanted. A bumblebee the size of a conker droned across the path and Allison held out a hopeful hand, as if it might settle on her finger.

'Oh, who's that?' said Zena, her eye caught by a figure emerging from the clump of trees that lay beyond the Pavilion of the Four Winds, but it wasn't one of Lady Barbara's daughters, it was a man in an ill-fitting brown suit, carrying a cardboard box. A salesman, possibly. Or a tramp. She took Allison's hand as he walked through the long grass towards them.

Kitty and Priss were at the top of the Wyvern Tower with a pair of binoculars.

'And now she's going towards that square building at the back with the big arch,' said Priss, adjusting the focus, her elbows on the narrow parapet.

'Those are the stables.'

'How do you know?'

'Because I remember them.'

'Well, I don't. I can't remember anything at all,' said Priss. 'I don't even really believe I ever lived here.'

'Oh, you're being dumb now. You weren't a baby when we left, you were nearly eight.'

'I am *not* being dumb. I only remember Brookford. Everything before that's a blank.'

'I expect you've repressed it.'

'What does that mean?'

'It's psychological. Harold said they're not interested in psychological matters in England. He says they don't have any subtlety.'

'I don't know what you're talking about, and I bet you don't know what you're talking about either. She's come out again, and she's going towards that little house covered in shells. And I can see that old dog of Grannie's too. It's doing a you-know-what.'

Kitty checked her wristwatch. 'I think we should stay up here another half an hour and then it'll be too late for us to go to that school meeting, and then we can tell her that we got lost.'

'Tell who?'

'Mother.'

'She said we should call her Mummy.'

'Well, I don't know about you, but I simply can't call her after a preserved Egyptian corpse.' Kitty had been honing and polishing this sentence in her imagination, with the intention of bringing it out during one of their appalling evening meals. She slightly hoped that an older member of the family might faint with shock when they heard it. It was the sort of remark that people said at cocktail parties; in Brookford, she had been allowed at one or two such gatherings since she'd turned sixteen, and had heard the bright flare of laughter that followed such a carefully produced opinion. She had worn a burnt-orange dress with a full petticoat underneath, and a proper, stiff brassiere which had made her bosoms look much larger than they actually were. 'My, you look nice,' Harold had said, in a way that she hadn't quite liked, though she *had* looked nice, especially since she'd been allowed a permanent wave. Not for much longer. 'Oh dear, that will have to be grown out,' had been Grannie Irene's very first words to her, followed by 'What an extraordinarily tall girl you are,' and her mother had made an awful breathy gushy noise somewhere between a protest and a laugh and had talked about how good and nutritious the food was in the States.

'But I ate the same food and *I'm* not tall,' Priss had said, and Kitty had pointed out that Priss hadn't been through puberty yet, and merry hell had broken loose, as if she'd shouted the word 'asshole', instead of using a correct biological term. Harold and Trina, with whom she and Priss had lived, were very modern in outlook. Their house had been modern too, with a flat roof, a huge Frigidaire and three bathrooms.

'Could I have a shower?' Kitty had asked on her first night back at Dimperley, and everyone had laughed, including that old bat Hersey who hovered around Grannie Irene like . . . well, like an old bat. Because, of course, there were no showers here, only huge, high-sided tubs into which lukewarm water trickled with incredible slowness. Even more incredible was the fact that there was only one toilet on the whole of the third floor and during the night they were supposed to use a china pot under the bed, as if they were cavemen.

'She's shouting our names,' said Priss. A faint shriek was audible. 'I don't mind calling her Mummy.'

'You tried calling Trina Mummy when we first arrived.'

'No I *didn't*.'

'Yes you did, but it doesn't matter,' she added, quickly, as red blotches started to appear on Priss's neck, the signal that she was about to perform one of her switchbacks, zipping from calm to fury in the snap of a finger. She'd never been like that till they were sent away, and then she'd spent their first three months in Brookford refusing to leave her room, ill with home-sickness, reading and re-reading the few letters from home that had managed to dodge the U-boats and weeping so hard and so often that her face had shrivelled up and she'd looked like a little old lady. Trina and Harold had been sympathetic at first, and then had started to lose patience. 'We're not running a nursing home,' Kitty had overheard Trina say. 'Of course I'm sorry for the kid, but what are we supposed to *do*?' They'd even talked about sending the girls back, but by then no-one was allowing evacuees on the Atlantic route, not since the *City of Benares* had been torpedoed and all those children had died.

In the end, Kitty had had to give her sister a talking-to. 'You can't go home, it's not allowed, so you can either stay in your room and bawl and make everyone think that

English children are chicken, or you can dry up and be brave and do nice things. You know you can buy ice-creams here even when it's snowing, and they've given us lots of new things to wear – they've bought us *bicycles*, for goodness' sake, and the school-work's easy-peasy. I've been moved up a year and I'm not even clever, so the teachers'll think you're an out-and-out genius.' This last appeal had been very cunning; Priss wasn't pretty or good at sport, but she was proud of being brainy. She was also acquisitive. 'And I'll give you five cents every day that you don't cry,' Kitty had added, in a spur-of-the-moment masterstroke.

It had worked, partially: Priss had stopped crying and come out of the bedroom and had eventually achieved fame, if not popularity, by being the youngest seventh grader ever to attend Brookford High, but she'd also lost all her old clingy admiration for Kitty and had instead become very humourless and pig-headed, as well as prone to terrible rages during which she threw things.

'*Why* don't we want the meeting with the headmistress?' asked Priss abruptly, lowering the binoculars.

'Because you may not have noticed but, so far, during the *six days* since we arrived, we've been told to grow our hair, throw away our blue jeans, speak properly instead of with "that ree-vole-ting accent", eat all the food on our plates, though I think it'll probably kill us, take our elbows off the table, avoid mentioning the names of any boys we knew at school because otherwise everyone will think we're street-walkers, and stop using the word "hygiene", even though people parade through the house carrying *pee* in a *giant cup*, and I am drawing a line, Priss, I am taking up a position. I am not going to go to a school where I have to wear a purple sack and long underwear and a hat like a *spittoon*.'

Her sister gave her a long, expressionless look and then shoved the binoculars back into their case.

'I don't care what I wear,' she said, 'and I want to go to school. You can stay stupid if you want.' She turned as she spoke and took a cautious step through the dark doorway that led to the spiral staircase.

'Don't go, Priss.'

'Shut up.'

'But we have to—'

'Shut up shut up shut up shut up . . .' The words faded around the curve of the stairs, and Kitty went back to the parapet. Her mother was still visible as a dot in the distance, hurrying past what looked like a ruined Greek temple. She never seemed to stop moving – half-running instead of walking, fidgeting whenever she sat down, forever taking out her handkerchief – clutching, wringing, dropping and then picking it up again – and whereas Priss hadn't cried once since arriving back in England, Barbara seemed to sob all the time. 'Oh, my girls, my girls, my little girls,' she'd shrieked, heading towards them at Liverpool Dock, and the sisters had instinctively pressed together, as if to ward off an attack.

'Hello, Mother,' Kitty had said, offering a hand before being enfolded into a damp embrace. In the train, Barbara had kept touching her daughters, stroking their arms, patting their hair – 'My girls, back from America,' she'd announced proudly to the other passengers in the compartment, 'aren't they beautiful?' and Kitty had sat, rigid with embarrassment, while Priss had stared at her mother with the expression of someone watching a movie with an incomprehensible plot.

'Did you have a nice time?' an elderly lady had asked, as if they'd been to California for the weekend, and Kitty had said, 'Yes,' just as Priss had said, 'No.'

Priss appeared now at the foot of the tower, where she looked around uncertainly and then ran off in the wrong direction. A moment or two later, the coping-stone on which Kitty was resting her forearms shifted suddenly. She jerked back and the stone tipped silently the other way and disappeared from view. It was so unexpected, so unbelievable, that she actually placed her hand in the gap to check that it had really gone, and felt the tickle of a spider crossing her fingers. From the ground came an oddly muffled thud.

'Hello, man,' shouted Allison, when the chap with the brown suit was still a few yards away. 'What's that?' she added, pointing at his sling.

'I hurt my hand.'

'How?'

'I expect this gentleman's in a hurry,' said Zena, trying to steer Allison away.

'No, I'm not particularly.' He had a slightly hoarse voice, and a surprisingly nobby accent for someone who looked as if he flogged vacuum cleaners for a living.

He stopped a polite few feet away, awkwardly lowered the box to the ground and removed his hat. His hair was army-length, his squarish, unremarkable face streaked with sweat.

'Someone hit it with a very large hammer,' he said, and Allison gave a bellow of laughter.

'That is *not* funny,' said Zena to her daughter.

'You might think that, but almost everyone I've told finds it hilarious,' he said. 'I blame Laurel and Hardy.'

'What's in that?' asked Allison.

'In this?' He gave the box a tap with his foot. 'Nothing very interesting. A raincoat, two shirts, a pair of boots, a couple of souvenirs of Sicily and my discharge papers.' He huffed a long sigh, put the hat back on and picked up the box again. 'Better go, I suppose,' he said, almost to himself; without moving, he stared pensively past Zena at the view.

'Oh!' she said, involuntarily.

'What?'

'Nothing. I mean – are you Mr Vere-Thissett's nephew?'

'Yes.'

'I'm his secretary. He has a photograph of you on his desk.'

'Oh God, is he still writing that awful book?'

Agreement seemed disloyal; Zena gave Allison's hand a little tug. 'We should go. We're on our way to the pets' graveyard.'

'Are you?' For the first time, his expression showed a speck of animation. 'Which grave do you like best?'

'My daughter likes the one with the painting of the angel dog on it.'

'I did that painting,' he said. 'Neddy was my dog.'

'What colour was he?' asked Allison.

'Brown with a black tail.'

'Neddy,' repeated Allison.

'Yes.'

'Sounds more like a donkey,' said Zena.

'He was actually quite like a donkey. He was stubborn and he ate carrots, and sometimes he – oh Lord.' The enthusiasm slid from his features as he caught sight of something over Zena's shoulder, and she turned to see Lady Barbara hurrying up the path towards them, calling out unintelligibly as she came, waving, breaking into a run, losing a shoe, turning back to put it on.

'It's the silly lady,' said Allison.

'I'd better go,' said Alaric's nephew. 'Very nice to meet you, Mrs . . .'

'Baxter.'

'Valentine!' The shoe was back on and Barbara was on the move again, now within earshot. 'You didn't tell us you were coming!'

'No, I thought I'd—'

She reached him and gave him a breathless kiss on the cheek. 'I'm so glad you're back – your poor arm, though. Why didn't you get a taxi?'

'I hitched a lift part of the way.' Though he'd baled out with two miles still to go, almost queasy at the prospect of arriving home, at the finality of it, as if his return was the end of everything, rather than a beginning. 'I wanted a walk,' he added. 'How are you, Barbara?'

'The thing is, the most awful thing's just happened. I mean, minutes ago.'

'Has it?' His sister-in-law was very pale, he realized, in spite of her exertions.

'I was trying to find my girls – you know they're back from America – in fact, that's another awful thing, because I haven't told them about Felix. Of course, they know he's missing, but I haven't mentioned the telegram yet because I can't bear to upset them when they're already so . . . so . . . I suppose I'd been hoping they'd be just the same as when they left, which was silly of me, obviously, but they won't even call me Mummy' – she started crying as she said the word and wiped her eyes with the handkerchief already balled in one hand – 'and Kitty's taller than I am, and she's been so' – she lowered her voice – '*rude* in front of your mother, and of course your mother blames me for . . .'

'What did Kitty say?'

'. . . for everything. Oh, "puberty", and "pants" and "bum", though that doesn't mean the same thing over there, apparently, and "goofy", which isn't anything to do with teeth and – anyway, I was trying to find the girls because—' She looked at her wristwatch and let out a bleat of distress. 'Oh, and it's much too late to go now, and someone told me that the headmistress always says that unpunctuality is exactly as bad as theft because it's stealing time. Anyway, I was looking for them, and I passed by the Wyvern Tower, and I noticed something on the ground, and it was a stone that must have dropped off the parapet, because this whole, entire place is falling to *pieces*!' The sudden, savage rise in the pitch of her voice startled a flock of corn bunting that had been feeding, invisibly, in the long grass nearby; they burst upward, like earth from a mortar. 'And there was something

48

underneath the stone, Valentine. There was a little hairy white tail sticking out.'

'Oh God,' said Valentine. 'Pollux?'

'Yes.'

'I had no idea he was still alive.'

'Well, he isn't, is he? Not any more.'

'No.'

'And how are we ever, ever going to tell your mother? Oh dear, it's just—' She took a couple of wavering breaths and then blew her nose. 'Anyway,' she added, with an unsuccessful attempt at a smile. 'Welcome home.'

Valentine managed to escape again after supper, walking with his brother as far as the silted lake and pausing by the Pavilion of the Four Winds to watch a barn owl ease itself from the stone mouth of Boreas and fly towards the woods.

'Why do I keep finding little piles of dog filth covered in sawdust?' he asked Ceddy on the way back, having trodden in yet another.

By the moat, they stopped again. Swallows were dipping to drink, scoring the surface as if with a razor.

'Shall we sit down for a while?' He lowered himself awkwardly on to the grass, the immobile arm throwing his balance off, and Ceddy dropped neatly and said, 'Aaaah,' as if he'd just got into a hot bath. 'Nanny Burton,' said Valentine. 'It was Nanny Burton who used to say "Aaaah" like that, every time she sat down, wasn't it?'

His brother leaned over to study the grass between his knees. Since Valentine's last visit, his mother's handsome features had sharpened and Alaric's had sagged, but Ceddy hadn't changed at all, his forehead remaining almost unlined, his expression a perpetual half-smile with averted gaze. When he'd seen Valentine walk into the Tapestry Room he'd carried on sorting through a box of spillikins but had added the soothing hissing sounds to his labour that the groom had used to make when curry-combing the horses.

Lady Irene, on the other hand, had risen to her feet and exclaimed, 'What on *earth* are you wearing?'

After breaking the ghastly news about the dog, Valentine had gone to his room to change and had discovered that none of the clothes in his wardrobe fitted him any longer, being too tight on the shoulders and too short in the leg. He'd come down in Felix's cricket flannels just in time to hear his mother informing Miss Hersey that the demob suit should be given to the poor or burned. After that they'd had luncheon and he'd almost broken a tooth on a pellet in the rabbit stew. 'Shot that one m'self,' Alaric had said, rather proudly. The whole day had been as exhausting as a route march with full pack.

'Yes, it was definitely Nanny Burton,' he said. 'Do you remember she kept a mouse skull in a locket around her neck?'

He lay back in the long grass. A dotted line, like a print-out of Morse code, was streaming from one of the turrets. Above the Great Lawn it flared into a constellation of dots – tens, dozens, hundreds of bats, wheeling and flitter-ing. And all in silence; he could, he realized, no longer hear the tiny chirrups that had punctuated the evenings of his childhood. Age, he supposed – age and the guns of Sicily.

'I am not a fanciful woman,' his mother had said, 'but it cannot be denied that he was Felix's dog, and a dog always follows his master ...' The implication being, Valentine supposed, that the terrier had committed suicide rather than accept a new owner. It was certainly true that Felix had *named* the dog, deliberately choosing a word that when called from a distance by someone who enunciated as clearly as Lady Irene sounded exactly like 'bollocks'.

There was a light splashing sound, and Valentine sat up to see Ceddy kneeling on the bank, reaching for something, fingers dabbing the surface.

'Don't fall in,' he said, automatically. He himself had tumbled into the moat as a three-year-old, and Ceddy had fished him out, and a week later his brother had been stricken with the brain fever that had ever after been blamed on the stagnant water. And also on Valentine, who had apparently been told several times not to go near the edge and who had ignored this injunction.

'What have you got there?'

It was a headless doll, pale in the half-light, draped with weed like a celluloid Ophelia.

Water poured out of the neck-hole.

'What are you going to do with that?'

There was, of course, no answer. Ceddy picked off the weed and then stood and raised himself on his toes a few times, like an athlete stretching before a race.

'Want to go in, old lad?' asked Valentine.

They walked side-by-side towards the lighted windows and an evening as strictly scheduled as any in the military: his mother had informed him that she needed 'a word' about

Pollux, Miss Hersey wanted to take his measurements so that she could begin wardrobe alterations and Alaric had promised to read him a chapter of The Dullest Book Ever Written ('or even two, if we have time').

And there wasn't even any alcohol in the house to blunt the pain.

5

Bucks Herald, 22nd September 1945

SAD NEWS OF BUCKS WAR HERO

The family and the many friends and admirers of Squadron Leader Sir Felix Vere-Thissett, Baronet, DFC, AFC, of Dimperley Manor, were saddened to hear the recent confirmation of his death, which occurred while on active service with the RAF in Singapore in 1942. After his Hurricane was observed to have been shot down, some hope had remained that he might have been captured, hope that was dashed after the Japanese surrender.

LOCAL FIGURE

Always at the ready with a smile and a cheerful wave, Sir Felix was a well-known and highly popular local figure, often seen driving between Dimperley Manor and Woodsley Airfield, and once memorably offering a flight in his aeroplane to the winner of the 1936 North Chilterns Ploughing Competition, a prize that is talked about to this day after its recipient, Caleb Glaser, lost his hat and upper plate when the pilot performed a 'loop the loop' over Farrow Hill. Interested in aircraft since his university days, Sir Felix joined the RAF on the day war was declared and was the recipient of numerous decorations, including the Distinguished Flying Cross (with bar) for his valour during the Battle of Britain.

The Baronet had survived a previous aeroplane crash unscathed, when his Curtiss Robin overshot Woodsley Airfield (of which he was part-owner) in 1938, demolishing a cowshed and killing two heifers belonging to G. Robinson of Hedges Farm, who subsequently received forty-five guineas in compensation for the cattle at Aylesbury Assizes. A claim for the cowshed was rejected, since it was said to already be on its last legs, an assertion denied by G. Robinson.

MOTOR-VEHICLE SMASH

Sir Felix had also survived more than one motor-vehicle smash, including a three-vehicle collision at the cross-roads just outside Woodsley Airfield in 1935 which resulted in a minor injury for the Baronet and the loss, by fire, of an entire wagon of hay belonging to Mr Frank Edgell of Four Elms Farm, Whittam, for which a financial arrangement was amicably reached.

WIDOW

Sir Felix, who inherited the Baronetcy after the death of his father (Sir Arthur Vere-Thissett) in 1933, leaves a widow and two daughters.

A memorial service will take place at St Aelfric's Church, Addenham, on Friday, 28th September.

★

Valentine was back in front of the Addenham Doom, his head angled as if listening to the vicar, his gaze directed surreptitiously up at the arch where the Wicked were still dropping into the flames with their little white legs waving while the Good watched smugly from the one and nines. His pose was so reminiscent of a hundred soporific Sundays that he kept having to remind himself of what – or, rather, of *whom* – the service was actually about; each of these reminders was accompanied by a jolt of anticipatory nerves.

He'd last seen Felix in 1941, outside Charing Cross Station on a twilit summer evening. They'd been crossing the Strand in different directions, and had halted, startled, in the middle of the road, taxis sputtering by on either side. Felix had been on his way to the Club, looking like a Brylcreem advertisement in a uniform that fitted and a stripe of medal ribbons that ran halfway across his chest, while Valentine, called up six months before, had been running to catch the train back to Pirbright Camp, with Miller and the others shouting 'Hurry up, you pongo,' from the pavement, and there hadn't been time for more than a mutual grin and a clap on the back, a 'Good luck, old fellow,' and yet it might have been the only time in their lives that they had met as something approaching equals, as men together. Before then, the twelve-year gap had always been unbridgeable, Felix more of a glamorous and joshing uncle than a brother.

Next to Valentine on the pew, Priss dropped her hymnbook and, bending to retrieve it, managed to kick it further away. 'You can share mine,' whispered Valentine. She gave him one of her odd looks, momentary blankness replaced by what looked like a willed change of expression, her features moving carefully into a small, tight smile. Beside her, Kitty sighed and crossed her legs. Neither of the girls appeared in any way grief-stricken – 'Harold explained to us years ago that when someone's "missing in action", it generally means they're dead, so we're used to the idea,' Kitty had said, with studied casualness, after Barbara had broken the news.

'And we don't remember him anyway,' Priss had added.

'Of course we remember him' – Kitty had been scornful – 'you told me yesterday that you dreamed about the time he let you steer the motor-car and you hit that statue. And we both went up in the aeroplane with him. You haven't forgotten that, have you?'

'But that's a . . . a *thing* I remember, not a person. It's like remembering only thunderstorms or days so hot the sidewalks melted, and none of the weather in between.'

And Valentine had found himself nodding, because Felix had always come and gone throughout his own childhood like the genie in the Aylesbury Players pantomime, with a flash-bang and a handful of sparkle-dust.

'And now let us stand and sing hymn number one hundred . . .' The smell of mothballs rose like incense above the creaks and coughs; the first notes of the organ slid from flat to true and Valentine turned slightly from his position in the front pew to glance across at the rows of half-familiar faces, hoping to pinpoint the glimpse of red hair he'd seen earlier and finding himself instead staring directly into the eyes of Eric Harwood, the son of the tenant of Home Farm, who had left Addenham as a ruddy nineteen-year-old and had returned only a week ago from the jungles of Burma with a face of crumpled paper and eyes like ink-blots.

'Uncle Val,' whispered Priss. He turned back to see her holding the hymn-book open between them, and he directed his gaze at the page in the usual automatic pretence, though in any case he had sung that dreary old clunker 'All People That On Earth Do Dwell' a thousand times and could have recited the words in his sleep. Further along the pew, he could see his uncle reaching into a pocket and taking out an ominously thick sheaf of paper; when the vicar, new and nervous, had called at Dimperley to discuss the service, Alaric had immediately volunteered to write a eulogy.

'And perhaps Sir Valentine could give a reading?' the vicar had suggested.

'No, no, no,' called Alaric, who had already crossed over to the writing-desk, to start making notes. 'You can't use the title, I'm afraid.'

The Reverend Fisher had looked confused.

'Apparently I'm not yet on the Official Roll,' said Valentine.

'He's not yet on the Official Roll, so you can't call him "Sir",' called Alaric, who was rather deaf. 'There was a Royal Warrant in 1910 that directed that no person whose name is not entered on the Official Roll of Baronets shall be received as a Baronet or shall be addressed or mentioned by the title in any civil or military Commission, Letters Patent or other official document.'

'Ah, I see,' said the vicar, uncertainly.

'Obviously, I've written a letter to the Registrar of Baronetage, and I hope that, in a few weeks . . .'

'There's no need for a reading,' said Lady Irene, cutting through the verbiage. 'Air Commodore Trewick will be giving an address.'

'I can do a reading,' said Valentine.

There was a familiar pause. His mother never argued; merely opined and then let the subsequent silence batter away at the same theme.

'Or one of the girls could do it,' said Alaric. 'Their father, after all . . .'

'I can do a reading,' repeated Valentine, rather loudly. 'Ecclesiastes Three.'

'Most suitable,' said the vicar, but his gaze had moved uneasily between the speakers, as if trying to locate the source of an unexpected smell.

He was looking at Valentine again now, giving him a tiny nod as the hymn dragged to its close, and Valentine's viscera seemed to shrivel like a punctured football. He stood, and eased past the others in the pew: the girls and Alaric and his mother and a red-eyed Barbara, and crossed to the lectern, where the Bible was already open and bookmarked with a narrow purple ribbon. The congregation sat. Valentine looked at the page. The print was very small, the lines doing their usual impression of a ploughed field, each furrow superficially indistinguishable from the next, their lumpy idiosyncrasies only revealed after prolonged squinting. He took a deep breath and heard his voice emerge, clear and fluent.

'To every thing there is a season, and a time to every

purpose under the heaven: a time to be born, and a time to die; a time to plant, and a time to pluck up that which is planted; a time to kill, and a time to heal; a time to break down, and a time to build up . . .' It had been Mr Harper, the only decent teacher at Umberton, who'd suggested that Valentine should attempt to learn poetry off by heart. 'Once it's stopped skipping about on the page and is sitting in your brain-box, you can begin to appreciate it, like the colours on a pinned butterfly.' And Valentine had found it no more difficult (though not much easier) to memorize words than to read them, and what he had chosen to memorize had fixed itself permanently, so that when the landing-craft had been bucketing through the darkness towards the Sicilian shore, the terror as intense as the nausea, the navy guns pounding so incessantly that there was no beginning and no end to the sound, he had recited Hardy's 'Weathers' ('This is the weather the cuckoo likes, and so do I. When showers betumble the chestnut spikes, and nestlings fly . . .') over and over again. 'Were you praying?' Miller had asked him afterwards, and he supposed that it had been a sort of prayer – an invocation of damp green fields and noisy rooks, that had accompanied him out of the grounded craft, through the chest-high waves, between the bodies that rolled and bobbed like lumber, and on to the shore.

He had kept Ecclesiastes 3, with its lullaby rhythm, for those nights when boredom or fear or mosquitos or Crockett's erratic, explosive snoring had kept him awake; here in St Aelfric's, the words flowed effortlessly – 'a time to weep, and a time to laugh; a time to mourn, and a time to dance; a time to cast away stones, and a time to gather stones together . . .' – so effortlessly, in fact, that as he spoke, he found himself looking up at the congregation to see the effect of his words.

Every pew was full, a sombre sea of black serge, and his gaze skipped between the more noticeable wavelets: the gold-braid-encrusted Admiral in the second row; the pallid bald head of Felix's godfather, Lord Carding; the large white handkerchief with which Mrs Procter, the Addenham post-mistress, was wiping her eyes. '. . . a time to embrace, and a time to refrain from embracing; a time to get, and a time to lose, a time to keep and a time to cast away . . .'

Seated next to the post-mistress was Alaric's secretary, Mrs Baxter, who was watching him with an expression that reminded him uncomfortably of an invigilator. Still speaking – '. . . a time to rend and a time to sew . . .' – he shifted his gaze across the aisle and immediately saw Deedee Manningford, her hair still the colour of a robin's breast (which wasn't actually red; people really didn't look properly – robins were *orange*), but it was cut shorter than he remembered, and brushed up around the edges of a natty black hat. He'd no sooner spotted her than, with solemn deliberation, she stuck out her tongue at him and then the next word didn't arrive.

'. . . a time to . . . to . . .'

A dreadful nothing. A silence that reminded him of the moment when a doodlebug engine cut out and the world below sat waiting for the smash. He looked down at the page, at the impenetrable thicket of lines, and spotted the word 'dance' tangled in the undergrowth, but surely he'd already said 'dance'? And hadn't he also said 'weep' and 'rend' and 'sew' and 'cast away stones'? Which left . . . what? His thoughts thrashed around and lighted on Felix.

'. . . a time to . . . to hunt and a time to . . . to shoot; a time to spend and a time to . . . refrain from spending; a time to . . . turn left and a time to turn right; a time to fly and a time to . . . to . . .' – he'd got himself into a mess with this one – '. . . to . . . to *perch*.' There was an uneasy stirring at the edges of his vision, but just as he thought he would have to cut and run, possibly as far as Watford, the real words came surging back again ('. . . a time to keep silence and a time to speak . . .'), and he rattled through the last few phrases at panicked speed and then flipped the Bible shut as if it were a hated text-book. Looking up, he saw the congregation staring at him with the expression of spectators at a fairground Wall of Death. Apart from his mother, who had her eyes shut.

'Jolly well done,' muttered his uncle, who had presumably heard none of it, as they crossed in the chancel.

As Alaric began to speak, Zena shifted a sleeping Allison into a more comfortable position on her lap. He had asked, after she'd finished typing up the seven pages, whether she thought it would 'do', and she'd ventured to suggest that it was a bit long. He'd actually cut a few paragraphs as a result, which made her wish she had also hinted at the monumental dullness of its content.

He had taken as his theme the continuity of family characteristics, beginning with bravery. After tracing Felix's

pluck through eleven generations, with examples in each,
he'd then repeated the same process for intelligence, ami-
ability and vehicular prowess (horses counting as 'vehicles'
for his purpose) so that the whole thing had a deadly pre-
dictability, like laps in a prison yard. And yet there was gold
in the straw, odd anecdotes and glimpses of character that
might have caught the imagination if only Alaric had been
able to view his family as intermittently intriguing rather
than *important*. Because Zena knew by now that they
weren't; not really, not in the scheme of things – no Vere-
Thissett had ever raised an army, or invented anything, or
written a proper book, or endowed an institution, or even
become a Member of Parliament. And although, when
she'd first arrived, she'd considered the inhabitants of
Dimperley Manor to be the poshest people imaginable
below the rank of royalty, it had turned out that she was
completely wrong. It had been Mrs Procter (who besides
being the post-mistress, and Zena's landlady, had been in
service to the Earl of Waxcombe before her marriage,
something she mentioned often) who had enlightened her:
Dukes came at the top of the pile, then Marquesses, then
Earls, then Viscounts and then Barons, this titled quintet
being the types who swished around in ermine in the House
of Lords. Baronets were in a lower league altogether – 'the
lesser nobility', as Mrs Procter referred to them – though
they were still above those who made their wealth from
trade, a word which Mrs Procter pronounced with disdain,
despite the fact that her brother was a greengrocer. 'And
the Vere-Thissetts are a very old family, of course,' she'd
added, as a concession.

'So what would happen if Lady Irene met a duchess?'
Zena had asked.

'Oh, she'd have to curtsey.'

'She'd snap in half!'

Mrs Procter's reaction to this comment – thin-lipped
disapproval – had been a lesson to Zena: despite their position on the lowest rung of the nobs' ladder, the inhabitants
of the Big House belonged to Addenham, and Addenham
was deeply offended if they were criticized by outsiders
(though quite prepared to give the odd dig itself). So Zena
had kept her opinions private, and merely watched with
fascination, like a spectator attempting to work out the
rules of an obscure sport. Though now there was a new
player on the pitch.

'What's he doing?' she'd mouthed to Mrs Procter, during
the mangling of Ecclesiastes.

'Shell shock, I expect,' Mrs Procter had whispered back,
twirling a finger beside her head to signify loopiness. 'He
might never be right. It happened to my uncle; it took him
five minutes to ask for a pint.'

In the ill-lit church, Valentine's bandaged hand was a
startling white, like a traffic policeman's glove; he no longer
had a sling, but kept the hand pressed defensively against
his midriff. Since their short conversation on the hillside,
Zena hadn't met him again, though she'd seen him in the
distance, wandering the grounds, binoculars round his
neck and his brother Cedric in tow. He'd looked aimless,
rather than loopy; more like a reluctant day-tripper than an
heir.

Alaric had just reached page five of his speech ('. . . which jocular remark of my nephew's reminds one of a merry sally from the lips of the first Baronet . . .') when Allison woke up and loudly demanded a drink. Zena took the chance to escape.

It was warm for late September, the sky the heavily laundered blue of Allison's frock. After they'd played for a while with the tap on the churchyard wall, her daughter set off barefoot through the grass, Zena following her, holding the damp socks and sandals in one hand, and her own hat in the other. From the open window of St Aelfric's leaked the innumerable verses of 'For All The Saints', the last hymn of the service, so there was no need for her to go back inside, thank goodness. She'd had enough of all that stuff; at various points in her childhood she had been required to attend Sunday services at St Dymphna's (Catholic), St Aiden's and St Luke's (both C of E), Pellett Lane Primitive Methodist Chapel, Hoxton Baptist Hall and once, very memorably, the East London Spiritualist Church, where the medium had asked if anyone there knew of a deceased lady with the initial 'P'. Mrs Bate, the woman with whom Zena and her brother, Raymond, had, at that point, been living, had given them a nudge and hissed, 'What was your mother's name?' and Raymond had said, 'That Bitch.' They hadn't stayed very long at *that* foster home.

'Look!' shouted Allison, joyfully, holding up a snail.

'Very nice.'

'I want my bucket.'

'Use this,' said Zena, spotting a flower-pot lying on its side by the wrought-iron cage that surrounded the Gryce family tomb. All the larger monuments were clustered on this side of the graveyard, and most were much uglier than the weathered headstones of the humbler occupants, though none quite as hideous as the Vere-Thissett mausoleum, which looked as if Dracula had commissioned a public convenience. Its door opened suddenly as Zena walked past and the elderly verger came out carrying a broom, a torch and a dust-pan.

'Startled you, did I, Mrs Baxter?' he asked, looking gratified.

'What were you doing?'

'Having a sweep round before they arrive. Making it look tidy.'

'But . . .' Zena peered round him at the slice of darkness. 'Nobody's going in there, are they? Since there's . . . no body.'

'No *body*. That's clever, that is.'

'Thank you.'

He shut the door, turned the key and pocketed it with an air of deliberate mystery.

'Well?' asked Zena.

'I can't say, can I?'

'What do you mean?'

'It's their tomb, they can do what they like with it. It's not up to me. Vicar says they may, so they may.'

'May what?'

He shook his head, mysteriously. 'What's your little maid up to?' he asked, looking past her to where Allison was squatting beside a headstone.

'She's collecting snails. Oh, go on, please tell me, Mr Hastings.'

He paused, as if considering his answer, and then spotted movement at the church door, the starched white of the vicar's surplice, the bobbing black of a top hat, and busied himself by tipping the gritty contents of the dust-pan on to the nearest grave. A breeze picked up the lighter particles and Zena turned away so as not to inhale a swirl of ancestral Vere-Thissett.

'Splendid to see you, Valentine,' said Lord Carding, as the congregation spilled from the porch on to the path, 'albeit on such a fearfully sad occasion. *Sir* Valentine, I should say now, of course.'

'No, no, no,' corrected Alaric, steaming into the conversation. 'The Royal Warrant of 1910 stipulated that no person whose name is not entered on the Official Roll of Baronets shall be received as a Baronet, so you can't yet call him . . .'

'And how's the hand?' asked Lady Carding, extending one of her own solicitously towards the bandage. Valentine reared back as if threatened by a cobra, accidentally shoulder-barging the curate.

'Sorry, sorry,' he said, to the world in general, since, yet again, everyone was staring at him; impossible to explain that his fingertips were so indescribably tender that even the *thought* of anyone touching them brought him out into an icy sweat. 'It's much better, thank you,' he added, to Lady Carding's retreating form.

'Hello, Valentine,' said a dry voice behind him. He turned to see Deedee Manningford and, in the first pleasant surprise of the day, realized that he must have grown since they'd last met and was now taller than her.

'Obviously I shouldn't have done that,' she said. It was more of a statement than an apology, though he found himself replying as if it were the latter.

'It's all right.'

'I don't think it *was* all right. You lost your place and made an absolute pig's bottom of Ecclesiastes. I imagine Felix would have roared.'

'He probably would have, yes.'

'There wasn't much of your brother in that service, was there? That's why I did it, I suppose – I was sitting there, thinking, "Who's this person they're all talking about?" I should have taken a 'plane up and buzzed the church, lobbed a couple of flour bombs at the verger.'

There was no smile accompanying the words, only a sardonic look from those long, narrow eyes that he'd once decided were exactly those of a faun in an Aubrey Beardsley print. He felt the familiar feeling of hopeless lust that her presence had always inspired in him as he'd stood on the fringe of one event or another, too young to dance or drink or even to talk with her. He supposed that she must be thirty or more now, though she didn't look any older than when he'd last seen her; only, he realized, unhappier.

'You've been demobbed?' he asked.

'Yes. In June.'

'I never saw you in uniform.' He realized, as soon as he spoke, how ridiculous that sounded.

'Poor you,' she said. 'Obviously, I looked fabulous.'

'I expect you did,' he said, humbly.

'Oh, come on, Valentine, you must have seen the ATA flying suits. We looked like barrage balloons.'

'What I meant was, we haven't met since I joined up. Could we – could you – I mean, would you like to go for a drink?'

'Now?'

'Well, no, I can't now.' His mood instantly plummeted, thinking of what awaited him at the other end of the churchyard. 'I have to . . .' He couldn't bring himself to tell her. 'A bit of a family occasion. Something my mother's arranged. But next week? Or . . . some time?'

'You're back for good, then?'

Valentine searched around for a word less definitive than 'yes'; something that didn't feel quite so much like the fastening of manacles.

'Yes,' he said.

'And what are you going to do? Now that you're' – she paused slightly – 'in charge.'

'Oh God,' said Valentine, involuntarily. 'Well, I have a meeting with the land agent next week. I suppose we'll have to sell some more fields. To cover the death duties. Someone said there might be gravel under the lake and elsewhere . . .'

She was only half listening, her gaze moving across the thinning crowd; behind them, Alaric was telling someone else about the Register of Baronetage.

'Where's Ceddy?'

'At home with Miss Hersey. Apparently he's developed a

habit of deliberately making . . . well . . . raspberry noises in public.'

She lowered her voice. 'We could have done with a few of those when your uncle was speaking.'

Valentine's snort was loud enough to swivel heads.

'I'm a bad influence,' said Deedee. 'Listen, I'm heading off now, but you must drop by. Inspect the damage.'

'What do you mean?'

'You haven't heard? We had half the army stationed at Chilverton and they . . . well, you'll get the idea when you see it. It's quite the eye-opener. Oh, hello, Barbara.'

'Hello, Deedee.'

There was the cool ruffle of a draught as one woman replaced the other.

'Could I borrow your handkerchief?' asked Barbara. 'Mine's sodden.' She took the proffered square and blotted her eyes. 'I didn't cry until I looked round during the Air Commodore's speech and saw Kitty looking *exactly* like Felix – well, exactly like him before he broke his nose in that smash at the Woodsley Cross-roads – and then I suddenly thought: "What if she takes after him?" She's been asking and asking to drive the Austin, and I saw myself having to start worrying all over again and jumping every time the telephone rang in case it was the police station – it was always that Sergeant with the little crack in his voice so it sounded as if he were about to burst into tears – "I'm afraid there's been another road-traffic accident, Lady Vere-Thissett," and I'd say, "He's dead, isn't he?" – I must have imagined Felix's funeral a dozen times and then, of course, he didn't ever have one . . .' She blew her nose, lengthily. 'Oh, by the way, your mother's asked me to tell you that it's time for the . . . the . . .'

'Right. Are you coming?'

'No, I'm taking the girls to Tring for a cream tea. Kitty was upset enough about the incident as it was, without this . . . this . . . I don't even know what to call it.'

'Ceremony?'

'Travesty,' she said, with unusual firmness.

The small group had assembled outside the Vere-Thissett mausoleum. The whole thing had been his mother's idea. 'He was, after all, Felix's dog. I am not a fanciful woman, but one thinks of the Crusader tombs, of the hound resting at the armoured feet, and it seems fitting.'

'Can you manage, Sir Valentine?' asked Epple, placing the casket on Valentine's outstretched arms.

'No, no, no, I'm afraid that you can't use the title until—'

'*Alaric*,' said Lady Irene. He subsided, and stood back as the verger unlocked the door.

Pollux had spent the last three weeks in the Pavilion of the Four Winds, arranged on a large block of ice delivered from the butcher in Wendover, and was now nailed into a specially made beechwood box, well packed with straw, but a smell of decay moved with him like a pall, and Valentine tried to breathe through his mouth as he followed the verger's torch into the interior.

He had never been inside the tomb before. Opposite the door was an altar, carved with the family crest and bearing a cross and two candlesticks; above it, a pierced window let in a little light. On either side of the narrow aisle were rows of shelves, like bunk-beds, reaching from floor to ceiling. The four on the left were each sealed, forming a flush wall of inscribed marble. The bottom shelf on the right was also sealed, the inscription fresher than the others:

Here lie the mortal remains of
Major Arthur Felix Radley Vere-Thissett MC
Fifth Baronet of Dimperley
Hero of Ypres
Born 4th March 1885
and departed this earth 5th March 1933
Survived by his sorrowing widow and sons.
'With Christ, which is far better'

'Put it on the next one up, Sir Valentine,' said the verger, in a hoarse whisper. Valentine went down on one knee and eased the box on to the second shelf. It looked pathetically small in the long space; where, he wondered, would Felix's feet have been? He pushed Pollux towards the end nearest the altar, and gave the lid a pat with his good hand.

'We brought nothing into this world, neither may we carry anything out of this world,' said the vicar, from the open doorway.

His mother had come in now, holding a sheaf of late roses, followed by Alaric, so that the mausoleum resembled the corridor of a crowded train.

'The Lord giveth and the Lord taketh away. Even as it hath pleased the Lord, so cometh things to pass: blessed be the name of the Lord.'

As his mother placed the flowers on the second shelf,

Valentine stood up and found himself eye-level with the third. He felt the flutter of a passing thought – delicate, ungraspable – and then the breakneck jolt of its return: he was, he realized, staring into his grave. This was the exact surface on which his own coffin would rest; he could almost hear the slither of wood on stone as it was pushed into place, the clink of the marble that bore his epitaph, the scrape of the mortar: Valentine Vere-Thissett, seventh Baronet, no achievements of note, an unmemorable link in an interminable chain. Or perhaps they wouldn't waste a shelf, and he'd be put in with Pollux, walled up for eternity with a Jack Russell. Either way, there'd be no green turf above, no sapling springing from his innards, just a box of bones on a shelf, useless in life, useless in death. Might as well climb in now – in fact, in some ways it was almost tempting; no more expectations, no responsibilities, no-one telling him what to—

'Come along, Valentine,' said his mother.

'Coming.' He unglued himself and walked, blinking, into the sunlight. A few villagers were watching over the churchyard wall, and a small figure stared at him from a couple of yards away, and then pointed.

'Dead doggie man,' she said, and he thought, yes – yes, fair enough; that was a title he could live up to.

It was when they had left the churchyard and were walking towards the tubcart that a man in a blue suit and a trilby came up to Valentine.

'Are you Sir Vere-Thissett?'

'Yes,' said Valentine, before his uncle could interrupt.

Blue Suit held out an envelope. Puzzled, Valentine took it.

'Delivered and accepted,' said the man, turning to go. 'It's from Maple.'

'Who's Maple?'

The chap checked his stride. 'Maple?' he asked over his shoulder, casually but quite loudly, clearly enjoying his work. 'You don't know who Maple is? Maple's the bailiff.'

6

Dear Lady Vere-Thissett,

I wonder whether we might arrange a meeting to discuss your daughters' progress at the school.

Last week, Miss Sudderby, a _very_ experienced teacher, came to me in some distress and showed me the enclosed story, written by Priscilla. Conversely, Kitty's teacher has been unable to provide me with any of her written work whatsoever, since none has been completed.

Yours sincerely,

N. Gilbert, Headmistress,

Gwendoline Chailey Day School for Girls

THE GHOST
By Priscilla Maud Jennifer Vere-Thissett, Class IIB

'Whatever you do, don't go down to the cellar,' said the faithful old retainer to Alicia Forbishore. Alicia, aged twelve, had recently moved with her family from a smart pied-à-terre in London to Eglemont Castle, high on a hill in a wild region of the North Country.

'Why shouldn't I go to the cellar?' she asked, with a merry, insouciant laugh. The old retainer shook her matted locks and looked at Alicia with rheumy eyes.

'The story goes that many a year ago, the Lord of the Castle borrowed three hundred gold pieces from a wicked friend of his to build a new jousting-list so that he could hold tournaments, but then the Lord went off to The Crusades and died from the cruel thrust of a Saracen sword and nobody wanted to rent or preferably buy the jousting-list so the family couldn't pay back the three hundred gold pieces. The wicked friend was shaken with rage and he put a curse on the Castle. The curse said that anyone who goes to the cellar after midnight will suffer a horrible fate.'

Alicia gave another merry laugh – she was a modern girl, and she wasn't afraid of silly ideas. That night she set her alarm-clock for 1 a.m., and when it rang, she got up, took her torch and quietly and carefully went down the stairs and all through the Castle to the cellar. The steps downwards were narrow and slippery, and when she reached the bottom, all she could see was a dark, empty stone dungeon. But then, from one of the shadowy corners, she heard a hideous rasping breath.

She shone the torch at it, but before she could scream, a huge grey, slimy lizard with razor-sharp teeth and claws like meat-skewers leaped towards her and started to attack her, crushing her neck between its hideous, blood-soaked, vicious jaws that dripped lethal venom into the gaping wounds and so Alicia died horribly.

THE END

'Who is that person?' asked Lady Irene, looking out of the West-facing window of her dressing-room. The sky was a hard, clear blue and blasts of cold air were forcing their way around the frame. On the far side of the moat,

on which the duck-weed had been herded to one end by an
overnight storm, Sir Valentine stood in conversation with a
sandy-haired young man who was holding a large bucket.

'That's Mr Epple's nephew,' said Hersey. 'He's helping
out in the garden. He left the Royal Navy last month.'
Where he'd served as the Captain of a minesweeper, though,
in the circumstances, Hersey thought it was tactful not to
mention his rank. 'He seems a nice, respectful young man,'
she added. 'He told me how very grateful he was to be
given this chance and how he'd always wanted to work at
Dimperley.' In actual fact, Roy Epple had said within her
earshot that it was only a fill-in while he looked around for
a proper job, but after the past, painful weeks, she felt it her
duty to lift Lady Irene's spirits.

'Will you be wearing a brooch with that, my Lady? Perhaps the tourmaline?'

There was a clatter from behind them, where Ceddy was
sorting through his treasure box. A tortoiseshell button
rolled across the floor and Hersey stooped to pick it up.

Lady Irene examined herself in the looking-glass, touching the collar of the grey georgette. 'No, the pearl pin, I
think. And the felt with the matching band.'

'That's still in my sewing room, my Lady – it needed a
steam. I'll go and fetch it now.'

Irene turned back to the window. The conversation
between the seventh Baronet and The Man with the Bucket
was continuing. Of course, it was entirely acceptable for
the head of the house to talk to an under-gardener, but
such an encounter should consist of instruction on one side
and deference on the other, and what she was witnessing

clearly came under the heading of a 'chat'. Either man could have been holding the bucket.

That could never have been said of Felix, whose easy, jovial authority had been visible, almost tangible, from a hundred yards. Nor of Cedric – the Cedric who lived forever in her mind, in parallel to the Cedric who was currently sorting buttons – the Cedric whose endearingly dreamy air belied the sharpness of his intellect and who had, in her imagination, spent the war engaged in crucial scientific research . . .

The window rattled again and a gust blew Valentine's cap off. He trudged away to retrieve it, while Epple's nephew put down the bucket and lit a cigarette.

Before the catastrophe of Ceddy's illness, before war began to wink on the horizon, it hadn't greatly mattered that the youngest of her boys was, from whichever angle one viewed him, faintly disappointing; by the time of Valentine's birth, she had already been twice blessed – the older two so lissom and bright, so thoroughly brushed with gold that perhaps there had been none left in the fairy paint-pot for a third. A page after two princes was no great disaster; the Vere-Thissett line was assured – so she had thought, so had they all thought, but, like a makeweight entry in the Grand National that had hung behind the field, steered through the thinner sections of hedge and ambled past the fallen champions, Valentine had scooped the prize. The future of the family was now in the hands of a young man who'd not only been described by his prep school headmaster as 'a complete blockhead, I'm afraid, Lady Vere-Thissett' but who was also unfortunately lacking in either personal magnetism or the sort of skills that were needed for the forging and maintenance of useful connections. He was, as his father had noted, a poor rider, a below-average shot, an indifferent golfer and 'rather unfortunately, the image of my Uncle Fenwick', though Irene had been unable to confirm the latter since every picture of Uncle Fenwick had been removed from the family album after the incident with the bearer bonds and he had died in Penang while in the company of a woman to whom he was not married.

So that now, when the urgent requirement was for confidence, leadership and shrewd alliance, all that Valentine had to offer was a parroting of official gloom, the refrain 'the solicitor told me' running through his every conversation, when clearly the required phrase should have been the emphatic 'I told the solicitor'. And Alaric was as useless as always, his sole suggestion having been to search the attics for saleable items, as if the Koh-i-noor diamond might be tucked away between the stuffed owls.

Amidst all the ridiculous talk of land sales and trusts and leases, the traditional method of saving a house seemed not to have occurred to anyone but herself. Not that it would be easy: she would need to take the reins, navigate the course and (to use a hideous phrase of Barbara's) make the best of a bad job.

She had a sudden urge to make a list.

'Hersey, could you bring me . . .' Her maid, she realized, had not yet returned. She rang the bell, and waited.

Hersey had been waylaid on her return from the sewing room; these days, her duties to Lady Irene were repeatedly overlapped and postponed by tasks that would once have fallen to others. Sometimes she felt like the dollies that she snipped for Mr Cedric from a pleated length of newspaper – a stretched chain of lady's maids, thinly hurrying.

'We're planning an *inventory*, but the West attic is locked,' Mr Alaric had said, and together with Mrs Baxter and her daughter, he had followed Hersey to the basement, passing through the green baize door and along the cork-lined corridor that was supposed to protect the ears of the upper house from the bustle and clatter, the constant bells and footsteps, the swish and clang of the kitchen.

The housekeeper would once have kept the keys on her belt, but they were now in a drawer in the butler's pantry, and Hersey sorted through the paper labels until she found the correct one. She could hear Allison running, unreproved, from room to room and shouting, 'Echo, ECHO,' in the empty servants' hall.

Imagine, thought Hersey, what Mr Lemons would have said about behaviour like that. Of course, the children of the house had sometimes been sent downstairs to deliver messages, or to beg for a handful of currants between meals, but even Felix had known better than to misbehave. Not that Mr Lemons had been a killjoy, of course, but like all butlers he had expected a certain propriety. No horseplay on the premises, and certainly no *bellowing*.

'Here it is,' she said, passing the key to Mr Alaric. 'I don't suppose it's been used for a while. Let me find you a little pot of grease, just in case.'

'Awfully kind.'

They passed through the kitchen and found Mrs Baxter

already in the scullery, twirling the handle of the Kent patent knife-grinder. 'I've never seen one of these in real life before,' she remarked. 'I once read a detective story where the murderer used it to sharpen his weapon.'

'You'll damage the mechanism if you don't put emery powder in first,' said Hersey. 'Excuse me,' she added, pointedly, feinting a step towards the supplies cupboard.

Mrs Baxter moved aside, but Hersey was conscious of her gaze as she searched for the grease pot amongst the remaining tins of polish (furniture, floor, boot, brass, silver), the half-empty jar of soft soap, the depleted packet of soda, the empty box of dried tea-leaves for the rugs, the single bar of yellow scrub where once there had been a shelf-full.

'How that woman *stares*,' Lady Irene had once remarked to Hersey. 'I suppose that if one has always lived in the most frightful slums then one might find one's current circumstances a source of awe.' But it never seemed to Hersey that Mrs Baxter's expression could be defined as 'awe', exactly. Curiosity, possibly. Fascination. Even bafflement. And sometimes, when Hersey had been hurrying past her, or had visited Alaric's study with a note or a message or a tray, she'd seen something that looked very much like condescension or even *pity* flitting across the woman's features, as if Hersey were a tweeny, as if all the current skimping and rushing and doubling-up was the way her life in service had been spent, as if the house had always been like this. 'You haven't the slightest idea,' she wanted to say, and she'd thought of showing Mrs Baxter the set of scrap-books in the sewing room that she'd been compiling since 1919, the photographs cut from the *Tatler* and *Country Life*, the wedding-parties attended, the shooting weekends, Lady Irene always so elegant (so *soignée*, as Sir Arthur had liked to say), always the focus of compliments that she would kindly and invariably pass on to Hersey – 'Lady Barnes was complaining about her own lady's maid, and asked if I would ever part with you, and I said, "Not for a thousand pounds." ' The sewing room had been a bower of silks and jacquards and feathers and trims, and if anyone had told her that one day she would be cutting up one of Sir Arthur's waistcoats to provide a new hat-band for her ladyship, or using re-dyed blackout material – actual *curtains*! – to make matching coats and dresses for the grand-children to wear at a memorial service, then she wouldn't have believed them. Until the start of the war she had not lit a fire, or cooked and served a meal, or answered a door, or washed a plate or used a mangle for more than twenty years. Her role had been exclusive and exacting and appreciated; it had had *glamour*.

She found the grease pot, and transferred a blob into an empty match-box.

'Thank you, Miss Hersey,' said Mr Alaric, who was always polite. Mrs Baxter called her daughter, and after a few seconds Allison trotted out of the pantry and was swung on to her mother's hip and carried up the stairs. 'Whatever have you been doing?' Hersey heard Mrs Baxter ask. 'Your hands are filthy,' and when Hersey went in to check, she found a row of keys on the floor. They were leaning against the skirting board in order of size, and there was a little heaped-up pinch of woolly dust in front of each of them, like a dinner plate.

As she returned to her ladyship's dressing-room, up the

West stairs and along the Gallery, every finger-mark on the bannister, every line of grime on the picture frames seemed more than ever noticeable. There was no point in saying anything to Mrs Parnaby, who was supposedly responsible for the cleaning, since she always responded to criticism not with the shame or embarrassment that might be expected, but by immediately handing in her notice and then having to be placated at length before rescinding; as she frequently pointed out, there were ten other ladies in the district who would employ her in an instant. She worked at the house three days a week, cycling from Addenham on a large black tricycle, while Mrs Skates walked over from the East Lodge on week-day mornings to do the rough, and Mrs Alley, the laundress, took the bus from Wendover on Tuesdays and Fridays and occasionally on Mondays.

When Hersey had first arrived at Dimperley as a fifteen-year-old, there had been an indoor-staff of twenty-seven, and now no-one outside the family (besides herself) actually lived at the house any longer. All the male servants had gone within weeks of the start of the war; the women had followed more slowly, some to factories and some to the forces, but even before the main house had been requisitioned, half the rooms had already been closed off, the furniture sheeted, the muslin-swathed chandeliers hanging like laundry bundles from the rafters.

When the expectant mothers had arrived, Hersey had been quite pleased to move to the Dower Wing, where some semblance of normal life had remained: the silver on the table, Lady Irene dressing for dinner, even though that dinner had usually consisted of rabbit in some form, or of vegetables with a cheese sauce, and had been prepared either by Lady Barbara or by Hersey herself.

All along, she had assumed – or perhaps merely hoped – that once the war was over, the house would resume its old life, but the page of the *Bucks Herald* on which, last month, Lady Barbara had placed an advertisement for an experienced cook with impeccable references was entirely filled with pleas for kitchenmaids and parlourmaids, companions and housekeepers, the same tempting wording repeated week after week – *cheerful family, modern house, electric vacuum-sweeper available* – and it seemed to Hersey that something vital had changed, like a sprung door that would never again close properly.

Nearing the dressing-room, she could hear the tinkle of the porcelain bell which, since the disconnection of the electric system, her ladyship was wont to use, unaware that it was completely inaudible from more than a dozen yards away.

'Sorry, my Lady,' she said, arriving a little breathless and inspecting the grey felt to make sure that it had remained pristine during its journey through the house. 'Mr Alaric needed an errand.'

'Can you remember the age of Viscount Brearley's younger daughter?'

'The one who married the French gentleman?'

'Oh, did she? Never mind, then.' Her ladyship crossed through something she'd written in a tiny silver-backed notebook of the sort young ladies used for listing dance partners. 'And could you bring me all the copies we have of *Country Life* and the *Bucks and Chiltern Observer*?'

'I'm afraid that most of them went in the last salvage drive.'

'Did they? How tiresome.'

'I'll see what I can find, my Lady.'

'Thank you, Hersey. I shall be in the Morning Room.' Her ladyship took the hat and, turning to her reflection, carefully put it on.

'What do you think?'

Hersey moved closer and tilted her head, so that she was looking into the mirror at almost the same angle as her ladyship, their faces side-by-side. They were much the same height, and age, their eyes almost the same shade of blue, their figures so similar that Hersey could use her own waist and hip size when adjusting patterns for her ladyship.

It had been Mr Lemons, the butler, who'd remarked that they could have been sisters. 'Separated at birth,' he'd said – just as a little joke, of course, in the privacy of the housekeeper's sitting room – but Hersey had carefully pre-served the phrase in her memory, taking it out occasionally, to wonder at and enjoy.

'It's very nice, my Lady. It matches perfectly.'

'It does, doesn't it?'

Their reflections smiled at each other.

'Now, Ceddy,' said Lady Irene, taking her gloves from the dressing-table, 'are you ready for your walk?'

From outside came the sound of tearing gravel.

'It's a horse,' said Ceddy, standing so suddenly that the treasure box tipped over.

'No, it's the motor-car,' said Irene. The baby Austin nosed round the corner from the stables and then stalled, jerking forward half a foot. The side window dropped, and a hatless Barbara stuck her head out.

'Yoo hoo!' she shouted across the moat. 'Are you coming, Valentine?'

Irene watched her son lope over to the ridiculous vehicle – more like a clockwork toy than a motor-car – and insert himself into the front seat. As it set off again, it became apparent that the back window was partially obscured by a piebald veil of bird-lime; thus adorned would the seventh Baronet and the Dowager Lady Vere-Thissett shortly be appearing in public view.

Irene turned away and began to fasten her glove-buttons; what her daughter-in-law (who had chosen the Austin) never seemed to understand was that, as a member of a titled family, one was forever on display. Each undignified appearance, each informality of speech, each pair of *slacks* was a piece chipped from the plinth on which the family stood. Without elevation, there was no respect; without respect, there was nothing to stop Mrs Featherstone, Deputy Head of the Preserves Committee, from loudly calling, 'Come on, Lady I, join in the fun!' from the conga line at the Wendover Victory Celebrations, a line in which Barbara could be observed clutching the waist of the post-mistress, while being herself clung to by a man who sold horse drench from a van.

'There we are,' said Hersey, straightening up. 'All the treasures back in the box. Though I'm afraid that one of the pretty snail shells got broken.'

'What a shame.' Irene held out her hand to Ceddy. 'Come along, then. Let's see if we can find another.'

7

The whole road surface as far as the East Lodge was in a dreadful state, and Valentine jammed his good hand against the roof to keep level as they lurched between the potholes. His sister-in-law steered with immense concentration, her knuckles white, her gaze rigid.

'When did you learn to drive?'

'When the chauffeur left. It was just before Dunkirk, I think, and he told everyone he was joining the marines, and then it turned out that he was driving a tea van around an air-base in Cheadle.'

A sheep was standing in the road next to the Pavilion of the Four Winds; Barbara pipped the absurd little horn and it gave a panicky leap and then hurtled ahead of them for twenty yards, before veering off towards the lake.

'I hate it, actually. I'm not very good at it. The Bentley was far too wide for me and then the garage lent me a Rover and I kept getting my foot stuck under the brake, and then they came up with this, which I can manage, though your mother always closes her eyes for the entire journey – in fact, she'd always much rather take the pony-trap.'

'Couldn't Uncle have learned?'

'He told me he didn't have the time. Did you drive in the army?'

'Only a Bren carrier. In the desert. It was quite fun.' He'd spent weeks training in Qassasin, racing up and down dunes, learning how to build a fire by pouring petrol into a jar of sand, and then the whole regiment had been shipped out again and sent to Caithness, having not heard so much as a rifle shot; most of the war had been like that for him – a succession of camps: boiling, freezing, dusty, knee-deep in mud, fizzing with insects or surrounded by damp crows. Orders would arrive and off they'd go, theirs not to reason why, theirs but to eat Spam pie, as Miller had liked to say.

'You know, I wanted to join the services,' said Barbara. 'There was no reason why I shouldn't have, with the girls away.'

'So why didn't you?'

She showed the whites of her eyes, like a fox-hound spotting the whip. 'Your mother said that Felix wouldn't approve.'

'Why wouldn't he?'

'He thought that uniforms made women look ridiculous.'

'Did he? Remind me to show you a sketch of my platoon in full desert kit, if you want to know the definition of "ridiculous".'

'And also she thought that it was our duty to set an example to the villagers by leading the local war effort.'

Valentine had a brief vision of his mother and Barbara running across Addenham Green with sharpened pikes. 'So what did you do?'

'I was – I still am – Chairman of the Savings Committee and the Preserves Committee and I'm Deputy Chairman of the Evacuees Entertainment Committee, though of course they've all gone back now, thank *God*, and I'm on the Salvage Committee and the Autumn Show Committee and I collect for the Spitfire Fund and I'm in the Forces Comforts Circle. Which is mostly knitting. Which I'm not very good at.'

'And what about my mother? What does she do?'

They were passing beneath the first trees of the lime avenue, bands of shade blinking across the interior of the Austin, and for a few moments Barbara drove in silence, moving her jaw as if sucking an unpleasant lozenge. 'She opens things,' she said, at last. 'Ploughing competitions. Fetes. Fund-raising musical evenings. Sometimes she presents the prizes. She says a few words and receives a bunch of flowers.'

'So she's not on any committ—'

'*No.* No, she is not on any committees. And what's so – so galling' – she slowed right down to negotiate the shallow crater that covered the entire drive between the griffon-topped gateposts – 'is that even though I'm the person spending hours and hours and hours going from one dreary thing to another, it's your mother that everyone thinks is marvellous. "Oh look, there's Lady Irene, doesn't she look lovely, isn't she splendid, so brave, such a brick to turn out for the Harvest Supper?" Meanwhile, I'm still in the kitchen at the Village Hall, chopping my three-hundredth apple and . . . oh *damn*!' The lurch this time was different in quality, the familiar slump and skid of a puncture. 'Oh bloody, bloody, bloody hell, I have to be at the school for twelve thirty.' She slapped the dashboard with the flat of her hand and the hooter gave a tiny bleat.

'Do you have a spare?'

'No.' Valentine felt a spurt of relief; at least he wouldn't have to stand around helplessly while Barbara attempted to change the wheel. In the sudden silence, he could hear a chaffinch, just feet away. He levered himself out of the car and saw the rose blur of it, springing from the hedgerow and alighting again, a few yards further along.

'We'll just have to walk to Addenham,' said Barbara. 'The butcher's son runs a taxi service when he can get the petrol.' She took her handbag and set off at a determined lick, and Valentine had to hurry to catch her up. The lane rounded a corner and dived downhill, sinking between hedges that were just beginning to turn, the hazel leaves freckled and perforated, a field maple like a spill of yellow paint. Birds fidgeted amongst the haws.

'There's a motor coming,' said Valentine, hearing a sputter from behind, 'maybe it can give us a lift,' and he stood in the centre of the lane as a grey van appeared over the brow of the hill.

It came to a halt a few yards away, and there was a long pause before the driver – a squarely built man in his forties, with a head of frothy grey curls – opened the door. 'Good morning,' he said cautiously, his gaze shifting from Valentine to Barbara and then swiftly back again.

'We've had a puncture – you probably saw the Austin by the road – and my sister-in-law has quite an important meeting to get to. Could you possibly drive us at least as far as Addenham? Sorry, the name's Vere-Thissett.'

'Haxall,' said the man. 'Yes. Yes, I can do that. Of course I can. Climb in.' He sounded curiously wooden, as if he were reading the words from a script.

'Thank you.' Valentine had already opened the passenger door before he realized that Barbara was still standing a few yards away, by the side of the lane.

'What's the matter?' he asked.

'Oh, nothing.' She walked towards him rather stiffly.

'After you,' said Valentine, gesturing to the door.

'No, you get in first.'

'But I'll probably get *out* first.'

'But you're going to Chilverton – that's further.'

'Yes, but I can get out at the crossroads and walk across the Common.'

Barbara pulled an unreadable face and then lowered her voice. 'I *don't want* to go in the middle.'

'Oh.' Valentine glanced across at Haxall, who was sitting behind the wheel, staring straight ahead. 'OK.'

It was quite a small van, and Valentine sat thigh to meaty thigh with the driver. A heavy chemical smell hung in the air, and underneath it a delicate whiff of animal shit.

'Are you . . . er . . . delivering?' he asked, after no-one had spoken for at least a minute.

'I am, yes.'

'Delivering what?'

'Fourteen boxes of Poultry Spice for Ashford Farm and a case of horse drench for a stable in Bradfield. And a basket of puppies, though that's just a favour for a customer.'

'So you're in the business of . . .'

'Haxall's Reliable Remedies for Livestock and Poultry, Conditioning and Anti-Parasite Treatment a speciality.'

'Ah.'

'Long name, isn't it?'

'Yes, it's pretty long.'

'Ask Benny.'

'What?'

'That's what everyone calls the business. "Ask Benny".'

'Who's Benny?'

'It's me. Benny Haxall. After I started up, someone said nobody would remember all those words and I ought to have a motto. Like the ones they have in advertisements: "Bovril for Strength" – you know the sort of thing?'

' "My Goodness My Guinness".'

'That's it! So I thought of one and had it painted on the van: "Ask Benny". It was the best thing I ever did.'

'And what do you get asked about?'

Haxall gave an easy grin, his earlier awkwardness all forgotten. 'Everything. I'd swear to God, you'd laugh if you knew. I get asked about blimmin' everything, don't I, Babs? And when I—'

He stopped speaking abruptly, his remark terminating in a sort of strangulated croak, while, on the other side of Valentine, Barbara jerked back as if pinned to the seat by an Apache arrow. The word 'Babs' seemed to dangle in the air between them, almost visible.

'Oh look, here's the crossroads,' said Valentine, with relief.

He watched the van drive off; the puppies had apparently woken during the last halt, and a thin yapping accompanied the diminishing noise of the engine; when the sound had entirely disappeared, to be replaced by the low moan of sheep, he found himself laughing.

There were donkeys on the Common as well as sheep,

and one of them placed itself ahead of him, so that he had to stop and rub the downy nose that butted at his pocket. Miss Hersey had this week presented him with a right-hand chamois-leather glove, the three middle fingers padded at the end with cotton wool, and as he walked on, along one of the narrow paths that webbed the cropped grass, he realized that his fingertips no longer flared with pain at every footfall and that he could swing his arms naturally for the first time since Miller had wielded the mallet. He still, however, couldn't do anything remotely delicate or useful: he held his dinner knife as though it were a poker, and when he'd had to sign a couple of letters at the solicitor's, his nib wavering across the paper like a dowsing rod, he'd wondered fleetingly whether he'd be the first Vere-Thissett to have to mark his name with an X. Drawing was impossible. He would have liked to draw.

The donkey, he realized, was following him, keeping pace as the path skirted a series of low, grassy mounds that interleaved, so that the brambled ditch that ran between them was a tight zig-zag. He'd played there as a little boy – could remember stumping through the decayed leaves at the bottom while Felix jumped back and forth over his head. It had been years before he'd found out that they were trenches, dug during the Great War by officers in training, and even longer before he'd linked those muddy hollows to his father's dreadfully slow walk, to the soft rattle of his exhalations, to the dugout in Belgium where his lungs had been fretted by mustard gas. Even his speech had been slow, a wheezy pause between every sentence, so that the discussion of something important, a poor school report for instance, might stretch out over a great many minutes. By the time that Valentine was ten, a wheeled chair had been kept downstairs, and his father had had no breath left for conversations with small boys. Alaric had pushed him back and forth in the Orangery, back and forth, for hours at a time, neither of the men speaking.

'Off you go,' said Valentine, to the donkey, after it had nudged him in the back; it stood and watched as he climbed over the stile into Malden's Wood, and took a path that led downhill between colossal beeches, the ground beneath them pebbled with mast. Where the trees gave way to a shrubby slope, he caught a glimpse of Chilverton, the long, pale, pillared frontage reflected in a perfect oval lake, a view famous from a thousand prints and tea-pots, but it wasn't until he ducked under the low branches of a hawthorn and reached the parkland edge that he saw what was on the opposite side of the lake: row upon row of Nissen huts, the dark green paint etched with rust, the tracks of vehicles like muddy calligraphy looping across the greensward. The faint plink of metal on metal was audible.

'How did you find me?' asked Deedee, when he tracked her down to the stables. She was sitting in the driving seat of a wheel-less, roofless Daimler, smoking a cigarette.

'There was an old fellow trying to dismantle a Nissen and he suggested looking here.'

'How's he getting on?'

'I don't think his heart's in it. He needs a crowbar and he only has a claw hammer.'

'I've been trying to fix that thing,' she said, nodding over at an Alvis that stood with its bonnet open. 'Are you any good with engines?'

'No.'

'I think it's the points. Can't do much without a feeler gauge.' She stood up abruptly. 'Come on, I'll show you round.'

She was wearing a stained boiler suit, belted with a length of twine, and he wanted to sketch her exactly as she was, rising from the Daimler like Venus from her shell.

'So who was stationed here?' he asked, following her out of the stables.

'Who wasn't? Eighteen different regiments, Parry thinks. That's the man you saw – he's supposed to be the gardener. He was the only person who stayed. The army requisitioned the whole place, inside and out. See Long Wood over there?' She gestured at a fir plantation that curved around the North side of the park. 'They used it as an ammunition dump – it's completely sealed off, full of phosphorus bombs, apparently.' The intermittent clang of Parry's hammer continued as they walked around the outside of the house towards the exterior double staircase that led to the main entrance; Chilverton was built on a grand scale and lacked the barnacled effect of Dimperley, where a new wing or turret had been glued on every century or so; here all was height, uniformity and golden-grey harmony, the careful symmetry broken only by a run of boarded-up windows.

'The Lancasters played indoor cricket,' said Deedee, nodding her head at the damage. She pushed open the front door.

'Oh, we have those too,' said Valentine: a semi-circle of marble nymphs gazed down from their alcoves at a thicket of iron bedsteads, 'though not quite so many.'

'They were supposed to be picked up last week. Nobody came. Smell anything?'

'Mould?'

'They only used half the house so no-one noticed when a down-pipe got blocked.' She led him through a succession of state rooms, the walls bare, the furniture often pushed into a corner to make room for desks, the blackouts still fixed, with just a corner or two pulled away to let in the light. The smell grew stronger.

'Here,' she said, easing open one of a pair of enormous doors. 'Don't go in, it's too dangerous.'

Cautiously, he peered round. It was the ballroom, its floor mounded with broken plaster and filth, its ceiling, thirty feet above, largely missing, exposing ranks of blackened laths. Although the windows were unshuttered, the light within the room seemed tinged with green, as if in a submerged wreck.

'Christ.'

'The damp's made the floor lift so that it feels like a mattress if you try to walk across it.' She closed the door again. 'The same thing's happened to all the rooms in the South corridor upstairs. One of them's entirely full of orange mushrooms.'

'But what will happen? Will there be any compensation?'

'Supposedly, but apparently Francis says it's a drop in the ocean compared to what's needed and he'll probably sell.'

'Sell what?'

'The *house*. So you can regard this as a valedictory visit.' She was off again, heading up a corridor that led to a back staircase.

'I don't understand. I don't know who Francis is,' said Valentine.

'My second cousin. The one who's going to inherit when Daddy dies.'

'Oh. Oh, I see. So where would you go?'

'Haven't the foggiest.'

'And . . . how is your father?'

'He didn't recognize me the last time I went to see him. The nursing home says that visitors agitate him and they'd rather I didn't go. Unless I'm called. Which will probably be rather soon.' She continued up a second flight of stairs and then led him along a narrow, uncarpeted corridor. At the end was another staircase.

'Where are we going?' asked Valentine.

'The only bit of the house that hasn't changed.'

The steps ended at a blank doorway. Deedee opened it and they were on the roof, in a blast of breezy sunlight. Startled, a crow launched itself from the leads just beside them and balanced for a moment at eye-height before tilting away to settle on one of the chimneys. It had left a wing feather behind, and Valentine stooped to pick it up before looking round to see where Deedee had gone.

'Don't,' he said.

'Don't what?'

A waist-high balustrade ran all the way around the perimeter of the house, punctuated at ten-foot intervals by winged classical statues. Deedee had stepped on to the pedestal of the nearest and was standing with an arm round its lichened waist.

'Please get down,' said Valentine.

'You don't mind heights, do you?'

'You've just spent twenty minutes showing me how the house is falling apart. I don't suppose anyone's cemented that thing in two hundred years.'

'I climbed on its shoulders once, when I was a child. Do you think I could still do that?'

'Of course not.'

'Is that a dare?'

'*No.*' He thought of Pollux, two-dimensional in death. 'Please get down, Deedee.'

'This is where I saw my first aeroplane, when I was about eight. A Curtiss Robin. It flew right over the house, and the pilot waved at me.' She jumped back on to the tiles and started walking clockwise around the perimeter. Valentine followed her. 'I don't know what to do with myself,' she said. 'The days seem about a hundred hours long. In the Auxiliary, every time I blinked it was a different month. Do you ever miss the army?'

'Miss it? No. At least not the square-bashing, or the drill or the . . .' He tailed off; the shabby truth was that the only thing he truly missed was the ease of not having to make any decisions, of being borne along without effort, like two legs of a millipede. 'You can still go flying, though,' he said. 'Can't you?'

'Yes, I could take an aircraft up, but that's just a jaunt, isn't it? It's not important, it doesn't matter, I don't have a deadline, I don't have to plot a route to avoid being shot down by my own side, I won't be flying that particular model for the very first time, I won't have to strap the instruction manual to my leg so I can read it in flight, I won't have to deliver it to Ayrshire and land there at twilight and then take a night train all the way back to London and arrive at Waltham still carrying my kit and my parachute just in time to get a chit to take another one up. I won't be flying something that's urgently needed. I won't be useful or welcomed. I won't see the shock on the chaps' faces when they see who's just climbed out of a Halifax after a landing in filthy weather. I won't fly a Spitfire straight out of the factory and feel as if I could loop the moon. It won't be a *job*, it'll be a hobby, it'll only ever be a hobby – I was stupid enough to think I could transfer to a commercial airline, but now there are queues of pilots, aren't there? Hordes of them. Men who trained during the war. No-one's going to employ a woman when they can give a job to a returning hero. So what am I going to do?'

She turned, unexpectedly, so that Valentine almost bumped into her. 'I mean, really, what am I going to *do*?' she demanded, and though she was so close that he could smell the cigarette smoke on her breath, she seemed to be staring straight through him and out the other side, as if the answer might be sky-written over Long Wood.

'Well, you could . . .' He groped unproductively for an answer; here was Deedee Manningford, clearly unhappy and asking, *begging*, for his help, and all he could think about was the tiny freckle that he'd never noticed before, just above her upper lip.

He tried again. 'You could – I mean, I expect you could . . .' The wind kept lifting and then dropping a strand of her hair, fanning the fine copper threads across her cheek. '. . . you could – if you wanted to – you could get married? We could. I mean. Get married. If you wanted.'

Had he said that? Had he actually said that? For a moment he wasn't sure, but then Deedee's gaze shifted and she was looking at him, properly, intensely, her pupils widening. A tiny blister of hope formed on his heart.

And burst. 'Oh, don't be so ridiculous, Valentine. I don't want *you*,' she said, and abruptly started weeping.

He took a step back. 'I'm sorry. God, I'm sorry.' He felt around in his pocket for a handkerchief, found only a bent crow feather, and stood there, helpless, useless. For what felt like an hour, she stayed with her hands over her face, little gasps of pain escaping between the fingers, and then she turned away and wiped her eyes on a sleeve.

'I'm sorry,' said Valentine, yet again. 'I wasn't thinking. All this time . . . I mean, I suppose there must have been someone – someone you lost.'

She jerked her head round to look at him. 'It was Felix, you fathead,' she said. 'Didn't you know?'

'No.'

'We've been lovers for years. And years. Ever since I learned to fly at Woodsley. Look, I have to wash my face and then I need to go and hit something or drive somewhere. So if you could find your own . . .' She was crying again. She turned and walked away and Valentine watched her go, and then cautiously rested his elbows on the balustrade and listened to Parry's hammer. After a while, he dropped the feather he'd been holding. Instead of wafting poetically to earth, it fell in a straight line and lodged in the guttering a couple of yards below him. He watched it twitch in the wind.

Concealed by the bus shelter, Kitty saw her mother climb inelegantly out of a grey van, straighten her coat, drop her gloves, pick them up and then head towards the visitors' gate of the Gwendoline Chailey Day School for Girls. It was the same gate through which Kitty had exited just ten minutes before, while the lunch-time bell was still ringing.

Pupils were not allowed to leave the school premises during the day for any reason whatsoever, short of being carried off in an ambulance, something that had actually happened to Kitty's classmate Bonita Astley just a week ago, after she'd been knocked unconscious by a lacrosse throw-in. Kitty, who on her second day at the school had pointed out that in the USA the sport was played only by grown men, had felt vindicated as a moaning Bonita was loaded on to the stretcher. Play, meanwhile, had continued, girls with mottled blue legs thundering like hippos over the frozen mud, grunting as they hurled the ball across the crowded pitch at head height.

The lacrosse sticks themselves were horrible objects, the leather lattice slathered with grease, the wooden frame scarred and stained (almost certainly with blood). 'Those are not hygienic,' she'd said to the PE teacher, who had laughed and sent her to detention again. The girls in her form had used this as yet another example of her gutlessness – 'Kitty Severe-Cissy', as she'd been dubbed, as soon as it was discovered that she'd 'run away' to America during the war. They had no interest in her experiences and in fact two of them had made up a song to which a new verse was added whenever she mentioned anything about her life there.

> When I was in Californ-i-a
> There was steak for every meal.
> We all had fifteen bathrooms
> And my school taught sex-appeal.

This was after she told them about the sophomore class in which, for once, girls and boys had been separated, and they'd been taught about the personal grooming necessary for adolescents. She'd intended the anecdote as a hint, aimed at the universal spotty lumpishness of her formmates, the swinging plaits that ended in a puff of split ends, the flaky partings, the ink-stained fingers, the odour billowing from arm-pits that had never encountered an anti-perspirant. 'A dee-odey-*what*?' Carys Clark had screeched, derisively, when Kitty had tried to explain about Odorono and the first rule of long-lasting charm. In this country, it seemed, grooming was only for horses and guinea-pigs.

Her mother disappeared through the visitors' gate and the grey van drove off. A few minutes later, exactly as the second hand on the school clock jerked to half past, Kitty spotted the boy from the grammar school. He was crossing the road by the post-box, hands in the pockets of his blue blazer, long, thin neck thrust forward like the arm of a crane. She left the bus shelter and hurried to meet him.

'Oh, you came!' he said, looking thrilled.

'Yes. Can we stand a bit further along the sidewalk?'

'All right. I like the way you say "sidewalk".'

Kitty glanced up at a pointed window halfway along the school building and then herded the boy a few yards downhill.

'So I've got a list—' he started to say.

'Just a second, George.'

She put a hand on his arm and moved him slightly, so that he was at right-angles to the road.

'It's Geoffrey, actually.'

'OK.' She stepped back and smiled. He was still looking at his arm, where she'd touched him, and his ears turned slowly pink. 'You were saying you had a list,' she said.

'Yes.' He took a stub of pencil and a notebook out of his blazer pocket and thumbed through the pages. 'Right. The first line is "Hey there, punk, what are you saying about my old lady?"' He looked down at Kitty expectantly. He was almost a head taller than her, though emphatically younger – fourteen, perhaps, or even thirteen. She hadn't actually asked him his age, because it wasn't important; it was his height and sex that mattered. She'd met him in Tring the week before, after he'd overheard her in Boots, discussing depilatory cream with the woman behind the counter (entire conversation: 'Do you stock depilatory cream?' 'What's that, then?'), and when she'd exited, he'd been waiting outside, and had tentatively raised a hand to gain her attention, as though in class.

He was, he'd said, playing an American in a Wendover Amateur Dramatic Society production of *Dangerous Business*, and wanted to 'nail the accent'. Could she possibly help him?

The idea had come to her in a second. She knew that no-one thought she was clever, but there were different sorts of cleverness; in the States, people who had ambition, people with big plans, were admired just as much as those who could work out the square root of a hundred and doodah. She hadn't been bold enough; her strategy of not clapping at matches, failing to hand in prep or feigning cramps during country dancing was not going to win the prize. What she needed was a knockout blow.

'Hey there, punk, what are you saying about my old lady?' repeated Kitty, looking towards the arched window again; this time, she could see a pale shape against the glass. 'Is this character supposed to be from New York?'

'I don't know, really. The script just says "Two American gangsters enter".' He made a note and muttered the word 'punk' a couple of times. 'And could you say the line after it for me?' He turned the notebook around for her to see.

'That just says "Aaagh".'

'Yes. He's been coshed.'

'What does that mean?'

'Hit on the head with something.'

'Aaagh!' said Kitty, jerking forward so violently that Geoffrey stuck out his hands to save her. 'I don't know if that sounded very American,' she said. 'You'd need to put in some words.'

'Which words?'

'Oh, something like "You Goddam son-of-a-bitch".'

Geoffrey goggled at her, admiringly. 'I'd probably be thrown out of the Players if I said that.'

'You could save it for the first night.'

He gave a nervous laugh, apparently unsure of whether she was joking or not.

'What's the next line?' asked Kitty.

'There isn't another. Only those two, but I thought if I acquitted myself well, then they might give me a larger part next time. I'd like to be an actor when I'm older, you see.' He closed the notebook. 'Thank you.'

'That's OK.' She risked another glance at the window. A face was pressed against it.

'Would you like to come and see it?'

'See what?'

'The production. It's at St Margaret's Hall on the twenty-ninth and thirtieth of November, tickets are two-and-six on the door, but I could—' His gaze wavered over her shoulder and then he took a step back; Kitty turned and saw her mother hurtling across the road towards her, with Priss just behind.

'Oh, hello,' said Kitty.

'You're in the most terrible, terrible trouble,' called Priss.

'Am I?'

'Come along, Kitty,' said her mother, taking her arm and pulling her along the pavement; Geoffrey leaped out of their path as if avoiding a runaway bus.

'Miss Gilbert's still looking out of the window,' reported Priss.

'Where are we going?' asked Kitty. 'What about afternoon school?'

'There won't be any for you,' said Priss. 'You've been expelled for meeting a boy while in school uniform.'

'Have I?' Kitty couldn't keep the delight out of her voice.

'I knew it,' said Priss. 'I knew you'd done it deliberately.'

'Priscilla, you need to go back to school,' said their mother.

'But I want to see you tell her off.'

'Go back, please.'

'That meeting was supposed to be about *me*, but you didn't talk about *me* at all, you just talked about *her*.'

'Well, I'll just have to arrange another meeting.'

'Miss Saul thinks I might need to see a brain doctor.'

'The whole school thinks that,' said Kitty.

'The whole school thinks you're sex-mad.'

'Oh, shut up.'

'No, *you* shut up,' said Priss, lunging at her sister, aiming for her purple-and-yellow-striped tie and grabbing instead a handful of hair.

'Stop it!' shouted Barbara, trying to separate them, fending off the hand with which Kitty was trying to slap Priss, the headmistress's gaze burning through her back. 'Stop it now. Stop it! WOULD YOU BOTH LIKE A PUPPY?'

Priss slackened her grip, and both girls turned to look at her.

'What?'

'Would you both like a puppy?'

'What colour?' asked Priss.

'I don't know. I haven't actually seen them.'

'Could we choose?'

'I expect so.'

'All right, then. Thank you, Mummy.' Doing one of her

lightning mood-switches, Priss hugged her mother round the waist and then turned and sprinted back across the road towards the school.

'She can have my puppy,' said Kitty. 'I don't even like dogs. I murdered one, didn't I?' She started to adjust her tie, and then removed it altogether and tossed it on to the verge.

'Go on, then,' she said, with deliberate rudeness. 'Tell me off.'

Barbara stooped and picked up the tie and smoothed it over her hand. 'I don't know what to do with you,' she said, her voice barely audible. 'Either of you.'

'You don't have to *do* anything with me. I'm nearly seventeen. How old were you when you left school?'

'Well, I was . . . very young. But I went to a finishing school for a year. Would you like to do that?'

'No. I only liked school in Brookford because I met my friends there. And after school we sang in the glee club, we went for sodas, we swam, we curled each other's hair, there was TV.' Oh, the lovely ordinariness of it all, before she'd been dragged off to live in a creaking ruin a million miles from the nearest modern method of removing underarm hair.

'I wish I'd seen you,' said Barbara.

'Seen me what?'

'Being happy.' Her mother was embarrassingly close to tears, her voice beginning to waver. 'I should have come with you. I wanted to, but I—'

Kitty glanced around; there were people nearby. 'Well, you know I wasn't *always* happy,' she said, hastily.

'Weren't you?'

'No. I mean, if I had a bad report card or cramps or something, or I wasn't asked to a formal by someone. Also, I didn't get on with Trina so well.'

'Didn't you?' asked her mother, brightening, as if she'd been offered a small gift.

'Well, she was OK at first and then later on she wasn't OK. I thought it was because she and Harold only agreed to take us in the first place because it was fashionable and she hadn't thought it would last for so long. She said we were a lot of work. But then my girlfriends said she was getting jealous because Harold kept giving me compliments and saying what a nice figure I had and wanting to take me out to meet his golf buddies.'

Her mother's expression, which had started to verge on the hopeful, became fixed.

'He didn't *do* anything,' said Kitty. 'And anyway, it might just have been because Trina was going through The Change. Can we go?'

Further down the hill, Geoffrey was still visible, scuttling back to safety.

'And is that boy your . . . your boyfriend?' Barbara's tone was so apprehensive that Kitty wanted to laugh.

'Of course not, he's just a kid. In the States, girls speak to boys all the time – it's normal.'

'But you really have to understand that things are different over here.'

Well, no *shit*, thought Kitty. Out loud, she said, 'Can we go home now, because I think that old skunk is still watching us – you didn't come in the Austin, did you?'

'How do you know?'

'Because I saw you getting out of that grey truck. Who does it belong to?'

They spotted the bus at this point, and had to run uphill thirty yards, an exertion that might, thought Kitty, as she watched the endless dull greenness unwind past the window, account for the intensity of her mother's blush, still vivid after five minutes. Or, alternatively, it might be something to do with Barbara's age.

'Trina takes tablets made of monkey glands,' she said, conversationally, as they passed another bunch of sheep. 'She said it helps.'

8

4th October 1945

Dear Zena,
I fervently hope that this finds you well, and of course Alison
too. I know that this letter will have come as a shock. I
shouldn't have stopped writing to you so abruptly and I feel
awfully bad about it. I'm so very, very sorry, Zena. As
you'll see from the postmark, I am back in London, and have
been demobbed. I desperately need to talk to you, preferably
somewhere private where I can explain matters. Please let
me know where would be best for you.
 Yours, with all fond regards, and deepest apologies,
 Truly,
 Chris

He had spelled his daughter's name wrong; this was the thought to which Zena kept returning as she stood outside Madame Tussaud's, waiting for Chris. It was the single point of clarity upon which she could focus, whereas the rest of the coming encounter was all shifting blurs. What did he want? What were his plans, and did they include her and Allison? If so, what should she do? What would be best? What would be *right*? Her uncertainty felt physical, her body seemed to lack solidity, her thoughts – usually stacked like clean plates on a shelf – kept sliding dangerously.

He was late. She re-tied her headscarf and checked her lipstick in the compact mirror. The view was awful, a brownish pall of mist hanging over the Euston Road, the sky and the pavements identically dull, every intact building in need of paint or roof slates, blind boarded windows still chequering the facades, a bomb-site directly opposite her, bristling with dead weeds; it was three years since she'd last been to London, and it all looked even worse than she remembered, the gaps from the Blitz still unfilled, the more recent rocket damage no longer raw but drearily established. There was a smell of coal gas and motor-exhaust and everyone she saw looked irritable; a woman with a pram had barged into her outside Baker Street Station and the baby had given her the same pale, crusty-eyed stare as the mother.

For the second or third time since leaving Addenham, Zena looked around in momentary panic before remembering that Allison wasn't with her. Her daughter, seated on the floor behind the post-office counter, had barely looked up when she'd called goodbye, being intent on working Mrs Procter's official hole-punch across a page from an old telephone directory. 'Take as long as you like,' Mrs Procter had said. 'I've some lovely tripe for her lunch, and I'll make sure she has a nap in the afternoon.' Even in the midst of her worry, Zena had almost laughed at the idea of Allison taking an afternoon nap.

I fervently hope that this finds you well, and of course Alison too. She was certain she'd explained the spelling to Chris in a letter, written the week after she'd given birth. Miss Allison had been the deputy headmistress of Hackney School for Girls. 'You have the brains for university,' she'd said to Zena, at fifteen. 'I know that your circumstances are straitened, but you could compete for a scholarship.'

'I'd rather earn my own living. I want to be independent.'

'I see. Well, that's very much to your credit. But you should aim high. In an ideal world, what would you like to achieve?'

The phrase 'in an ideal world' was not one that Zena had heard Miss Allison use before. As a geography teacher, she avoided airy sentiment: the action of glaciers upon volcanic rock was entirely responsible for the so-called 'romantic' appearance of the Lake District, while the bloomy plums of the Vale of Evesham were down to mudstone deposits. Miss Allison's ideal world would be constructed on bedrock.

'I'd like to be in charge of something,' Zena had said, discovering the ambition as she spoke, as if the words had unveiled a plaque that had always been there, its inscription engraved more deeply by every new foster home, every change of school, each unheralded visit from a representative of the Board of Guardians. 'I'd like to be the one who makes the decisions.'

Miss Allison had nodded, approvingly. 'A manageress, perhaps. Or a businesswoman. Would you like to start in a shop or in an office?'

And when Zena had been promoted at Dawson's, Miss Allison had taken her out to tea at a Lyons Corner House, and had said, 'As you are no longer my pupil, you may call me Edna,' but there was something rather dispiriting about the name 'Edna' whereas 'Allison' sounded like a bunch of sunflowers and 'I think it suits her', Zena had written to Chris, as the baby lay wide-awake in her cot at the end of the bed, odd little creaks and smacks issuing from the pursed mouth, the sliding gaze seeming to trace the path of the plaster ribbons that wreathed the ceiling of the Dimperley music room.

'Zena!'

And here was Chris, walking along the pavement towards her, wearing a mackintosh rather than the volunteer ambulance uniform in which she still always pictured him, his hair too short to show its natural wave, his figure more thickset than she remembered, a hint of jowl beneath the jawline.

'Zena,' he said again, halting a couple of feet away, smiling but clearly nervous. 'You haven't changed a bit.'

She nodded, unable to return the compliment. He swayed forward, as if about to embrace her, and she took a step back and folded her arms. He still looked a little like Jimmy Stewart, which was the very first thing she had noticed when he'd helped her out of the basement of the bombed hostel in Hackney and she'd handed him the list she'd drawn up of the girls who should have been in the shelter, but who weren't, and who might yet be buried beneath the rubble. And it was still a likeable face, attentive, a little bashful.

'You didn't bring Allison, then?'

'Bring her? To a serious talk? Have you ever tried to have a discussion with a three-year-old in the room?'

He looked embarrassed. 'I spelled her name wrong,' he

said. 'I realized as soon as I posted the letter – I remembered you'd called her after the teacher who helped you.'

'Yes, that's right.' Slightly mollified, she unfolded her arms.

'You're still wearing them, then,' he said, looking at her left hand and sounding relieved.

'Of course I am. Look, shall we go somewhere?' She was conscious of the Tussaud's queue snaking along the wall behind her, its members no doubt bored enough to watch any slight scene occurring nearby.

'A café?'

'I'd rather stay outdoors, somewhere we can't be overheard.'

'Regent's Park? It's only round the corner.'

They walked in silence until they'd left the heavy traffic behind. A street of cream stucco houses led towards the first greenery she'd seen since leaving the station.

'When I wrote, I wasn't even sure if you were still at the big house,' he said. 'I wondered if you'd moved back to London.'

'Moved back to the rockets? Why ever would I do that?'

'Since the war ended, I mean.' He was sounding very humble. She nipped her tongue between her teeth before she could give him another sharp answer; she needed this to be a conversation, not an argument. The odd thing was that they had never quarrelled; in the bright, dusty summer after the Blitz, when Londoners had felt like convalescents recovering from a near-fatal illness, limp with relief and inclined to general bonhomie, she and Chris had recognized each other in Hackney Library – one borrowing, one shelving – had dined and danced and gone to bed together a few times, taking precautions on each occasion, and then the Royal Army Medical Corps had claimed Chris, and Zena had been promoted again at Dawson's and on her first morning as Acting Chief Assistant had counted the days on her calendar and realized that her monthly was late. She and Chris had already exchanged letters by that point, hers a cheerful page or two of news and description, ending with the phrase 'I hope you are keeping safe and well', and his a disconcertingly emotional treatise on how helpless he was feeling without her warm strength to lean on, her firm wisdom to support him, etc., and in other circumstances she'd probably have begun to edge away at this point. She'd noticed in the past that the men she attracted seemed chiefly to admire her ability to prop them up, as if she were a padded splint or a corset of some kind, and now that she couldn't actually admire Chris's eyes, or be swung around a dance-floor by his surprisingly muscular arms, he sounded disappointingly like another of those types. But then the doctor had confirmed her pregnancy, and she had made two decisions, the first taken in an instant: she would never, ever let this baby go – and the second after a few days of thought. Her letter to Chris had been brief and unre-proachful, a simple stating of the facts, and his reply had been swift and ardent and followed shortly by his actual presence, on a twenty-four-hour embarkation leave. He had brought with him a bunch of anemones and his deceased mother's rings, and when he'd proposed to Zena she had said yes, without visible hesitation, because he seemed a decent man and an amiable one, with a good job in civilian life, and she knew it was the right thing to do for their future child. But also because it was impossible – even for someone as clear-headed as herself – to resist the romance of the moment.

There'd been no time for an actual ceremony, of course, but Chris had suggested that she wear the rings and take his name, and later on, at Dimperley, when she was served tea by the unmarried mothers, and saw them having to help the nurses to change the beds and take the nappies to be boiled, she was very glad of the surprisingly heavy gold band and matching engagement ring with solitaire dia-mond and four tiny rubies.

'Go on, then,' she said. 'You say what you need to say.'

They were almost at the park now. Ahead of them, a dog hopped over the stumps of the railings and on to the grass; most people were still dutifully using the main entrance ten yards further along, from which a broad avenue ran between flower-beds still planted with cabbages.

'Well, I . . .' His voice dried up. 'I'm not sure where to begin.'

'You went to Malta. You wrote to me regularly. And then you wrote to me less regularly, and then, about six months after Allison was born, you stopped writing altogether.'

'Yes.'

'Obviously, I didn't know if you'd been killed.'

He ran a hand over his face. 'I'm sorry. God, I'm sorry.'

'I knew they were still bombing Malta to pieces. And I realized that if you were dead then no-one would inform me, unless you'd listed me as next-of-kin, which didn't seem very likely. So I didn't know if I was a widow or not – or whatever the word for a widow is when you're not married. There isn't one, of course; that's the whole point.' She was managing to keep her voice quiet and level, but she could remember the queasy realization that she was in limbo, without official status, without access to a pension, and strapped to a lie. 'And then I found out that you were still alive.'

'Did you?' He stopped walking. 'How did you?'

'It wasn't hard.' She didn't feel that she particularly owed him an explanation. Credit went to Mrs Procter, who had noticed that Zena was no longer receiving letters, and had deduced from her silence that the situation was not straightforward. It so happened, Mrs Procter had announced, that a Mrs Slater of Addenham Parva had a daughter in the Wrens, stationed in Valletta and a good correspondent. Perhaps the daughter could make a bit of a general enquiry? And lo, it had turned out that the occupants of the Advanced Dressing Station in Cospicua, including Lance Corporal C. T. Baxter, were all very much alive.

Zena had first been angry and then relieved and then she had shoved him aside in her thoughts – more fool him, for not wanting her or Allison – but it had underscored, more than ever, that her present idyll was only temporary. One way or another, there'd be complications ahead, and difficulties and explanations; she'd heard gossip, even in tiny Addenham, of lifelong sweethearts estranged, of soldiers returning to children not their own, of husbands back from the dead to find their wives remarried, of kind men turned nasty, of strong men enfeebled, of abandonment and of reconciliation; you couldn't give half the population a gun and send them away for five years and then expect their slippers still to fit when they came home. The arrival of Chris's letter, sodden with apologies, had had the inevitability of an unpaid bill.

'Go on, then,' she said. They'd reached a fork in the avenue and she nodded towards the empty path that led past a Tudor-beamed tea-house, shuttered for the season.

'You see, I didn't want to be a hypocrite,' said Chris. 'I didn't want to write to you as if nothing had changed; I *couldn't* write as if nothing had changed, because every-thing had changed.'

'Everything had changed because I'd had a baby, do you mean?'

'No!' He sounded stricken. 'No, it wasn't that at all. God, no. I mean, it really wasn't about . . .' He glanced around uneasily, as if planning to leg it across the balding lawns; ahead of them the path veered to the left and ran alongside a tall, spiked fence.

'It really wasn't about what?' asked Zena.

'About you.'

'It wasn't about *me*? Then what was it about?'

Chris spoke so quietly in reply that for a moment she doubted her own hearing.

'You fell in love?' she repeated.

'Yes.'

'Again? That was quick.'

'What?'

'You said you were in love with *me* when I wrote to you that I was expecting.'

'Yes, but—'

'So was this girl in the Wrens?'

'No. No, she's Maltese – she's the daughter of a

117

stretcher-bearer in our unit. Honestly, Zena, you've no idea what the Maltese people went through.'

'No, I don't expect I have.'

'It was far worse than our Blitz. When we first arrived in Valletta I couldn't believe there were still people living there – it was all ruins, smoking ruins, it was still being bombed almost every night. And yet Cesar invited me to his home – they were living in a cellar, an awful hole, but his wife cooked for me, they welcomed me in.'

He left an expectant pause. Was she supposed to applaud?

'And that's where I met her.'

'That's where you met me too.'

'What?'

'A bombed cellar.'

'Oh. Yes, so I did.' He seemed a little thrown by this. 'Anyway, it turned out that she – Mary – was working as a nurse at the hospital our unit was attached to and so we kept . . . meeting. And then gradually – it really was gradual, Zena, I wouldn't want you to think that there was anything deliberate about it, it was as if there was a . . . a current slowly drawing us together.'

'But that's almost the same thing you said to me – you said you felt that we'd been linked by invisible forces.'

'I know, but—'

'But what?'

'This was different.'

'How?'

It took him a second or two to answer. 'Because she felt the same way about me.'

It was a casual slap, the more painful for being

unexpected. She thought of all the letters she'd written to him, in which she'd done her best to be a fondly waiting wife, to conjure and shape a future that might one day be real, a home together, Chris building a sand-pit in the garden for Allison, a roast in the oven, but she had clearly aimed awry. He'd wanted passion and she'd offered a family. She looked away so that he couldn't see her expression, and saw a camel, staring through the fence at her. 'What the heck . . .' She moved closer to the railings; it was taller than she was, chewing slowly. 'What's that doing here?'

'It's the Regent's Park Zoo,' said Chris. 'Haven't you ever been?'

'No, never.' It was far hairier than she'd imagined and had two humps, the second one hanging flaccidly, like an empty straw bag; she wished Allison could see it, so that she could prove to her that not every exotic animal was stuffed, or made of wood. With an effort, she dragged her attention back to Chris. 'So why are you telling me this? I don't understand. That letter you sent was chock-full of apologies, and I thought, "Oh, he lost his nerve about marrying me when he was out there and now he's home again he's changed his mind and he wants to give it another chance." And I thought I probably ought to give you that chance; I'd have been willing to make a go of it, if you'd felt that way too. But it's not about that at all, is it? You've already decided on her rather than me.'

Chris was looking rather white around the gills.

'So what *is* it about? Do you want me to forgive you, is that it? Do you want my blessing so you can go off and marry her?'

His expression shifted.

'You've married her already? You're *married*?'

The 'yes' was so constricted that it sounded as if he were being strangled.

'When?'

'In, er . . . forty-three.'

'You've been married two years.'

'Yes. You see, we—'

'Where is she?'

'At home.'

'At home in Malta?'

'No.'

'At *your* home? You have a home with her?'

'A flat in Homerton. It's not much of a place and it's bomb-damaged, but we can't afford anything better at the moment.' He was looking and sounding absolutely wretched, his gaze barely holding hers, his posture seeming to indicate that he might keel over unless he could find something to support him – something that offered the requisite warm strength and firm wisdom; a Maltese splint.

'She made you do this, didn't she?'

'What?'

'Mary. She told you to come and talk to me. You'd never have done this on your own.'

There was an awkward pause, which acted as an answer. He appeared to brace himself.

'The thing is, Zena, I have to ask you something.'

'Do you? What is it?'

'We . . . you see, we weren't able to have much of a wedding. And we don't have any money to spare, what with the . . . things. And Mary doesn't complain, but there's something that I *can* give her, that's actually hers. I mean, rightfully hers. It's—'

A shrieking bellow made Zena duck and she turned, cautiously, her shoulders round her ears. An elephant swayed past the railings, spattering a series of greenish pancakes in its wake, a keeper with a spade following at a distance.

'. . . and hoped you wouldn't mind,' said Chris.

'What? What wouldn't I mind?'

'About the rings.'

For a mad moment she thought of circus rings, ladies in spangles riding elephants, clowns tooting horns. Rings. He was looking at her left hand.

'You mean you want these?' she asked, incredulously, staring at the golden hoop and the solitaire diamond. 'You want them *back*?'

'They belonged to my mother.'

'The brass neck of you!'

'Zena—'

'My God, the nerve! How do you think I've managed, on my own, with a child? How do you think I'm *going* to manage? I've earned these rings; they're mine.'

'But they're my—'

'And do you know what? I'm glad you've found someone else, I'm glad it's not me who's got the job of steering you along, we're better off without you. And you haven't once asked about Allison, not once. You don't deserve her, you're about as much use as a . . . a . . .' For a moment she couldn't think of a suitable epithet, and then she heard the scrape of a shovel.

'. . . as a dose of *skitters*.'

His reaction was so much more Harpo Marx than James Stewart that she nearly laughed. She clasped her hands, enfolding the rings, and then abruptly turned and walked away, ignoring the path and taking a straight line across the greensward.

So that's that, she thought: that's the end, that's really the end. Three years with an anvil dangling over her head and now it had fallen and hit someone else, and it was astonishing – the speed of it and the finality. And what now? The future swung open like an unlatched door. Whatever came next was up to her, and only up to her; she was once again in charge and the realization seemed to lift her clear of the ground so that she sped just above it, the grass unfurling like a royal carpet.

9

Just past Great Missenden, the train stopped in a steep-sided cutting and showed no signs of re-starting. The man who had been talking to Valentine since Marylebone about the absolute necessity of punishing the German people showed no signs of changing the subject; outside, the bank was a tangle of leafless brambles. Occasional wisps of steam drifted past.

'Yes,' said Valentine, to some question or other. 'Though I never actually met any Germans. Apart from a couple of prisoners-of-war.'

He could hear footsteps in the corridor, knuckles against a door and an indistinct voice. The sound was repeated, nearer this time and then, finally, at their own compartment door. 'Sorry for the delay, gentlemen,' said the guard. ''Orse on the line.'

German reparations continued, with occasional forays into the state of the Stock Market. 'I might go and have a look at what's happening,' said Valentine. 'See if I can help.' He exited quickly before anyone could ask precisely how.

The train was near-empty. He walked the length of it and passed two small boys standing in the third-class corridor with their noses pressed to the window.

'Looking for the horse?' asked Valentine.

'No, we're waiting for the train to move because Mum says we can't use the WC till it goes again and Dudley's going to bust himself.'

'I'm going to bust myself,' confirmed Dudley.

'Oh dear,' said Valentine, inadequately. 'But doesn't that rule only apply if the train's standing in a station? And in any case, I'm sure you can use the lavatory if it's just a . . . a number one.'

'It's not,' said Dudley. He was looking rather pale. 'Mum says it all goes straight down the hole on to the track. And if they spot it, they make you pay *a hundred pounds*.'

'I just got an idea,' said his brother. 'You could go and then you could pretend it was the horse what done it.'

'Now that,' said Valentine, 'is clever.'

'You won't tell our mum, will you?'

'Absolutely not.'

They scuttled away. Valentine stared at nothing out of the window for a minute or two, wishing he'd brought the file of papers with him so he could move to a different compartment, but he'd left it in the rack above Mr Reparations. Reluctantly, he began to walk back along the corridor and immediately saw Alaric's secretary. She was the only occupant of a third-class compartment and she'd clearly already seen him through the glass because she raised a hand. He slid the door open.

'I was wondering if you'd seen the horse,' she said.

'Not yet.'

'I'm beginning to feel like Mrs Noah. I've already spotted a camel and an elephant today.'

'From the train?'

'No, I was in Regent's Park.' She placed a piece of wool between the pages of the book she'd been reading, and closed it. He'd only ever exchanged a couple of sentences with her before, but she looked ready for conversation. More than ready, really; she seemed as alert as a sprinter on the blocks, taut with purpose.

'I've just read *What was Down There*,' she said.

'I beg your pardon?'

'The ghost story that's set at Dimperley. The library had to order it from another branch – I've been waiting for months and months.'

'Oh yes, I've heard of it.'

'But you haven't read it?'

He shook his head and she looked astonished.

'Honestly? Weren't you curious?'

'I'm not much of a reader. What's it like?'

'Quite good. Though it's written by an American so the lady's maid says things like "I've gotten a fright down there, many a time." It all takes place in the tunnel between the kitchen and the Dower Wing. Shall I sum it up for you?'

'Er . . . yes.' He sat down opposite her.

'It's set in the thirteenth century, so actually before Dimperley was even built, which is why your uncle won't have a copy in the house. Anyway, it starts off in modern times – well, not modern, because it was written in eighteen something – it starts off in Victorian times, when a visitor's exploring the house and finds that someone's bolted the door to the tunnel. And then it goes back to the story of the lady of the manor, who used to meet her assignation down there – he was always standing waiting for her beneath the spiral staircase, and the first thing she'd see was his shadow, and then he'd run and embrace her. One day, though, his shadow doesn't move and she can hear a sort of bubbling, gulping sound – and when she brings the lit taper towards him, she sees he's being held upright by a lance through his neck, that's gone straight through and pierced the wall, and he's trying to warn her, but of course he can't speak. And then she's murdered too, by her husband, who's been lying in wait. And then it goes back to modern times again and the visitor finds a key and goes in and all he can hear is a gulping, gurgling, splattering sound. Quite good, as I said. Have you ever been down there?'

'Not for years. But I seem to remember there's a hole in the wall, which might have given him the idea.'

'I'll have to have a look. When I first came to the house we were told that there was a weeping ghostly housemaid down there, though no-one I spoke to ever saw it. Did you know there are two boys looking at you?'

'Oh . . .' Valentine turned to see Dudley and his brother, fogging up the glass. The door slid open.

'He's done it,' said the brother.

'I done it,' said Dudley. 'Just in time.'

'Good,' said Valentine.

'Only, can we ask you something?'

'Yes.'

'If the police come and see us and we say a horse done it, they won't believe us because we're only kids. But if *you* say you saw a horse done it, they'd believe you, wouldn't they?'

'I suppose they might.'

'So Graham wants you to sign something.'

'We didn't have no paper,' said Graham, unfurling a copy of the *Dandy*, 'but there's room on this.' He tilted the comic sideways, and Valentine saw the words 'I SOLLOMLY DECLARE THAT I SAW A HORSE DONE IT' written in capitals down the side of the Korky the Cat comic strip.

'You'd like me to sign this?'

'Yes, please.'

Graham held out a stub of pencil, and, rather than take off his glove and have the boys gape at the contents, Valentine reached for it with his left hand. He appended his signature with surprising neatness.

'Does that say "Sir"?' said Graham, peering at it.

'Yes.'

'They'll *definitely* believe it, then.'

The door shut again.

'I do hope I haven't witnessed something illegal,' said Mrs Baxter, primly. It took him a second to realize that she was joking.

'The thing is,' he said, 'I've spent most of the day signing documents and that's the only one I fully understood.'

'Lucky that you're left-handed,' she said, nodding at his glove.

'But I'm not.'

'Oh. I'm sorry. My daughter's left-handed, you see, and she holds a pencil exactly the way that you do.'

He looked at his ungloved hand and wiggled the fingers. Something stirred in his memory; a feeling of restriction, a twisted elbow. He pincered an invisible pencil and made an imaginary mark.

'Oh, look!' exclaimed Mrs Baxter.

An underfed piebald was ambling past the carriage, a frayed halter dangling.

'It's a horse,' said Valentine, automatically. 'Sorry,' he added, seeing her mouth twitch. 'That must sound idiotic, I know. It's my brother Cedric, you see; it's the only thing he ever says.'

'I know.'

'Though he makes other noises sometimes.'

'I've heard him tutting.'

'Yes, he does that when he's annoyed about something. We once had a housekeeper who did the same – oh, are we starting to move?' The train jerked forward and then stopped again; Valentine stood up. 'I think I should fetch my briefcase – I've left it in another compartment.'

'Yes, of course.'

Zena watched him fumble with the door and disappear along the corridor. Was he making an excuse to leave? Had she been over-familiar? Talking to him was so surprisingly similar to talking to a normal person that she'd almost forgotten how careful you had to be with the gentry; Alaric, for instance, might spend half his time praising her and the other half pretending that he wasn't staring at her bust, but their conversation had never moved beyond the courteously formal. Once, when he'd requested some help when Zena was in the middle of typing a sentence, she'd said, without thinking, 'Hang on a mo,' and he'd looked completely thrown, as if she'd spoken in Swahili. And Lady Vere-Thissett, in the unlucky event that you had to speak to her, always gave the impression that she should only be engaged in conversation by prior written request delivered a week in advance on a silver tray by a brace of uniformed heralds.

'Got it,' said Sir Valentine, opening the door again, a briefcase under his arm. He sat down and unclipped the strap. 'The very odd thing about meeting you here is that I actually have something for you. I'd forgotten about it.'

'For me?'

'For your daughter, rather. I'm sorry, I don't know her name.'

'It's Allison.'

'I passed a toy-shop earlier in the day and I went in to buy something for my brother and then I remembered the doll that he'd found in the moat.'

'A doll? Really? Did it have yellow hair?'

'Headless when I saw it, I'm afraid.'

'I'll bet it was hers. We've been searching for it everywhere – I thought she'd dropped it in the grounds.'

'It looked as if the dog might have got hold of it. Or a fox, perhaps. Anyway, I happened to see this.'

He took out a small blue cloth figure with a frilled bonnet, and gave it a doubtful look before handing it to Zena. A chubby, celluloid baby-face of startling hideousness leered back at her.

'The shop was rather dark,' he said, apologetically, and she laughed.

'It's very kind of you. She'll love it.'

'Really? Looking at it now, I wonder if it isn't on the frightening side.'

'Allison's not frightened of anything. Thank you. What did you get for your brother?'

'He likes sets of matching objects – things like counters and buttons. So I bought him dominoes.' He rattled the box. 'Apparently they were made by Italian prisoners-of-war.'

'Can he play the game?'

'No, no, he can't manage that. He lines them up and stacks them and so on.'

His tone was completely matter-of-fact, unlike the pained, lowered voice that Alaric always adopted when talking of his nephew.

'Do you remember him?' she asked, impulsively. 'I mean, the way he was before?'

'No. Not even slightly. I was only three when it happened.'

'My daughter's age.' It was strange and rather sad to think that Allison would retain so few memories of her current life.

'The only thing I remember is my father's valet carrying Ceddy downstairs, all wrapped in blankets. Perhaps he was convalescing then – there are photographs of him lying on a chair in the garden. They hadn't expected him to survive.'

'My little brother didn't,' she said, the words out of her mouth before she even knew they were there. 'He had a brain infection, but he died in hospital.'

'How old was he?'

'Nine. And I was eleven. He was called Raymond.' The cloth doll she was holding emitted a loud squeak, and she relaxed her grip. How many years was it since she'd spoken her brother's name? The past was pushing up everywhere today, thistles through the grass; she covered the hiatus by stowing the doll in her handbag.

'So, er . . . were you in town for a show?' asked Valentine, after the silence had become rather long.

'No. No, I was meeting someone. And you?'

'Oh, estate business. One piece of lousy news after another.' He slid open the box of dominoes and inspected the contents. Silence fell once more, broken by the sound of hooves as the piebald cantered past again, followed a few seconds later by a red-faced man holding a bridle.

'It's a bit like being at the pictures, isn't it?' said Zena, craning to watch them. 'I'm half expecting Buster Keaton to bring up the rear on one of those trolleys.' She leaned back. 'I wonder how long we'll be here? It could be hours.'

'You wouldn't care for a game of dominoes, would you?' asked Valentine. 'I mean, if you'd rather read, of course . . .'

'No, I like dominoes. We used to play it all the time during raids. Shall I come across?'

She seated herself on the same side as him, and he laid the briefcase between them and started to arrange the pieces on it, face down.

'Draw or block?' she asked.

He glanced up, caught by the casual expertise of her tone. She had that droll look again, like someone laughing behind a closed door.

'Draw,' he said.

'Seven or eight?'

'Seven.'

'All spinners to start?'

'Good for me. First to fifty?'

'You're on.'

He grinned. 'A needle match. If I can hold the damn

things,' he added, as he tried to grip his gloved hand around the tiles. 'You know, Mrs Baxter, I think you may have hit the mark about my left hand. I have a definite feeling that I might have started off that way.'

'Was it tied behind your back, to stop you using it?'

'Yes, I think it might have been.'

'By your teacher?'

'No, it would have been my nanny. I was already right-handed by the time I went away to school.'

'I have the double six,' she said, laying it down.

'Draw,' he said, picking up a piece from the boneyard.

'So how old were you then?'

'I was five.'

'I know they say that left-handers have terrible hand-writing because they smudge the ink as they write, but I read that Hans Christian Andersen was left-handed and so was Mark Twain, so it can't really be that bad a thing.' Impossible to imagine binding Allison's fat little hand, those kissable knuckles; impossible to imagine packing her off to school at five. She laid down another tile.

'Ah. Blanks at both ends,' said Valentine.

'Yes.'

'Draw again. Good thing we're not playing for money. In my platoon we put up imaginary stakes, and I'm pretty certain that a man called Briggs still owes me his house.'

'Do you need another one?'

'Well . . . since you mention it . . .' He stared at the tile in his hand, pricked by the urge to tell her exactly *how* lousy his London meeting had been – a dress rehearsal, of sorts, for the bruising family performance that would come later.

132

'I don't know how much you already know about the estate debts.'

Zena hesitated. What she already knew was gossip – Felix and his affairs, and his motor-cars and his generous tips and his jocular disregard for bills. 'Nothing official,' she said, carefully.

'I suppose it'll all be public before long, anyway. My brother – my oldest brother, I mean – borrowed a lot of money to open the airfield at Woodsley. And it was a going concern before the war, but once everything kicked off, there were hardly any civilian flights. He hoped the RAF would rent it, but it turned out the ground was no good for heavier aircraft, so the whole thing simply slid into disaster. And now that the debt's been called in, on top of the death duties, it's' – he groped for the euphemism that the solicitor had used – 'severely narrowed our options. To be honest, Mrs Baxter, the egg's hit the fan.'

'Has it? So you'll have to sell even more land?'

'It's actually much worse than that. We'll have to sell all the farmland, including Home Farm. The best hope is if a body called the National Trust agrees to take the house and grounds. Or rather, we'd give it to them. If they decide that they want it. We'd endow it to the Trust, and then they'd allow us to live in part of it, as long as it were open to the public for several days a month.'

' "Allow" you?'

'Yes.'

'So you'd be tenants?'

He had an apocalyptic vision of how his mother would react to that description. 'I suppose so. In a way.'

'But what if this Trust doesn't want it?'

'Well, then we'd . . . we'd have to let the house go.'

'Let it go?'

'Yes.'

'You mean, sell *Dimperley*?' Her tone was pure outrage, her straight gaze pinning him to the seat.

He found himself beginning to gabble. 'Without the farm-land, you see, there's no income, so there'd be no choice. The solicitor says there's a market for large houses for use as schools or as . . . er . . .' His imagination failed him. 'Or it might be bought solely for the land it's on. Gravel.'

'The land it's on?'

'Yes.'

'You mean . . . it might be *demolished*?'

He was silent.

'But you won't let that happen, will you?'

'Well, I . . . I, er . . .' It hadn't actually occurred to Valentine that he might have any agency in the matter; paperwork had been piled before him by people whose job it was to read paperwork, figures had been added and subtracted by those who relished figures. '. . . I obviously have to rely on what the solicitor told me.' She was sitting very upright, her hands curled around the dominoes so that she looked rather like a prize-fighter waiting for an opening. 'And there really doesn't seem a great deal I can do about it.' He heard and hated the shuffling defensiveness in his own voice.

She said nothing, switching her gaze back to the tiles, but he could feel her judgement, like a hand shoved in his face.

'It's all very complicated,' he added, sounding as pompous as Alaric.

'Yes, I'm sure it is.' She carried on playing, trying very hard not to show her anger – because she was, suddenly, very angry with him: to sit there like a boiled pudding and fail to fight for what was yours and let change push you over instead of pushing you forward.

There was a voice in the corridor, and the guard walked past, shouting that they'd be on their way shortly; seconds later the train jolted and all the dominoes slid off the briefcase. Zena helped to pick them up and dust them off and then she moved over to her side of the compartment again, and opened her book, and Valentine clumsily lit a cigarette and looked out of the window. The last part of the journey seemed terribly long.

'The general public? In *here*?' said his mother, aghast, glancing around the Morning Room as if it had suddenly filled with expectorating tramps. 'We obviously can't allow that.'

'But we don't have a choice,' said Valentine. 'I was shown the figures. The only alternative is to sell the house.'

'I'm sure that's an exaggeration. I have, in any case, been meaning to speak to you on this subject.'

'Which subject?'

'We'd be like the apes on the Rock of Gibraltar,' said Alaric. 'Stared at and goaded by ignorant trippers.'

'But the alternative is to sell the *house*.'

'No, no, no – I'm sure we have a trick or two up our sleeve.'

'Do we?' asked Valentine. 'What are they?'

Alaric tapped his nose.

'Come along to my little sitting room,' said his mother, 'and we'll discuss matters there.'

'Now? But I've only just . . .'

'I can't see why they'd goad us,' said Barbara. 'Doesn't that mean being poked with sticks, or something? What is it, Priss?'

Her daughter's head had appeared around the door.

'I heard shouting.'

'It's just a discussion.'

'About selling the house?'

'Are you selling it?' said Kitty, eagerly, coming in behind her sister. 'Truly? Can we buy somewhere in the town that has a shower? And central heating?'

'And no ghost,' added Priss. 'Did I tell you that one of my dogs can definitely see it?'

'There is no ghost at Dimperley,' said Alaric. 'The Larby story, as I have stated before on numerous occasions, was a complete invention. Surely you realize, Priscilla, that this house didn't exist at the time of the Crusades.'

'I don't care, because Toto can definitely see a ghost.'

'You mustn't be rude to your uncle,' said Barbara.

'In America, kids are educated that we're allowed to question our elderlies,' said Kitty.

'Elders.'

'So anyway,' said Valentine, raising his voice in an attempt to wrench back the subject, 'that's the solicitor's conclusion, and we'll be receiving a visit from a Mr Rhydderch-Jones from the National Trust.'

There was a brief pause.

'Shall we meet in my little sitting room, in an hour?' asked his mother. It wasn't actually a question.

She was seated at her desk, engaged in the Sisyphean task of serially re-pasting photographs into the albums, dusting the old dried glue off the backs with one little brush and applying the new adhesive with another.

'I need a moment to finish this page. This is your father's cousin Phyllida on her twenty-first birthday, beside the auricular theatre at Gribbets. Do you remember her?'

'I'm afraid not.'

'She was married to a Frenshaw and one of her daughters later married the Duc de Roscoff, which was a surprise. Rather a plain girl. Stop it, please, Ceddy.'

Valentine's brother had emptied the newly bought dominoes on to a table and was tapping two of them together.

'Can I have a turn?' asked Valentine. He built a little stack of tiles and then watched Ceddy methodically take it apart again. Most of the furniture in the room was dust-sheeted, including the glass dome containing four stuffed weasels playing whist, which had so fascinated Valentine as a child that his sketches of it had filled an entire notebook. He lifted a fold of cloth and saw that the weasel with the monocle had dropped its winning ace.

'Do come and sit down,' said his mother. The album was still open in front of her: sepia gatherings, women in hats like coal scuttles, blurred fox-hounds, palisades of servants.

Valentine sat and then awkwardly shuffled his chair back, so that they weren't positioned knee to knee. He could feel the formality of the situation beginning to work at him, uncovering a familiar but unhelpful seam of nervous flippancy.

'Okeydoke,' he said.

'*Must* you use that expression? I have had to correct Kitty several times and I would prefer that you set an example.'

His lips began to form the very same word again, and he forced himself to nod instead.

'We need,' said his mother, 'to talk about the future of Dimperley.'

'Yes. Yes, well, the fundamental problem, obviously, is that after my back pay's gone, there'll be nothing left beyond a very few rents and some dividends, and the solicitor told me—'

His mother tilted her head very slightly, a movement that he knew of old was the equivalent of a Sergeant-Major screaming, 'SHAAAADAAAP!' across the parade ground. It took an effort for him to continue: '. . . the solicitor told me that we've been left without options.'

'Which is, of course, nonsense.'

'Is it?'

'When I married your father, the estate was on its knees. Your grandmother had to sell her Holbein, and that still wasn't enough.'

'So what happened?'

'I have just told you what happened.'

'But how did the estate get *off* its knees?'

His mother looked perplexed. 'I married your father,' she said, again.

'You mean . . .'

'My dowry was quite sufficient to restore the estate. Of course, there had never been any question of either of us marrying anyone else – we had known each other since we were babes in arms. In fact, he first proposed to me at a children's party, using his father's regimental ring.' The memory caught and held her for a moment, the Long Gallery webbed with Christmas candlelight, ten-year-old Arthur dressed as Sir John Moore at Corunna, herself as Guinevere in white silk threaded with silver ribbons, the ring large enough to take two of her small fingers. 'Nevertheless . . .'

Valentine sat back and blinked a few times. 'Are you saying you want me to marry for money?'

'People are very silly about the idea. There's nothing at all wrong with the considered union of one well-bred family with another.'

'So you *are* saying that? You don't mean you have some-one in mind?'

Irene reached for a small notebook and opened it at a bookmark.

'You've got a list!' said Valentine. Glimpsing the double column, he wasn't sure whether to laugh or to bolt for the hills.

His mother picked up a pencil and scored through one of the names.

'Who was that?'

'The Manningford girl.'

'Deedee?'

'I've heard that she went to the colonies after her father died.'

139

The news was a poke in the stomach.

'Which colony?'

'Australia, I believe.' She crossed out another name. 'Agnes Pellew. *Not* suitable.'

'Why not?'

'There are rumours that I would rather not repeat about her service in the FANYs. The Honourable Minna Staithe?'

'I've never heard of her.'

'Her mother is one of the Gladwins. The Coddington sisters – I suppose it would have to be the older of the two, but I believe she's stopped wearing spectacles now. Alethea Winn-Preston. Beatrice Chett.'

'I've never heard of any of them.'

'Yvonne Maberly. Dodie Prax-Hetherton-Fyford. Well, of course, you would need to *get to know* the girl first.'

'You mean, before I blow her entire fortune on zinc guttering?' His mother's expression didn't change; she was not someone who ever found humour in serious matters. Or in any matters at all, really. Valentine thought of Deedee again, and replayed his farcical, impulsive proposal and the crushing response. *It was Felix, you fathead.* 'Anyway,' he added, glumly, 'why would she even want to?'

'Want to do what?'

'Marry me.'

His mother looked astonished. 'Because you're a *Vere-Thissett*.' There was a crash of dominoes from the card-table followed by a further cascade of tiles on to the rug. Ceddy tutted loudly and Valentine went over to help him to pick them up.

Irene watched her two sons crouching together, and

thought, as she often thought – sometimes hourly – of their missing brother. On this occasion, the thought was sharply regretful: why, *why*, hadn't she had exactly this conversation with Felix when he came down from Cambridge? She might have forestalled the passing fancy which had led to an embarrassingly hurried marriage, no very creditable or financially-useful family connection (Barbara's father had a large wireworks but he also had four other children) and the apparent end of the Vere-Thissett male line. Not that one could blame Barbara for having only daughters, of course, but nevertheless one couldn't shake off the feeling that she could have ... tried harder. She'd failed to understand that her role was just as much of a 'job' as picking oakum (or whatever it was that girls did in factories) and required a constant iteration of duty, posture, attention, foresight; one did not need to sweat in order to toil – sometimes one only needed to *endure*.

'I'm here to tell you that supper's ready,' said Priss, sticking her head round the door without knocking. 'It's disgusting kidney soup.'

She disappeared again, to be immediately replaced by Hersey, who had arrived to take Ceddy.

'I've just finished re-lining Sir Valentine's dinner jacket, my Lady,' she said. 'Oh, sorry, Sir Valentine, I didn't see you,' she added, as he reversed from under an ottoman, holding a double two.

'Why do I need a dinner jacket?' he asked, already guessing the thrust of the answer.

'The Wendover Hunt Ball,' said his mother. 'On Saturday.'

'And whom am I taking?'

She consulted her notebook again. 'Genevieve Mallet. She's extremely well bred – her mother was a Chandford – and I hear she's a very pretty girl. I really can't see why you'd have any objection to taking a very pretty girl to a dance.'

'Should I propose to her before or after the Paul Jones?'

His mother didn't reply. Instead, she bent her gaze to the album in front of her. 'Have you ever seen a photograph of Alaric when he was your age?' Valentine peered at the group of young people, togged up for a theatrical. It took him a few moments to recognize the large, happy youth right at the centre of the picture, dressed in a toga and wearing a wreath of greenery, a grin bursting through his attempt at sternness.

'A man really ought to have a wife,' said his mother, closing the album and looking up at her son. 'Or he simply falls to pieces.'

10

The tip had come from a fellow at the club. Alaric wasn't often in town, but he'd had a long-awaited appointment at the College of Arms to establish the authority of a Letter Patent, dated 1802, granting peculiar leave for the substitution on the Vere-Thissett escutcheon of three cormorants azure with a pair of squirrels gules, and after a satisfactory conversation with the Rouge Croix Pursuivant, he had dropped in at Pollet's. It had gone downhill since his last visit, the exterior shabby, the old head porter replaced by someone who had had to ask Alaric's name, a hatless woman in the dining room, but after luncheon, over the first decent whisky he'd tasted for more than five years, he'd found himself in conversation with a barrister called Parsons, a sensible chap in his forties. Of course, it was all gloom. What could one say about a government of savage philistines who understood nothing of tradition and lineage: men who would trample across fair Albion in their nailed boots, hurl aside her tax-ruined custodians, strip the greensward from her flesh and turn breeze-kissed blossom into coal dust? What could one say about the people who had voted for these yahoos, when even Stalin at Potsdam – even *Stalin* – had professed himself baffled at their ingratitude to the incumbent?

Parsons, in fact, had had plenty to say and had made the excellent point that the years of free food and accommodation in the services had given the working-classes the expectation that they'd never have to pay for anything ever again, hence the demand for a future in which complimentary spectacles and false teeth dropped into their outstretched hands; 'Attlee and his cohort will squeeze people like us as if we're oranges,' he'd said, 'and then hand round the juice to anyone who pays their union dues.' Parsons' neighbour in Worcestershire had been forced to give up his Queen Anne house and it had gone to the local council as a Youth Training Centre, so that the spotty sons of farm labourers could learn how to operate industrial lathes and drink milkshakes in the tapestry room. 'Of course, as soon as word got round it was being sold, there were greasy types from London calling at all hours, wanting to pay cash for the contents,' said Parsons. 'Pantechnicons queuing outside. Gawpers watching the poor chap's family portraits being carried out.'

'Heavens,' said Alaric.

'And, inevitably, they stiffed the poor chap. He was so keen for the whole business to be over with that he accepted anything offered. Sèvres tea-sets going for a song. Five pounds for a landscape that was very likely a Hobbema.'

'Dastardly,' said Alaric. 'So, er . . . what *should* your neighbour have done?'

'Do what the farmers do – take a list to a dealer on market day, bring a sample or two, get a price. Keep it discreet.'

After a lot of thought, Alaric had decided on Bicester, where he'd once spent a pleasant few hours searching through parish records for details of a cadet branch of the Vere family (who, interestingly, had styled themselves 'Verry'). It was only a half-hour train-ride from Princes Risborough but far enough from Dimperley to make it unlikely that he'd bump into anyone he knew, although he found himself bumping into a great many people that he *didn't* know as he tried to manoeuvre a fishing basket through the market-day crowds, raising his voice above a gusting wind and the incessant bleat of penned sheep, in order to make enquiries. Three separate tweed-clad arms waved him in the direction of the King George Hotel, and the pretty little thing at the desk nodded him towards the back quarters without a second look.

Alaric knocked at a half-open door.

'Mr Sherwell?'

'Five minutes while I finish this. Sit down if you like.'

The dealer, a large, bearded man of about his own age, with a ponderous Midlands accent, was at a table near the window, eating sausages from a plate, his knife clacking against the china, a full cup of tea trembling at his elbow. There was a fire in the hearth, though it wasn't yet ten in the morning, and in front of it lay a tortoiseshell cat, sprawled like an odalisque in the riper sort of painting.

Alaric seated himself and took his notebook from an inside pocket. In it, Mrs Baxter had itemized and categorized the attic inventory, her well-formed hand-writing transforming a simple list into the acme of clarity.

'Right, then,' said Sherwell, plate cleared, tea drunk in one long pull, 'what can I do for you, Mr . . .'

There was a pause. 'Bicesterly,' said Alaric, wishing he'd thought about this in advance. 'I have a highly interesting selection of historical items that could possibly be for sale, at the right price.'

'With you?'

'I beg your pardon?'

'Do you have them with you?'

'One or two of the more portable ones, yes.'

'Let's see.'

There was nothing eager, or oleaginous about Sherwell. As he dipped into the fishing basket, his face was as unreadable as a tin tray; his hands, as he examined and then opened the small leather box, were a workman's, skilful but lacking any reverence.

'Nothing much in here,' said Sherwell, looking up from the felt-lined interior, empty but for a clot of threads in one corner.

'You'll see there is a label pasted inside the lid.'

The dealer tilted the box so that the paper caught the grey light from the window. 'Edward the Seventh?' he read, frowning.

'Yes. It was the box in which he kept his trout flies. He left it at the house when he visited in 1872, when he was still the Prince of Wales, obviously.'

Sherwell looked again at the inscription. 'He didn't write this, though.'

'No, it was written by my grandfather, who fished on the upper reaches of the Wye with His Royal Highness and said that he was the finest wrist caster he had ever had the privilege of watching. His Royal Highness was a proponent of the Clyde-style wet fly, of which you can see an example in the box – it's a Hen Blackie, I believe.'

146

Sherwell dabbed at the Hen Blackie with a broad finger and then put the box on the table and took a cloth-wrapped object from the basket.

'A pincushion,' he said, unwrapping it. 'Georgian.'

'Originally belonging to Princess Adelaide of Saxe-Meiningen. Later the wife of William the Fourth.' It had a carved rosewood base and a neat dome of blue velvet on which the rusty heads of two pins were visible.

'How do we know it was hers?' asked Sherwell.

'Oh, there's no doubt. My family's particular royal connection means that a representative has attended every coronation since that of Henry the Fifth, and it was at William the Fourth's coronation that . . . that . . .'

The pincushion had already joined the box on the table and Sherwell was peering into the basket again. 'So what else is there? Just this candlestick?'

'One of six given by the Duke of Rutland on the occasion of the wedding of my great-great-great-great uncle. Solid silver.'

Sherwell reached in and weighed it with a hand. 'Plated, not solid. And it's got a dent.'

'Ah, but that's *precisely* why I brought it. Imagine the scene: that very candlestick was knocked from the table on the eleventh of May, 1812 – an extraordinarily cold evening, apparently – when the uncle in question rose suddenly in shock, having just been told of the assassination of the Prime Minister. He'd been dining with—'

'Are the others damaged?'

'No. No they're not.'

'If there are six of them, I could give you thirty quid.

The box and the pincushion aren't worth anything.' The last sentence was spoken without contempt, but also without regret; those objects that reached from the past, that plucked at one's shoulder and whispered: 'Turn your ear to us – we can tell you of others who lived and breathed just as you live and breathe, can you not hear us?', were clearly intangible and inaudible to Sherwell. Offered romance, he looked around for a set of scales.

'Is that the lot?'

'No, no, far from it. I have here a list of other available objects.' Alaric opened the notebook and cleared his throat. 'Items of taxidermy. Walrus, one; Arctic fox, one; moose head, one; raccoons, five – it's a tableau, in fact—'

'Stuffed animals? I can't do anything with those.'

'Wooden coffer containing an embroidered bedspread, never used, part of the 1642 dowry of Lady Eleanor du Plis, when she—'

'Can I look at that notebook myself?'

Alaric hesitated and then handed it across. Sherwell glanced expressionlessly through the contents.

'Helmet? What sort?'

'It's a leather bascinet, clearly damaged in combat. The story goes that—'

'No suits of armour?'

'No.'

'I can always shift military gear, any age. Muskets? Swords? Pistols?'

'No, I'm afraid not.'

'Any medals?'

'I beg your pardon?'

'Always a market for medals – Crimean, Boer War, Great War. VCs, DSOs, obviously, but American collectors'll take all sorts. I was offered fifty quid for my Military Medal. Not that I'd sell it.' Sherwell closed the book and handed it back. 'Can't help you with these, I'm afraid – you might want to try an auction house. Now, excuse me.' He reached down beside his chair and lifted a walking stick. 'Have to see a man about a dog.' Levering himself up, he limped away, and Alaric heard the creak of an artificial limb and the slap of the wooden foot on the floor.

Outside, it was pouring. Alaric had neglected to bring an umbrella, and he stood in the hotel porch, watching through the streaming glass as a farmer and his sodden collie guided a trio of ewes across the square. Alongside his irritation at the wasted journey, he could sense the slow return of a darker feeling, the spreading bruise beneath the graze.

There was no sign of the rain letting up, and after a few minutes he found his way to the bar-room and bought a brandy, sipping it at a corner table, penned in by livestock talk and the miasma of damp tweed. The alcohol did nothing to slow the familiar, inexorable slide into what he thought of as his 'gloom'. It had been a few years since its last, horrid visit, but he recognized each stage: the colour leaching from his vision so that the world began to resemble a woodcut, the creeping heaviness, as if he'd been harnessed to a cart full of clay.

Here was the reason that he rarely went to the club, or to the cricket, why he avoided Old Carthusian dinners and Masonic evenings and local shoots, why he had refused the honorary position offered by the Bucks Historical Society. Because sooner or later, men of his own age always talked about the Great War. The subject was broached in a thousand ways: the casual geographic reference, the shell-case cigarette-lighter, the military jargon, the pinned sleeve, the scar that disappeared into the hairline – like boys swapping slang from a school that they had all attended. Or nearly all.

His brother Arthur, considerably older than himself, had volunteered right at the start, and there had been no question but that Alaric would join him in the Ox and Bucks when he came of service age, but instead, when that date had arrived, he had unexpectedly received orders to report to a military camp in Norfolk. By that point, Arthur had been wounded, gassed and decorated and had twice returned to the front against medical advice. His continued survival seemed a miracle; their widowed mother had become a wisp of herself, a pale watcher at the window, scarcely able to face yet another day that might bring a telegram instead of a letter.

The military camp had turned out to be the Army PE centre for the East of England, and Alaric had found himself shouting encouraging comments as twig-limbed recruits attempted to climb ropes or scale netting; having always carried a little too much weight himself, he had not been a popular figure amongst the men. There had been nicknames. After a few months he was moved to the office, where he'd had to write letters to wives and mothers expressing regret for the serious or occasionally fatal injuries their husbands or offspring had received while training.

The CO was a Boer War veteran with a stiff knee; he

seldom spoke to Alaric, and when he did there was some-thing indefinably unpleasant about his expression. This was eventually explained when the CO's sister visited the camp, and turned out to be Alaric's godmother. She'd fluttered into the office, patted his cheek and promised to write to his mama to say how well he was getting on, and thus the puzzle of why and how he'd ended up in Thetford had been solved. Solved, also, was the mystery of the CO's expression; it was contempt.

Alaric could, of course, have requested a transfer to another regiment, but as he perused the daily casualty lists in *The Times*, recognizing name after name from his school-days, the act of *choosing* to go to the front seemed more and more impossible; had he been under orders, he felt he could have stood it: it was like the difference between having one's ears boxed in class, and the long, solitary walk through the school corridors in order to knock on the headmaster's door and hand over a note which actually *asked* for twenty strokes.

He stayed. Word inevitably leaked out about Thissett's Fairy Godmother and 'Cinderella' was added to the roster of nicknames.

The war ended with Arthur having survived. Alaric went up to Cambridge, but the college was full of chaps who had been at the front, parts missing, much the same age as him but seemingly years older. No-one ever challenged him, or demanded an explanation of his easy war, but he found himself more and more often avoiding their company, afraid that his shame would somehow be visible. In Michaelmas Term in his second year he'd been unable to get out of bed

one morning, and the doctor had diagnosed nervous col-
lapse secondary to overwork. He'd never returned to
college. It was really very fortunate that his researches had
proved so absorbing; the years had shuffled by.

In the bar-room the crowd was beginning to thin out.
Alaric finished his brandy and stood, with an effort; the
journey ahead (two trains and then a taxi from Aylesbury)
felt as impossibly elaborate as a trek through the Hindu
Kush, without bearers. And it was still raining.

He ordered another brandy.

11

ADDENHAM AND DISTRICT
PLOUGHING MATCH and NOVELTY DOG
SHOW

3rd November 1945, 9 a.m. – 3 p.m. in Fowler's Piece,
entrance at Gearman Lane.

Ploughing classes: Horse-drawn plough, Under-14 horse-
drawn plough, High-cut ploughing, Trailed ploughing,
Open conventional ploughing, Two-furrow mounted plough-
ing, Reversible ploughing, Standard three-furrow reversible
ploughing.

Judges: Major S. Akerham, Mr Cresby, Mr S. Torford,
Mr Mick Himwich, Mr W. Glee.

Dog classes (in tent, from 11 a.m.):

Happiest Dog, Saddest Dog, Cleverest Dog, Longest Sit-
up Beg, Waggiest Tail, Loudest Woof, Most Comical Trick,
Dog Most Resembling a Well-known Personage.

Judges: Sir Valentine Vere-Thissett Bt, Miss Yvonne
Maberly

The Airedale was wearing an ATS cap with the badge removed, and had a tobacco pipe tucked into its collar.

'Right,' said Valentine, massaging his own forehead; his head felt like a dinner-gong. 'So this is supposed to be . . .'

'Stalin,' said the small girl holding the lead. Her tone was defiant.

'Ah.'

'He had a moustache I made out of cardboard, but he ate it.'

'Right, yes, I can imagine that the moustache would have made quite a difference.'

The dog shook itself and both hat and pipe fell to the ground. The girl gave her pet a vindictive look and folded her arms. 'I know he's not going to win,' she said. 'I should've done Winston Churchill, but my dad said he bet everyone would do Winston Churchill.'

'Well, er . . .'

'Anyway, I speck *she'll* win.' The girl jerked her head towards the end of the line, where Priss stood. 'Again.'

'What's your dog's name?' asked Yvonne, brightly, holding a tentative hand towards the Airedale.

'Shredder,' said the girl. Yvonne withdrew her hand.

It was quite a small tent, and the barking had been incessant even before the 'Loudest Woof' category had been awarded jointly to a Jack Russell and a mastiff, but the main reason for Valentine's headache was the unexpected pressure of maintaining a balance between fair competition and perceived nepotism. Because, really, Priss should have won at least five out of the previous seven categories. Her dogs, Toto and Sinbad, were barely out of puppyhood, but she had worked with single-minded intensity on their training and they were already able to obey more than twenty

154

commands; Toto could even pretend to cry by lifting a handkerchief (tied to a paw) towards his eyes. It had been impossible to award the 'Saddest Dog' rosette to any other competitor, and exactly the same thing had applied to 'Cleverest Dog' (Sinbad saluting a photograph of the King and barking at one of Hitler; his nearest rival had been a Labrador who had reluctantly Died for His Country after being given a sharp push). It was at this point that Valentine had become aware of a restive atmosphere in the tent.

'The rest of them might as well go home,' one of the mothers had remarked, loudly, to muttered agreement. 'All the prizes going to the big house. Poor kiddies.'

And so he'd had no choice; *noblesse oblige*. 'Longest Sit-up Beg', 'Waggiest Tail' and 'Most Comical Trick' went to un-deserving winners and he could almost feel Priss's gaze of hurt bafflement pursuing him around the tent.

'Right, now who's this?' he asked, moving on to a morose-looking lurcher-cross, recently whelped, judging by the size of her tits.

Its owner, a very small boy buttoned into a jacket much too large for him, groped around in one of the pockets and withdrew a piece of card on a string, which he hung round the lurcher's neck. It bore the words 'WINSTON CHURCHILL' in wobbly capitals. A fumble in the other pocket produced a cigarette, painted brown, which he held to the dog's mouth as if it were a cigar.

'Oh yes,' said Valentine. 'Yes. Now that I come to look at her . . .'

'And what's this doggie's name?' asked Yvonne.

Valentine could tell that she was slightly afraid of dogs,

but she had accompanied him round the tent all the same, and had gamely patted some of the friendlier ones. She had also nodded whenever he'd given an opinion and had smilingly agreed with all his decisions, which had had the unexpected effect of making him instantly doubt their wisdom.

'Now, do you remember the Maberly girl?' his mother had asked, just before Yvonne and her mother had suddenly arrived for afternoon tea, and he hadn't, although he could recall a long-ago children's party at her house, because that had been the first time that he'd ever seen a radiator; they were in every room at Maberly Hall and he'd put a chocolate biscuit on one to see what would happen, with terrible consequences.

The tea invitation had, of course, been the latest advance in his mother's Blitzkrieg. The Maberlys, he gathered, had a quite tremendous amount of money, thanks to the Great War and tinned beef, but they had no title and Yvonne had no siblings. And now here she was again – no doubt a command had zinged along the wires from Dimperley to Major Akerham of the Competition Committee, an old friend of his father's.

Yvonne had seemed unexpectedly pleased to see him again – or, at least, not *dis*pleased; this was an advance on Genevieve Mallet at the Hunt Ball, who had abandoned Valentine immediately and spent the evening shrieking with laughter in the company of a handsome older man who had subsequently driven her off in his Jaguar. Similarly, the elder Coddington sister, at 'An Evening of Light Opera' in Aylesbury Town Hall, had firmly informed him at the interval that she had no intention of 'wallowing in Buckinghamshire' for the rest of her life. 'I can't tell you where I spent the war,' she'd said, 'but I never want to see another large, damp country house as long as I live.' Both encounters had smacked of duty; a tick on a joint parental list.

Yvonne seemed very different, and Valentine didn't quite know what to make of her. She was only nineteen and had spent most of the war at school somewhere near Wales; she had a pretty face, framed by short, curly hair, and she didn't seem to resent having to spend half a day in a draughty tent awash with canine urine. There had been little chance for conversation but during their few exchanges she hadn't made him feel boring or stupid or awkward and it had all been quite pleasant, really. A charade, but a bearable one.

'Oh, this is splendid,' said Yvonne. 'Look, Valentine.' He peeled himself away from the last Churchill in the line – a sheepdog in a homburg hat – and turned to see the blaze of glory that was Toto. The small white-faced spaniel-cross was wearing a starched lace ruff, a russet wig studded with pearls and a ruby clip on one ear.

'It's Queen Elizabeth,' said Priss. 'They're not real pearls, they're hatpins, the ruff's a dressing-table cloth and the hair's made out of one of your old mittens. It had holes in anyway, and Miss Hersey said I could unravel it. She helped me to starch the ruff. And look!' She unfolded a stained velvet wrap and, with a low bow, spread it on the grass in front of Toto. The dog stepped on to the cloth.

'I was being Sir Walter Raleigh,' said Priss, rewarding Toto with a peanut. 'Have you heard of him?'

'Yes. Yes, I have, very good,' said Valentine. 'Very detailed.' He paused, sensing a certain stiffness in the air – the spectators bracing themselves for yet another gentry-favouring decision. The sheepdog in the homburg hat gave an audible fart. The mother of its owner folded her meaty arms. Priss looked at Valentine, flung a glance at the other competitors and then looked at him again, imploringly. Valentine felt around in his pockets.

'Well, it's going to be very, very hard to decide on a winner in this category,' he said. 'So hard that I think we should have *two* winners – no, *three*,' he added, finding a third half-crown. 'Three winners. So I think . . .'

'We need a hand out here!' shouted someone. 'A lorry's stuck.'

'Er . . . I really should go and help. Perhaps Miss Maberly could make the final decision. Could you, Miss Maberly?'

'Yes, of course I could,' said Yvonne.

It was raining yet again. The field, which had been green when he'd first gone into the tent, was scored with furrows. Over the noise of tractor engines, Valentine could hear shouting from the lane, and he crossed over to the gate. A flatbed lorry, carrying an army bulldozer, was stationary at an angle along the road; as he approached he saw that the rear wheels on one side had slid into the ditch as the lorry had tried to follow the curve of the lane. The whole tarmacadam surface was thick with mud. 'Again!' shouted someone, and the lorry revved horribly, a thin veil of blue exhaust obscuring the cluster of men who were pushing at the rear of the flatbed.

'NO, no no no!' shouted someone as Valentine hurried to help. 'Not going to work. We'll just have to wait for the tractor.'

Someone banged on the cab door and the revving stopped. Puzzled, Valentine glanced round at the field full of tractors that was just behind him.

'We can't get one past the damn thing, Sir Valentine,' shouted Major Akerham, watching from the hedge. 'Blocking the whole lane. Fullshaw's taking his Massey Ferguson round the long way, via Milton Parva.'

'Ah yes, of course.'

The lorry driver jumped down from his cab and went to inspect the back wheels, and Valentine stared at the tall figure in oil-stained overalls.

'Miller?'

The man turned. He'd grown a moustache, but it was Dusty Miller all right, his strained expression cracking in a grin.

'Toff! Bloody hell, Toff, what are you doing here? Haven't seen you since – well, you know.' He nodded at Valentine's gloved hand. 'I still get nightmares, finding your fuc—' He caught himself: 'Top of your finger down my shirt. Horrible. How you managing?'

'It's not so bad.'

'This is a bloody nuisance, though, isn't it? I'm supposed to be in Northampton by four.'

'Who are you working for?'

'Delivering for a builder. He bought the dozer off the Swavely camp; they're flogging surplus. I wasn't even going fast. Mud all over the bloody place; I hate the bloody countryside.'

He clapped Valentine on the shoulder and went round to look at the back of the lorry again. Valentine followed him.

The next hour was the most enjoyable he'd had since returning to Dimperley – first helping to pass straw bales from hand to hand to pack the ditch beneath the hanging wheels while spectators watched over the bare hedge, Priss and Yvonne waving; then the Massey Ferguson edging to and fro, unable to achieve the correct angle of pull in the curving lane, Miller letting down the ramp and backing the dozer off the flatbed and on to the road to relieve the lorry's weight and then – in front of at least thirty tractor drivers – asking Valentine to take the controls. 'It's pretty much like a Universal, apart from the blade,' he had shouted, getting back into the cab, and Valentine had clambered into the bulldozer straight away, before he could lose his nerve or worry about looking a fool, and it was like climbing back into his old self, a person who actually knew (more or less) what they were doing. He let his hands remember the gears; the engine started with the familiar blatting roar. He could see people's mouths moving but could hear nothing.

At the front end of the lorry they'd given up on the tractor and were using a short tow-rope and two plough horses. Miller's arm snaked out of the cab and beckoned, and Valentine eased the dozer forward until the blade was just under the flatbed. He had to use his right hand for the long rod that controlled the height, and the judder of it drove spikes of pain through his fingertips and up his arm and he shouted a word that he hadn't used since Sicily, and followed it up with a string of others, richly obscene, that somehow helped him keep his grip. The blade rose and lifted the back of the truck as easily as a spoon lifting sugar and the men shoved another bale into the opened gap between wheel and ditch.

Miller's arm signalled him away, and he lowered the blade and edged back again and saw the lorry begin to move, the wheels gripping and bumping over the bales, and it was back on the road again. Valentine turned off the engine, and climbed out into a world of back-slaps and terse admiration. 'Neat enough.' 'Sweet as a nut.' 'Tidily done, Sir Valentine.' He felt as if he'd grown six inches.

'Sir Valentine,' said Miller, reflectively, easing the rig on to the Watford road. The window on Valentine's side was jammed halfway, and rain blew on to the seat. 'But you've not been knighted, have you?'

'No, it's an inherited title.'

'So what happens if someone calls you "Mr" by accident? They get their balls chopped off?'

'No, I think nowadays it's just a short prison sentence.'

Miller made the snorting noise he used for a laugh. 'So, you enjoying civvy street?'

'Are you?' asked Valentine, swerving the question.

'I am and I'm not. I'll be honest with you, Toff, sometimes it all feels a bit flat. Once I'd been down the pub a few times and got used to Mum bringing me tea and not being screamed at by a fucking nutter because he can't bounce a penny off the bed, I started to wonder if that was it. My bit of adventure. I don't suppose I'll ever ride a camel again, will

I, or fire a mortar, or see a flying fish? I mean, maybe if I'd had a wife and a kid to come back to, it might have felt different, but as it is – DON'T DO IT bloody GOD WALLAH trying to meet his bloody MAKER' – he'd stamped on the brake as a vicar on a bicycle wavered out of a side road, followed, opportunistically, by a maroon Bedford van.

'Actually, this is a good place to drop me,' said Valentine. 'I can walk home from here.'

'What's the name of your gaff?'

'Dimperley Manor. Will you be back this way?'

'Maybe, it's not up to me. *That* bit hasn't changed.'

'All right. Well, if you get the chance, just call in.'

'White tie, is it?'

'Definitely.'

'All right, then.'

Valentine clambered out into drizzle. Over the noise of the engine, he caught the shouted words 'Nice work today, SIR,' and, grinning, he vaulted a stile and set off for Dimperley at a fast clip.

He arrived home via the back drive; it was in a worse state, even, than the carriage road, flooded potholes forming a chain from the gate all the way to the house. The maroon van he'd seen earlier was parked in the stable-yard, and as he rounded the corner he saw a couple of overalled workmen standing with folded arms, a low trolley piled with ropes and tackle on the cobbles in front of them. Their gazes flicked towards him and then moved uncomfortably away. From the stable came an ugly noise that Valentine couldn't identify, a repeated sound, agonized and staccato.

'What's happening?'

One of the workmen took off his hat, attempted to say something and then gestured towards the open arch that led to the stalls.

'Sir Valentine!' It was Miss Hersey, standing in the arch and beckoning, urgently, and he ran towards and then straight past her, heading for the source of the noise, and saw in the semi-darkness Epple, the gardener, and beside him a rocking, wailing figure, one hand gripping the door of the loose-box and the other smacking his forehead over and over.

'Oh God, Ceddy. Oh God.' Valentine wrapped one arm round Ceddy's chest from behind and grabbed the moving hand with his own. The cry continued, vibrating through both of them.

'He ran ahead of your ladyship and found the horse here,' said Epple, and over his brother's shoulder Valentine could see the slumped dark shape of Smokey, as slack as a bag of wet sand. 'I called the knacker, but your young fellow won't leave.'

Valentine leaned his chin on Ceddy's shoulder, tightened his grip on his chest and swivelled the two of them round, so that they were facing the tack rail where Smokey's harness hung.

'Shhh, shhh, shhhh, old chap.' He kept his head tight against his brother's, and tried to remember what Murray, the groom, had used to say to quiet the horses. 'Easy now, easy now, whisht the lad, whisht now.' He inched an unresisting Ceddy forward so that the two of them were right up against the rail, their foreheads resting against the saddle.

The cries were longer now, more broken, more human. 'Epple, you should get the men in,' he said.

It must have been thirty minutes that they stood there; long enough, anyway, for Ceddy to quieten and Valentine's arms to have stiffened so much that they stayed at an angle when he loosened them. He could hear the van driving away.

The door to the loose-box was open, and straw had been dragged along the flags as far as the stable arch. Epple, broom in hand, leaned towards Valentine's ear. 'Not a scratch on the poor old girl. They said she most likely dropped on the spot, an ambulism, gone between one breath and the next.'

'Come along, Mr Ceddy,' said Miss Hersey, gently taking his arm. 'I'll make you some cocoa and then we'll go and see your mother. Her ladyship was so very upset,' she added, over her shoulder to Valentine. 'I sent her indoors.'

'Horse,' said Ceddy, the syllable a slur of grief.

'I'll get you another horse. I will. I promise,' said Valentine. Miss Hersey cast him a look that he couldn't interpret – hope? doubt? disbelief? – and led his brother away. Valentine followed slowly; during that long half-hour of holding Ceddy he'd recalled other occasions when his brother's usual mood of mild recalcitrance had shattered into something darker: the day after Blott's Spinney had been cut and sold for timber, when the morning walk had taken Ceddy past the splintered stumps; the time when a flooded road had necessitated a different route to the usual on his way to the dentist in Addenham; occasions when the world had shifted a little without Ceddy's permission and he'd protested in the only way that he could. 'My God,' said Valentine, out loud. Why hadn't he *thought*? Taking his brother from Dimperley would be like moving him to Mars . . .

12

From *Bring Me My Bow*: Volume Two of the B. M. Rhydderch-Jones Diaries, 1944–1952:

7th November 1945

*I am worn out today. Meeting of the Historic Buildings Society this morning, and then motored to a Trust assessment in Buckinghamshire through a dirty mist which only cleared when the road began to rise beyond Amersham. Had to stop and ask directions twice (road-signs **still** not restored) and realized on the second occasion that I'd run over a hedgehog and its head was jammed under one mudguard like a heraldic symbol.*

The approach to Dimperley is undoubtedly romantic, the long lime avenue intact, follies dotting the greensward, but the grounds are overgrown and the driveway so potholed that I was surprised to arrive with all four wheels still attached.

The frontage is an extraordinary hotch-potch of styles, with the central early-Tudor section wedged between a sub-Strawberry Hill Dower Wing and a strangely proportioned Indian wing with a vast copper dome and an Orangery almost the same breadth as the entire rest of the house; the words 'blind architect' spring to mind. The guttering looks in a frightful state.

The current Baronet met me outside and advised re-parking my motor-car as he couldn't be certain that the drawbridge (on which I'd left it) wouldn't give way suddenly. He's a strongly built, rather blunt-featured young man, with none of the handsome grace of his brother Felix (lost in the war, alas). I met the latter in '38 on the occasion of the Torrington/Strand-Fitzroy-Blair wedding in West Charlesford, when he drove me from the railway station to the church in an utterly hair-raising journey that still, occasionally, has the power to wrench me from sleep in a cold sweat.

Vere-Thissett was very apologetic: his uncle, an apparently bottomless well of historical information, was prevented by illness from showing me around the house and answering any questions that I might have. 'So you're stuck with me,' he said, somewhat endearingly. The truth is that I always prefer a paucity to an excess of information, so my expressions of regret lacked sincerity.

We began with luncheon, served in a long, thin, Adamesque dining room, the ceiling encrusted with dangling bunches of stucco grapes like purple buboes ('We call it The Vineyard,' the elder Lady Vere-Thissett informed me), the walls lined with anaglypta the colour of Tangee lipstick. The room was so cold that the jacketed potato (containing an egg) with which I was served was steaming like a kettle, rendering my spectacles completely opaque for the first half of the meal. It was followed by large, thick pancakes containing custard and treacle, and when I stood up afterwards, I felt as if I'd swallowed a couple of cannonballs.

Lady Irene radiated disapproval throughout, barely chipping off the odd reply to my attempts at conversation; I gather that she thinks the National Trust is in league with the Unions and our only intention is to remove the house from her family and fill it with Bolshevik Youth Groups, so that the latter can practise throwing Molotov cocktails in the Long Gallery. Felix's widow was there, a very pretty woman with an air of strained desperation and a bored-looking adolescent daughter who ate her meal entirely with a fork.

The house is very peculiar, with odd charming corners and features of real interest – a wide Jacobean oak staircase; an Empire room with pink-damask walls; an extraordinary Italian marble fireplace in the shape of a gaping lion's mouth; exquisite Indian pastoral scenes flaking away on the Orangery ceiling – unbalanced by successive generations of ham-fisted extension and redecoration. Twin Tudor courtyards were roofed over during the last century and a series of haphazard attics and windowless corridors created above; great rooms have been chopped into little ones; panelling has been lined with imitation Spanish leather (to ghastly effect); friezes of mustard-coloured lincrusta render the entrance hall hideous, and everywhere – everywhere – there are what I can only term as curios, *many of the stuffed variety. The Baronet kept saying about each dust-sheeted object: 'My uncle could have told you much more about it than I can.'*

We were joined on the tour by the uncle's secretary, a large-breasted young woman who wrote in a notebook whenever I opened my mouth, something which made me extremely self-conscious. She was silent until I began speculating on the provenance of an equestrian portrait, at which point she crisply corrected me and offered to show me the original bill of sale. The paintings, incidentally, are as variable as the decor, with daubs of staggering ineptitude cheek-by-jowl with something which I am almost certain is a rather good Zoffany.

Afterwards, we walked around the grounds. There are only two gardeners working at present, and most of the pruning seems to be left to the rabbits; however, the various grots, cots, towers, temples and hermitages (all, obviously, in a state of disrepair) add a pleasingly eccentric element to every view. Vere-Thissett asked me, with touching hope, whether the Trust would take the property and I told him that I would need to take various aspects of the case into consideration before a decision was made. This, I'm afraid, was cowardice on my part, since the combination of the lack of any endowment (most of the farmland has already gone and the contents – with the exception of the possible Zoffany – are worth threepence-halfpenny) together with the total architectural salmagundi of the property means that I will be strongly advising against its acquisition. God knows what they'll do with it; it would be unsuitable as either a school, an asylum or council offices and I suspect that its fate will be decided by a combination of bulldozers and land-prices: in years to come, woolly lambs will graze on the pulverized remains of five centuries of patronage while the living Vere-Thissetts peer resentfully from the windows of a jerry-built mock-Tudor 'gentleman's villa' on the outskirts of Watford.

Returned home with a stiff neck, the car window having stuck halfway. Dined at the Haverstones' but could only turn my head to the left; Princess Galitzine was there and appeared to gaze fixedly at my trousers for the entire evening. I realized afterwards that there was a smear of custard on the fly.

13

'... seventeen, eighteen, nineteen, twenty. Coming, ready or not!' Zena opened her eyes and instantly spotted her daughter's red wellington boots beneath the oilcloth that hung from the kitchen table. For the second day running, it had been too wet for a walk in the grounds and out of desperation she had brought Allison through the garden door and down into the servants' hall.

There was no urgency about getting back to her desk in the library; her employer had not come in for a fortnight. Miss Hersey, after persistent questioning, had vouchsafed that his absence wasn't due to an actual *illness*, but more of a 'low mood', a condition that came upon Mr Alaric every now and again. 'I'm sure he'll be more himself in a few days,' she'd added. 'Or perhaps a little longer.'

Zena had seen him only once, in the distance, walking very slowly through the Stumpery, looking painfully older and baggier, his gaze fixed on the ground just beyond his feet.

He had sent her a note asking her to 'carry on as usual', but it had taken only a couple of days for her to rattle through her entire list of tasks and, after typing up the concluding paragraphs of Chapter Fourteen of *Woodsman to the King*, she'd boldly decided to attempt a draft of Chapter Fifteen, based on Alaric's notes. Six pages into ''ware Boney:

Dimperley during the Napoleonic Wars', she'd found herself too bored to continue and had instead started roughing out a plot for a detective novel set in a requisitioned country house. The truth was that, since returning from London, she couldn't settle to anything. The easy stasis of the last three years was over. It had never been more than a temporary perch, sheltered and with a fine view, and she knew that now she needed to think ahead: a fresh start in a new town, a neat flat, a nursery for Allison, a job for herself, Mrs Baxter, a widow with considerable administrative experience. It was a realistic and sensible plan. Her spirits slumped whenever she thought of it.

'Where on earth can Allison *be*?' she asked, loudly, turning her back on the kitchen table and randomly opening a cupboard to reveal a frying pan the size of a coracle. 'No, she's not in there. I think she *might* have gone through here . . .' She crossed into the scullery, gave the Kent patent knife-grinder a pat, and, on a whim, tried the door to the Dower Wing tunnel. It opened.

She stood for a moment, startled. The watery light in the scullery flowed only a yard or two into the interior, revealing a broken chair and a floor of quarry tiles. The air reeked of damp.

Zena looked back and saw the red wellies still in position; feeling like the heroine of a school-girl mystery, she opened the door more widely and crossed the puddle of light, trailing a cautious hand along the wall as the tunnel curved into darkness. After four or five hesitant paces, she froze. Ahead – an indefinable distance ahead – a crescent of light trembled across the low ceiling and she could also hear

171

something; she could hear the impossible: a gulping, chok-ing, breathless gurgle . . .

Did she scream? If she did, it was drowned out by Alli-son bellowing 'WHERE ARE YOU GONE?' and then there was only the panicky patter of her own footsteps, her uneven breaths as she closed the door and herded her daughter towards the kitchen.

'Nothing, nothing's the matter,' she said, her voice so unconvincing and squeaky that Allison stared at her, open-mouthed, and then switched her round blue gaze to something behind her. Zena turned and saw the tunnel door slowly opening . . . to reveal Miss Hersey, holding a torch in one hand and a handkerchief in the other.

'Oh!' They spoke simultaneously.

'I thought you were the daily,' said Miss Hersey, drop-ping the hanky and then stooping to pick it up, face averted. 'I must have scared you. I'm sorry.' She walked quickly past them and out of the kitchen.

'She's *crying*!' said Allison, astounded.

'Why don't you' – Zena glanced around – 'search in all the cupboards until you find the biggest frying pan you ever saw in your life?' Allison looked at her with suspicion, but the offer was too thrillingly unusual to argue with, and the banging of cupboard doors accompanied Zena as she hurried out; she caught up with Miss Hersey at the foot of the back stairs.

'Is something the matter? Can I help?'

The older woman turned to her, tried to answer and then tightened her lips as they started to tremble, compos-ing her features as if smoothing a bedsheet.

'I have a flask of coffee with me,' said Zena. 'And a clean handkerchief.'

They sat in the housekeeper's room, with the door half open. In the corridor, Allison was making what appeared to be a train out of saucepans, placing an item of cutlery in each as a passenger.

The faint shine of salt was still visible on Miss Hersey's cheeks.

'It wasn't anything in particular, Mrs Baxter. Just one thing after another. Mr Ceddy not at all himself and then today Sir Valentine showing me a letter, and for a moment it all seemed to get on top of me.' She took an extremely small sip of the lukewarm coffee. 'I feel rather silly now.'

'I'm the silly one. I thought you were a ghost.'

'There isn't a ghost at Dimperley.'

'Oh, I know, and I don't believe in them anyway. But what's odd is that when I first came here, one of the things the other women told me – you know, there were always lots of rumours, just like in any institution – they told me that the tunnel was haunted by the spirit of a . . . a . . .' She realized what she was about to say, and was suddenly embarrassed.

'. . . of a weeping servant girl,' said Hersey.

'Well, yes. Yes, that's what they said.'

Out in the corridor, Allison was shouting 'Tickets, please!' at the row of pans. Miss Hersey started to speak and then checked herself.

'Do say,' said Zena.

'There is a reason for that particular rumour.'

'Oh, go on!'

'The tunnel was only ever used if guests were staying in the

Dower Wing, and meals needed to be taken through to them. So it was a place that was quite private. And it wasn't possible for maids to go back to their rooms during the day, so if anyone was ever a little upset about something, then that's where they went. "Taking a hankie holiday", they called it.'

'We had a place like that in the women's hostel I lived in – we called it the Howling Room, except it wasn't really a room, just a little curtained-off corner where the caretaker kept his bucket. So, is that why you went there?'

'I suppose it must have been.' Miss Hersey's feet had chosen it, not her head. They'd taken her there when she'd realized that she was about to burst into tears in front of the daily and she'd almost run the last few yards, as if carrying a heavy dish that was sliding through her hands. She hadn't cried that fiercely in years; not since the butler, Mr Lemons, a good man and a good friend, had died suddenly during one of his day-trips to Brighton. It had transpired that he'd left his body to medical science so that there'd be no funeral and it had been months before she'd stopped expecting him to walk through the green baize door again.

She took another mouthful of the horrid coffee. 'I really should get on.'

'You mentioned a letter,' said Zena, quickly. 'I know I'm being nosy, but was it from the National Trust? I was here when the man came and he was very snooty. He wasn't interested in any of the good bits and he spent ages looking at the picture on the middle staircase – the clergyman that looks like Mussolini.'

'Yes, he mentioned that it might be by a famous painter.'

'But what about the house?'

Hersey looked down at her clasped hands. Sir Valentine had found her in the sewing room just after breakfast and had held out the letter. 'Could you possibly, Miss Hersey? It's in this lousy, spidery hand-writing and I can hardly make out a word.' His expression, as she'd read it to him, had slowly flattened from hope to resignation.

'Don't tell anyone I told you,' she said to Zena, 'but they won't take Dimperley. It's not a good enough example of the architecture of the . . . the various periods.'

'More fool them,' said Zena. 'It's beautiful. Isn't that enough?' and Hersey found herself being silly again, and having to dab her eyes with Allison's yellow-and-blue handkerchief.

'I do apologize, Mrs Baxter,' she said.

'Zena. Please do call me Zena. Since the other mothers left, nobody here ever calls me that.'

'Zena.' She blew her nose. 'It's a very . . . *modern* . . . name.'

'It was after Zena Dare – she was a film star my father admired. I know that hardly anyone ever likes their own name, but I've always loved mine.' She paused expectantly.

'Thelma,' said Hersey. 'It was the title of my mother's favourite book.' *My mother*; the sweetness of those long-unspoken words. She'd forgotten that it could be so easy to talk. 'In my first place of service, I was always called Alice. Because "Thelma" was considered too fancy for a parlourmaid.'

'Where was that?'

'A small household near Oxford – two maids and a cook. And then I came here.' She made a little, rounded gesture, as if to say: the world.

'Tickets, please!'

Allison came into the room wearing a bracelet of biscuit cutters.

'How much are they?' asked Zena.

'Five. Pennies. A pound is blue tickets.'

'Here you go, then: five pennies.' Zena handed over some imaginary cash and received a crinkle-edged circle in return.

'And a blue ticket for me, please,' said Miss Hersey, unfolding an invisible banknote. Allison deliberated before choosing a copper star – 'This is the best one' – and returning to her passengers.

'I wonder how much they would have charged visitors to Dimperley?' asked Zena, idly.

'There's a lady in Great Bilstead who allows people to look around her house for a shilling and sixpence, I think it is. My friend is the cook-general there. She says that visitors are sometimes quite critical of the furnishings.'

Zena frowned. 'I don't understand.'

'Well, for instance, one of them suggested to Mrs Blackstone – the owner – that she should really think about wall-papering the entrance hall.'

'No, I mean, you're saying that she sells tickets? To her own house? How long has she been doing that for?' She could feel her thoughts darting ahead, as if they'd slipped a leash and dived along an unmarked path.

'Since before the war, I believe.'

'Where *is* Great Bilstead?'

'It's quite near St Albans.'

'Is there a bus from here?'

'Yes, I think so.'

'What day would suit you?'

'Me?'

'You'd like to come, wouldn't you? We could have an outing – I'm sure we deserve one. I could ask my landlady to mind Allison and you could see your friend. When is your day off?'

There was a pause.

'You do . . . have a day off, don't you?' And Hersey saw that it was back again: that baffled, slightly pitying expression.

She bridled. 'I am quite able to take time away from my duties if I feel it *necessary*, Mrs Baxter. And now I think I had better—'

'Oh no, don't,' said Zena, putting a hand on her arm. 'Please don't, I didn't mean to offend you. It's been so nice talking to you. Honestly. This past couple of weeks it's only been me and Allison in the library, all day, every day, and if you'd told me before then that I'd miss hearing all about the 1780 Bedford and Buckingham Roads Act, I wouldn't have believed you. But I have. Because even though Allison's always—'

There was a clang from the corridor and then a commanding shout of 'Mummy!'

'In a moment,' called Zena. She smiled, a little ruefully, at Miss Hersey, and, after a moment, Miss Hersey smiled back.

There was a notice nailed to the gate:

Visitors to Great Bilstead Hall are admitted on week-days
(Wednesday excepted) between 2 p.m. and 4 p.m. for the price

of one shilling and ninepence.
Ring the bell ONCE and then wait.

The butler who eventually came to the door after Zena and Kitty had been standing outside for at least three minutes, shifting from foot to frozen foot in the pale sunlight, was wearing a tailcoat with brass buttons and a striped waistcoat, like an illustration in *Punch* magazine. 'Yes?' he asked, repressively, as if they were toting baskets of lucky heather.

'We're here to see the house,' said Zena.

Grudgingly, he stood aside, and they edged through the gap and into an entrance hall in which suits of armour alternated with gas lamps mounted on iron sconces. At the foot of a stone staircase a group of about twenty people stood in a cowed huddle. Without speaking, the butler closed the door and then exited along an unlit passage.

'What's happening?' asked Zena, who had taken a notebook out of her bag.

'We're supposed to stand over here,' said an elderly lady, in a whisper.

'Why?'

'I don't know, but that's what he said.'

'Yes, that's what he said,' echoed one of her companions.

'Perhaps they're waiting until there's enough of us to show around,' said the lady.

Zena looked at her wristwatch. 'But it's already half past two. What if nobody else turns up?'

Kitty folded her arms. 'It'll be a nice day out for you,' her mother had said. 'I worry that you're on your own so much – it seems so sad at your age,' and now here she was, standing in yet another prehistoric Frigidaire full of old people. She curled one of her hands round so that she could see the nails. She wasn't allowed to use nail polish at home, but in the bus she'd had a double seat to herself, behind Zena and Miss Hersey, who'd gassed the whole way – Dimperley this, Dimperley that – and she'd been able to apply a coat of Gadabout by Cutex during the straighter stretches of road, something that had taken considerable skill. The polish had been a present from a GI she'd gone for a coffee with in Tring, something about which she hadn't told her mother, since Barbara would certainly regard it as the equivalent of having sexual intercourse in the middle of the Market Place ('You have no idea how people *gossip* – the least thing sets them off. You have to be so careful!'). Which was rich, considering that nearly everyone in Buckinghamshire seemed to know that Barbara was seeing 'Ask Benny' Haxall, the driver of the grey van that Kitty had spotted on the day she'd been expelled. The proprietress of 'À La Mode', the gown shop where Kitty had recently begun to model new acquisitions, had seen them at the Oxford racecourse, where apparently a horse part-owned by 'Ask Benny' had come second. He also had a motor-cycle and side-car and was building a large modern house outside Addenham, and altogether it seemed typical of this country that someone who made money and liked to spend it was regarded as Joe Blow because he didn't live in a place where the drains hadn't worked since Shakespeare.

'Oh, at *last*,' muttered Zena, as the butler returned, this time carrying a small box.

'Visitors are required to pay one and ninepence,' he said, addressing a gas mantle just above their heads. 'I have spoken to Mrs Blackstone, and I am delighted to inform you that she will be honouring you with her presence later in the tour.' He paused, and one of the ladies made an appreciative noise, as seemed required. Coins rattled into the butler's box.

'Follow me,' he said, setting off up the stairs. 'Visitors are requested not to touch or sit down on or lean against any items of furniture. Mrs Blackstone is currently at work in her study so should not be disturbed with any unnecessary noise.' As if, thought Kitty, they were letting off firecrackers.

There was almost nothing to look at in the vast, cold room at the top of the stairs. 'This is the solar,' said the butler. 'The ceiling is the finest example of barrel vaulting in East Buckinghamshire.'

The group looked upward in respectful silence.

'It's high, isn't it?' whispered one of the women.

'What is the definition of a solar?' asked Zena.

The butler appeared not to have heard her and moved on into the next room.

'*He doesn't know,*' whispered Kitty.

'This is the Tapestry Chamber.' The room was in semi-darkness, the walls covered with yellowed sheets. The butler took a long stick from a corner and lifted one of the coverings to reveal a lumpy embroidery in various shades of mud. Dimly discernible was a unicorn with knees that went the wrong way and a woman with no neck.

'Such a lot of work,' said one of the ladies, obviously struggling to think of a compliment.

The butler lowered the sheet again and moved slowly along to the next section of wall, and Kitty realized that they were going to have to look at every single one of these God-awful tapestries, and that the day was going to be just as dull as she'd imagined. Lucky Miss Hersey, sitting in a warm kitchen with her friend the cook, probably eating cakes straight from the oven. Zena had her notebook out again and was drawing a firm line under something.

'*What are you writing?*'

She tilted the page and Kitty read the words 'Very boring' and snickered and felt a death ray shooting out of the back of the butler's head. Zena remained perfectly composed; she reminded Kitty of a store detective — someone you assumed was just a part of the crowd until you realized they weren't missing a thing.

The tour continued. Kitty worked out what she was going to wear for her imminent audition with the Aylesbury Music and Drama Society (all black, apart from a coloured silk scarf around the neck; she'd seen a photograph of Lauren Bacall dressed similarly) and trailed after the others through a succession of rooms where they were ordered to stand and admire things that (with good reason) you wouldn't normally even glance at in passing — like walls and the middle bit of windows. Eventually, when even the lady who'd said 'Fascinating!' when informed that the stone for the Great Bilstead gatehouse had been quarried near Watford had fallen silent, they arrived in a hall where there was an actual fire in the fireplace. The butler left for a moment and then returned accompanied by a tiny old lady who was wearing a fur coat. 'Mrs Blackstone,' he said, reverently, and she came twinkling across to the group, who were all standing right next to the fire, and said, 'How *lovely* of you all to have come to see my home. I so much hope that you found it as charming as I do. Did you enjoy your visit?' and she was so smiley and enthusiastic that everyone said, 'Oh yes, it was marvellous,' and other big lies.

They had to wait half an hour for a bus on the way back, which meant that Kitty missed her secret Wednesday driving lesson with Mr Epple's nephew, so all in all the whole trip was a complete waste of time.

14

Bucks Herald, Classified Advertisements

Piebald filly (black and white), 2 years old in March. Stands approximately 13.2 hands; gentled to halter and bridle; make ideal mount for a young lady or gent; 35 gns; property of working man – Barber, Ivy Cottage, Stockwell Lane, Meadle, Aylesbury.

The coping-stone that had killed Pollux was so heavy that Valentine could only take it to the top of the Wyvern Tower ten steps at a time. Once up there, he gingerly tested all the other stones and found that nine of them were loose, so that what had appeared to be a discrete task ended up stretching over the rest of the day: the chiselling of the old cement, the repeated toting of the bucket of lime mortar from where he mixed it at the foot of the tower, the slap and gritty scrape of the trowel. It was sufficiently physically taxing to remind him of how unfit he'd become since leaving the army, and required just enough concentration to push his thoughts away from the whole current lousy mess.

The weather was cold but bright. Each time he looked up from his work, the view had changed, the pockets of frost gradually melting, rooks peppering the newly damp grass, a kestrel riding the air at his own eye-level. Once or twice he took off his heavy gloves in order to make a sketch. The discovery that he could write better with his left hand than his right did not extend to drawing: a kestrel drawn with his still-clumsy right hand looked merely inept; drawn with his left it was as lifeless as a brick.

When he heard light footsteps on the stairs he assumed it was Priss, probably carrying at least one dog, probably keen to show him a new trick, and he straightened up, trowel in hand, and saw Yvonne Maberly emerge from the darkened doorway. She was carrying two mugs and she held one out to him.

'Cocoa.'

'Oh. Right. Thank you very much. I didn't realize that you were visiting.' He was conscious of his sweat-stained shirt. She was wearing a red coat and a matching pixie hat, and looked dazzlingly fresh and pretty.

'It's a wonderful view from up here, isn't it?' she said. 'What's that little pink house with the hole in the roof?'

'It's the Shell Grotto.'

'And that huge brown patch behind it? What *is* it? It looks like a nasty old rug.'

'That's the lake – it's silted up, just a mass of dead weed and about an inch of water. And beyond that – can you see, over the hedgerow – there's a crater in the clover field?'

'Yes. Another grotto?'

'No, it's where Dimperley's only bomb fell.'

'Oh gosh! Was that scary?'

'I wasn't here.'

'No, nor me. My school was evacuated to Shropshire and I didn't hear any bombs at all.' She took a sip of cocoa and made a face. 'Horrid. You don't have to drink it.'

'I've probably tasted worse.' He sipped it and changed his mind. 'So, er . . .'

'We were on our way back from seeing my cousins and then my mother said she wanted to lend your mother a novel that they'd been talking about.'

'Really? But my mother never reads novels.'

'Nor mine! I think it was just an excuse.'

'An excuse for what?'

'Well, they're trying to match-make us, aren't they?' She smiled with perfect candour, and Valentine took a large swallow of cocoa and burned the roof of his mouth.

'Why?' he said. 'I mean, why does your mother want you to . . .'

'Marry you? Oh, because she's worried I'll become a nun. Are there any bits of this I can lean on safely?' She patted the parapet.

'I'd rather you didn't.'

'Not even just my elbows?' She lowered them cautiously on to the nearest stone and then cupped her face in her hands and looked across at the back elevation of Dimperley. 'Did you know there's a great big piece of guttering hanging off over there?'

'Yes, yes, I did. You said . . . a nun?'

'Yes. My school was evacuated to a Catholic school and it was attached to a convent and two years ago I was received into the Church and after that I decided to become a nun, a Benedictine, but then Mother said I was too young – by

"Mother", I mean the Mother Superior at the convent, not *my* mother, although obviously *my* mother thinks I'm too young as well – anyway, Mother said that if God wants me to become a nun then He'll make it absolutely clear by sending me a sign, but it's also quite possible that He wants me to serve Him by being a good wife and mother, so she told me – this is still the Mother Superior, not my mother – that I should do what my parents wanted and go home with them, and that God will let me know in due course what He needs me to do. So that's what I did. But obviously my mother – that's *my* mother, not the Mother Superior – is very keen that I take the second option and get married. Gosh, that's a big puddle on your roof, isn't it? Do you get leaks?'

'Yes, we do. So you'd prefer the first option?'

She turned back to him, her expression serious. 'Well, I want to do what God wants for me, but I'm hoping that that's what He chooses.'

'But how will you know? What sort of sign would you get?'

'Oh, something terribly clear, I hope – for instance, St Wilgefortis was the daughter of the pagan King of Portugal, and he ordered her to get married, but Wilgefortis had taken a vow of chastity, so she prayed for a sign that would release her from her betrothal and when she woke up the next morning she'd grown an enormous beard. Obviously, I wouldn't want' – she started giggling – 'I wouldn't want that to happen, and perhaps it would be more of a feeling, a still, small voice, you know, like the one that spoke to Elijah, but it would be easier if it were a definite sign, because that would put it beyond all doubt and even Mother – I mean *my* mother, not the Mother Superior – would have to accept it.'

'An invisible hand, writing on the wall, as at Belshazzar's feast.'

'Yes, gosh, that would be perfect.' Her face glowed at the idea. 'Or a raven coming to eat out of my hand, because a raven's a symbol of St Benedict.'

'You know they're about the size of a spaniel?'

'Really?' She held out her hand and eyed an imaginary raven. 'Well, it wouldn't leave any room for doubt, would it?' She giggled again – she seemed a remarkably cheerful girl; he would have expected a prospective nun to be droopier, more pensive. The extraordinary thought occurred to him that if Jesus didn't want her for a sunbeam then there was actually no particular reason why he shouldn't, at some point, ask this nice-looking, good-natured (extremely wealthy) girl to marry him. Apart, that is, from the fact that he didn't really want to, and since when had *that* ever made any difference?

'I'm to tell you, incidentally,' she added, 'that we're having a party on New Year's Eve to which, of course, you're invited.'

She turned as she spoke: an odd noise – very like Alaric's distinctive laugh, but much higher in pitch – had emanated from ground-level. 'It's a little girl,' said Yvonne, craning over the parapet.

'Don't!' Valentine lunged forward and grabbed at her arm, pushing down on the coping-stone with his other hand. 'I've only just cemented that one.'

'Oh, sorry. Gosh.' She blushed and they stepped away from each other.

'I didn't mean to startle you.'

'No, that's all right. It was silly of me.'

'Sorry.'

'No, *I'm* sorry.'

He was aware, throughout the piecemeal, flustered exchange, that the child Yvonne had spotted was Allison Baxter, being kept at a safe distance by her mother, who was looking up at them with apparent interest.

'I'm stopping you from doing your work,' said Yvonne.

'No, no.'

'I'd better be off, anyway. Mummy will want to go.'

'I'll come down with you. I need to mix some more mortar.'

She'd recovered her composure by the bottom of the staircase, and waved at him as she left along the gravel walk before disappearing from view behind the statue of Zeus and the Cow.

'Hello, man,' said Allison, who was holding her celluloid doll by the neck. 'Ha ha *haaa*!'

Valentine looked at Zena. 'Is that meant to be . . .'

'Ha ha *haaa*!'

'Yes, I'm afraid it is. Stop it now, Allison. Why don't you see if you can walk Baby along the path? You know that this gentleman very kindly bought her for you?'

Allison nodded perfunctorily, as if showered daily with gifts, and trudged off towards the gravel path.

'Could I speak to you for a moment?' asked Zena, as Valentine hefted the bucket of lime. She had never seen him in his shirt-sleeves, physically working, before; he looked unexpectedly competent.

'Yes, of course.' He put the bucket down.

'I know it's not really my place . . .' *I sound like a parlour-maid*, she thought, and started again. 'What I mean is, I know it's not strictly my business, but I wanted to tell you something. Last week I visited a house called Great Bilstead Hall. It's about the same size as Dimperley, but it looks' – she groped for a description that would sum up the cold perfection, the ash-grey symmetry of the exterior – 'it looks all of a piece, all built at the same time, and all the rooms are *just so*, and everything matches, and apparently it's the best example of Elizabethan architecture in the whole of the South of England.'

'She's jumping!' shouted Allison, slamming Baby up and down on the gravel.

'Good,' said Zena. 'Jumpy, jumpy! And, to be honest, it was a very dull tour and the butler who was showing us around didn't answer any questions, there was no lavatory for visitors, there were no refreshments available and it was miles to the nearest bus stop, but in spite of all that, there were about twenty people there, on a freezing winter day, and none of them complained afterwards. They all seemed to think it was a privilege that they'd been allowed to look around, even though they'd been charged for it and – excuse me a moment.' She walked rapidly towards the empty space where she'd last seen Allison, called out, 'Coming, ready or not,' spotted her daughter peering out from behind the sundial, ushered her back towards the path, said, 'I bet you can't make Baby a lovely bed out of stones,' and returned to where Valentine was still waiting for her to continue, his expression polite but mystified.

'Sorry. There's an important reason why I'm telling you this. Great Bilstead isn't owned by the National Trust, it's owned by an old lady called Mrs Blackstone, who inherited it in 1937. *She* owns it, *she* decided to open it to the public and *she* gets all the money. Which can't be much, because it's only open for two hours a day, four days a week. But yesterday I went to Aylesbury Library and I found a list of other private houses that allow visitors, and there's one called Burleigh, in Surrey, that puts on charabancs from the station and charges eight and six. *Eight and six!* Admittedly, it's about the size of Buckingham Palace, but even so . . .'
There was a nudge at her elbow.

'My coat felled off.'

'I think you took it off, didn't you?'

'Yes, I did.'

'Well, let's put it back on again, because it's very cold. So,' she continued, stuffing Allison's arm into a sleeve, '*if* the National Trust should decide not to take Dimperley—'

'They have. Or rather, they haven't. They've said that they don't want it.'

'In that case, there's nothing to stop you from opening it to the public yourself. It would mean you'd be in charge and you could decide which rooms you want to keep private and which ones you let people see and what days they come and how much the tickets cost.'

'This is my Baby,' said Allison, pushing the doll into Valentine's leg. He stooped to defend his knee-cap, his gaze still fixed on Zena, hope and doubt mingled, as if she'd just taken something that appeared to be key-shaped out of her handbag and was waggling it at him through the prison bars.

'*Could* we?' he asked.

'Yes, you could. In fact, I hope you don't mind, but I did a bit of work on the possibility – your uncle's still not back at his desk and, to be honest, I don't have a lot to do. I typed up some thoughts on what visitors might require and which rooms could be shown and what you might need in terms of facilities, and I also compiled some costings. It's only a few pages . . .' She pulled a wedge of folded paper out of her coat pocket. 'It's more or less what I used to do when I was at Dawson's,' she said, holding it out to him. 'Feasibility. So it didn't take very long.'

'Dawson's?'

'Industrial and military glass.'

Reluctantly, he reached out a hand. 'I'm not, er . . . the paperwork type, generally.' He unfolded the sheets, and saw the lines shift and huddle in their usual fashion. A preposterously long word beginning with a capital F straddled the top line. 'Do you really think enough visitors would want to come here?' he asked.

'Yes, of course!'

'But the letter from the Trust said that Dimperley wasn't a good enough example of – well – of anything at all.'

'But people don't care about that, what they want is to nose around in somebody else's very grand house. They want to think "Would I like to live here?" or "This staircase gives me the shivers," or "I'd have that bedroom because it's got the best view." They want to say, "Ooh, I bet the breakfast is cold every morning if they have to bring it all the way from downstairs." '

He nodded, unconvinced.

'Is it?' she added. 'Cold?'

'Yes, always.'

'You see, Great Bilstead might be impressive, but there's no variety – the outside is perfect and the inside is perfect; you see one bit, you've seen it all. Whereas Dimperley . . .'

'. . . is nothing but a hotch-potch.'

'But that's what makes it *glorious*,' said Zena, so indignantly that Allison looked up at her, mouth open. 'Perhaps it's hard for you to see that, because you've always been here. You've never lived in an ordinary house, have you?'

'No.'

'Have you ever . . . *been* to an ordinary house?'

'Yes,' he said, rather defensively. 'On leave, I stayed with parents of another soldier. A semi-detached in Crawley.'

'And what did you think of it?'

'I thought it was . . . convenient.'

'Convenient?'

'The way that you could talk to someone who was in another room.'

'Oh, I see.' Her lips tightened.

'You're laughing at me.'

'No.'

'Ha ha *haaa*!' remarked Allison. Zena stooped to pick her up, and buried her face momentarily in her daughter's tam-o'-shanter.

'And obviously the breakfast was always hot,' added

Valentine. Zena laughed openly, then, and he found that he didn't mind.

'What sort of house did you grow up in?' he asked.

'Houses,' she corrected. 'And flats. And lodgings. And even a sort of mansion.'

'How come?'

'Because my mother ran off when I was three and my father couldn't manage on his own so we were sent to relatives and then to foster homes and then my . . . well, I told you about my brother, didn't I? Anyway, I was put in a charity home after that.'

'Oh,' said Valentine. And then, feeling that the response was inadequate, 'How dreadful.'

'It wasn't, as a matter of fact, it was just about the best thing that ever happened to me. It was a Georgian house in Clapton – quite shabby but enormous. Compared to what I was used to, anyway. It was called the Gertrude May Foundation for the Relief, Welfare and Continued Education of Indigent Young Women.' She enunciated the title with affectionate mock-formality. 'Gertrude May was a Suffragette and we called ourselves the Gertie Girls. I was there for four years, until I left school, and that's the longest I've ever lived anywhere, until now.'

She lowered her daughter to the ground again, and Allison made straight for Valentine's bucket of lime.

'No,' he said, snatching it away and dropping the folded papers as he did so. Allison picked them up. ' "F" for "Fish"!' she shouted, triumphantly, pointing at the top line.

'Well done,' said Zena. 'Clever girl!'

Valentine stooped to pick up his shovel. 'I'm stupid

193

about reading,' he said, quickly, tonelessly, the way he had spoken to the CO when asked why he hadn't applied for a commission. 'There's something wrong with my head, or with my eyes. I can't think and read at the same time so it would take me hours to go through what you've written. But if I come to the library when I've finished here, could you tell me more about your idea?'

'Yes,' said Zena, startled more by the honesty of his speech than by its content. 'Of course.' She remembered, then, the free-wheeling version of Ecclesiastes at the memorial service – a time to read and a time to feign reading – and she felt a peculiar shift in her thoughts. It was as if she'd wiped the glass on a dusty museum cabinet and seen, for the first time, that it contained something unexpected; something uncommon.

In the momentary silence, they all heard the grind of distant gears and turned simultaneously to see what looked like a furniture van travelling at cautious speed along the back drive.

'Oh, now,' said Valentine, in quite a different voice. 'I know what this is. Why don't you stay and watch, and I'll go and get my brother? Could you tell the driver to park in the stable-yard and wait for us?'

It was Miss Hersey who had found the advertisement in the *Bucks Herald* and had shown it to Valentine. And when the man from Sotheby's had opined that the portrait on the middle staircase of the vicar who looked like Mussolini was not by Zoffany after all, but by someone 'moderately talented but obscure', and would therefore be worth no more than thirty or forty guineas at auction, the same price as the advertised filly, the alignment of sums had seemed too perfect to ignore.

'What do you think's in there, Ceddy?' asked Valentine. A couple of muted thuds, iron on packed straw, came from the interior of the van. The driver shot the second bolt and opened the rear door.

Ceddy, who had been shifting from foot to foot on the cobbles, suddenly lifted his head like a pointer.

'It's a—'

'—horse!' shouted Allison. 'It's a horse!'

Ceddy rocked on his toes a couple of times. 'It's a horse,' he agreed.

'Horse,' said Allison, enjoying the game. 'It's a horsey!'

The piebald regarded them calmly, white breaths curling around her nostrils.

'She's nice-mannered,' said the driver.

'She's beautiful,' said Zena.

Ceddy's half-smile had returned, his oblique gaze at something that was almost too good to look at directly.

'Do you like her?' asked Valentine.

'It's a horse.'

'It is, yes.'

'It's a horsey,' repeated Allison. 'Horsey, Horsey, don't you stop, jess let your feet go Clippy Clop!'

Ceddy flicked a glance at the child and then tapped his fingertips together, meditatively.

'It's a girl,' he said.

15

The headmistress hesitated when she saw who was standing in the foyer beneath the school honours board – as well she might, thought Barbara, given that the invitation had been extended to one woman, and two had arrived.

'Ah, Lady Vere-Thissett,' said Miss Gilbert, recovering herself, 'and . . . er . . . Lady Vere-Thissett. How very kind of you to come to our Christmas concert.'

'Oh, I wouldn't have missed it for anything,' said Barbara, as Irene silently, graciously, inclined her head.

'Would you both like to step into my office, where I can offer you refreshment?' Miss Gilbert lingered outside the door for a moment, and Barbara heard her speak sotto voce to someone about seating arrangements for the concert. Ahead, with the inexorability of a berthing liner, her mother-in-law moved towards the most prominent visitor's chair.

It had, inevitably, been Irene who had opened the envelope addressed to the Dowager Lady Vere-Thissett, and she had been reading the enclosed invitation out loud to Priss when Barbara had arrived in the breakfast room carrying a tray of lukewarm scrambled eggs and a jug of coffee.

'Well, obviously that's meant for me,' Barbara had said, 'because my daughter is at the school.'

'*One* of your daughters. Where is the other one, by the way?'

'Still in bed,' said Priss, always keen to split on her sister.

Irene studied the invitation she was still holding. 'This clearly states that they wish to make a presentation at the end of the concert. To the retiring music mistress.'

'Which I'm perfectly capable of doing!'

Irene shifted her gaze towards her daughter-in-law, carefully inserting the little pause that always had the effect of making Barbara's last utterance sound hysterical.

'Very well, then. It does seem rather a shame to disappoint an elderly teacher who has given a lifetime of splendid service, and who may be hoping for someone rather more . . . But if you're certain that that's what the wording implies.'

Priss was looking between them, as if trying to gauge the potential winner. With a vast effort, Barbara kept her voice on the level. 'Don't you think they would have sent two invitations if they'd wanted both of us?'

Irene smiled, in a way that someone who didn't know her might perceive as warm. 'Indeed.'

Barbara heard herself give a little grunt; out-manoeuvred, as usual.

'Well, I shall definitely be going,' she said. 'It's up to you whether you want to come too.'

'Oh, do come, Grannie,' said Priss. 'I'm in one of the tableaux and my form is singing "Personent Hodie", though just for a lark I'm planning to sing "Personent *Doggy*-ay". No-one will notice.'

'Your daughter certainly does seem to be very keen on dogs,' said Miss Sudderby, who despite a hand-knitted cardigan looked just like Princess May of Teck and who was seated next to Barbara in the front row of the audience.

The curtains had closed after the medley of Latin carols; several minutes of clunks and scrapes, hissed commands and hurrying footsteps had followed, presumably indicating that something significant was now happening backstage. The headmistress, seated on Barbara's other side, had twice turned a quelling eye on the more restless sections of the audience.

'She has two of her own,' said Barbara. 'Toto and Sinbad.'

'Yes, they've both made several appearances in her English essays.'

'Have they? How funny!'

Miss Sudderby nodded, but without conviction, her expression uneasy. *Oh, what now*, thought Barbara, dread seeping through the momentary pleasantness, as if she'd sat on an unexpectedly damp cushion – *what am I going to find out now, just when I thought I'd got something right? What worrying new trait is going to be irrevocably my fault and the cause of yet more sleepless nights?*

'I wasn't going to mention it,' said Miss Sudderby, 'and obviously it's not as disturbing as Priscilla's essay about the ... the ...'

'Slimy grey flesh-eating lizard.'

'Yes. It's only that her stories have all become a little bit too ... canine. Even when I'm quite explicit about the required subject. So that when I asked the girls to write exactly two pages entitled "A Visit to the Shops", the shops in Priscilla's story were all staffed by dogs. Different breeds of dogs. The greengrocer was a Pomeranian and the butcher was a Great Dane, and so on.'

'It all sounds quite imaginative,' said Barbara, attempting a gay smile.

'But then it turned out in the last paragraph that all the people had been sent to a kennels in the countryside because nobody wanted to look after them.'

The gay smile shrivelled.

'Her hand-writing and grammar are excellent,' added Miss Sudderby, rather hastily.

There was a 'Shhh' from the audience as the curtains opened on the first tableau. To one side of the stage stood an easel bearing a board on which the words 'SCENE 1. OLD BETHLEHEM' had been chalked. An off-stage choir sang 'Once In Royal David's City', a blanket-draped pommel-horse with a cardboard head supported a weary Mary, while Joseph (a well-built girl with a full beard) stood with arms lifted beseechingly in the direction of the inn-keeper. In the background, above a painted stable, a star twisted slowly on a wire. Thirty seconds went by, during which the choir sang a descant on the second verse, and Joseph's outstretched arms wavered only slightly, and then the curtains closed again, to respectful applause. The backstage noises resumed.

'And how is your older daughter?' asked Miss Sudderby.

'Such a striking girl, and of course, school doesn't suit everyone.'

'She's quite well,' said Barbara, guardedly.

A woman on the other side of Miss Sudderby leaned forward to join in the conversation. 'I gather, Lady Vere-Thissett, that she's very musical.'

'Kitty?'

'Yes, she——'

The curtains began to open again and the woman leaned back just as 'SCENE 2. AND GLORY SHONE AROUND' became visible.

It was a moment or two before Barbara was able to pay any heed to the second tableau (*musical?*) and then a giggle from somewhere behind her was joined by another from the actual stage, and she focused her attention on the Nativity: Joseph and Mary kneeling beside the babe, the Kings in an orderly queue, Gabriel on a draped ladder behind the stable roof and the shepherds clustered to one side, all holding their crooks, with the exception of the smallest shepherd, who had a clockwork Scottie dog with a tartan collar tucked under her arm, its little legs marching roughly in time to the angelic rendition of 'Silent Night'.

'I think I must have flooded the carburettor,' said Barbara. 'I'm sorry. I'll try it again in a minute or two.'

She had noticed in the past that suppressed emotion almost always caused her to stall the Austin, and since she'd forgotten to park it on a slope, there was no choice but to sit in the gathering dusk while the engine pulled itself together again. Home-going pupils and their families streamed past, one or two glancing at the dickie seat, where Priss sat, swathed in a tartan blanket.

'Are you warm enough, darling?' called Barbara, out of the window. 'Would you like my scarf?'

'I'm fine, Mummy.'

'Could you close the window?' asked Irene, shifting her large tissue-wrapped bouquet to shield herself from the draught. When the headmistress had taken to the stage at the end of the concert, to thank the cast and eulogize the retiring music teacher, Barbara had deliberately avoided catching her eye, relieved, for once, that a second Lady Vere-Thissett was available to graciously hand over the envelope, mantel clock and framed embroidery of the first two bars of 'Au Clair de la Lune' ('by the senior handicrafts club') and to receive in return a large bunch of copper chrysanthemums.

Across the road, a pupil gestured towards Priss and made an obviously derisive comment to her companion. Laughter followed. Barbara twisted round to look at her daughter; she was writing assiduously in a school-book, mouthing the odd word, her face as animated as if she were mid-conversation. Beside her, the Scottie dog peered out from a fold in the blanket.

'I wish I knew what to do,' said Barbara.

'To do about what?'

'About Priss.'

'Well, she certainly behaved in rather a silly fashion this evening, didn't she? Perhaps you ought to stop her pocket money for the next month.'

'What? No. No, it's far more than being silly. It's

nothing to *do* with being silly.' That awful word. She knew that people used it – or, at least, thought it – about herself: silly Barbara Vere-Thissett, always forgetting things and stalling her car and hurrying to catch up, and the more she saw them thinking it, the more flustered she became – she simply didn't possess the natural dignity that enabled her mother-in-law to enter the jam tent at the County Show as if to the sound of trumpets. But it pierced more deeply than that: if you were seen as 'silly' then no-one seemed to think that you ever really suffered – your tragedies somehow didn't count: if there'd been a scene in *Romeo and Juliet* where Juliet had accidentally run over her own hat when visiting the Montagus, then no-one would have cried at the ending.

The phrase 'poor Lady Vere-Thissett', which she occasionally overheard in paddocks or at fetes or Services of Thanksgiving, was always about Irene, who had lost her oldest son in the war, and never about Barbara, who had lost him long before, apparently to half the girls in Buckinghamshire. And perhaps 'silly' really *had* been the right word for her at seventeen, straight out of finishing school, first dance, first proper kiss, bowled into bed by the most wonderful man she'd ever met. As she'd walked up the aisle in a deeply unfashionable empire-line dress, chosen to camouflage her waistline, her mother-in-law's expression might have been carved in marble and labelled 'Fortitude'.

Barbara pressed the starter button and gave the accelerator a savage dig. There was a faint whine and then nothing.

'Have you perhaps thought of sending Priscilla to a boarding school?'

'*Sending her* . . .' With an effort, Barbara lowered her voice. 'Of course not – she's only just come back, and if she hadn't been sent away in the first place then I'm certain she wouldn't be so out of step and so . . . so unlike all the other girls. Obviously, I should have gone with them to America. I wanted to – you know that I wanted to, I shouldn't have let myself be talked round.'

She could remember the word 'duty' being repeated so often that the sound had become meaningless: they all had to do their *duty*, and Felix was doing his *duty*, and her *duty* was to stay because a man shouldn't come home on leave after defending his country to find that his wife had fled to safer shores, and though she'd strongly suspected all along that the real *duty* in question was her availability to conceive a last-minute heir, she'd let herself be persuaded because everyone seemed so certain that the war was going to end in a few months and that the girls were merely going on an exciting, extended holiday. And then, of course, Felix had only come home a handful of times before being sent to the Far East. She was glad, now, that there had been no heir, because if she'd had a son then she would have been chained to Dimperley for life.

There was a click on the windscreen, like the noise of a clipped fingernail, and then another: the first of a flurry of tiny, icy snowflakes.

Barbara opened the window again. 'Would you like to squash in here with us, darling? You'll freeze out there.'

'No, I like it. I'm imagining I'm in a troika and we're being chased by ravening wolves.'

'I'll try the motor again.'

This time there was nothing at all.

'*Damn* it.'

Next to her, there was a slight rustle from Lady Fortitude. 'There is someone coming towards us,' she said. 'I believe it's the man who delivers horse chemicals.'

'Oh, hello, Mr Haxall,' said Barbara, hastily exiting the car and shutting the door behind her. She could see the van parked further down the road.

'Hello, Lady Vere-Thissett,' said Benny, who, since accidentally calling her 'Babs' in front of her brother-in-law, had stuck to rigid formality during their occasional, usually unplanned public meetings, though he called her 'Hottie Bottie' when they were in bed together.

'This is Mr Haxall,' she said to Priss. 'The person who gave you the dogs.'

'Thank you very much, Mr Haxall,' called Priss. 'They're in tip-top health and Toto can distinguish between four different tones of voice for the word "beg".'

'Is Toto the brown-and-white one?' asked Benny.

'No, the black one.'

'What have you called the other one?'

'Sinbad. I wanted to name him White Fang, but Mummy thought it might give the wrong impression, didn't you, Mummy?'

'Yes. Anyway, how can I help you, Mr Haxall?'

'I was passing by and I noticed you couldn't seem to start your car. Thought I might be of help.'

'Thank you. I think I used too much choke. Mr Haxall is just going to try and start the car,' she called to Irene.

Benny inserted himself into the front seat and Barbara waited, shivering; snow had settled on the road like a dusting of face powder. After the briefest of pauses he climbed out again.

'No petrol.'

'What?'

'I've got a can in the back of mine. Won't be a moment.' He returned in half a minute, and unscrewed the petrol cap.

'But I filled it on Monday and I've only been to Tring and back a couple of times. I can't possibly have used it all up. Might there be a leak?'

'There might be. Or is anyone else using it?'

'No. No-one.'

There was a noise from under the blanket.

'What was that, Priss?'

'I said Kitty is.'

'*Kitty* is?'

'Should be all right now, Lady Vere-Thissett,' said Benny.

'Thank you. Thank you very much.'

'I'll just stay till you drive off, to make sure.' He leaned towards her and lowered his voice in pitch but not in volume, something that he always seemed to think was the equivalent of whispering. 'New Year's Eve dance.'

'Shhh.' She glanced round to see if anyone could hear, but the street had emptied and Priss was hunched over her school-book again. Barbara moved a step further from the car, and Benny followed. 'Where is it?'

'Near Wantage. It'll be quite a drive, but far enough so we won't bump into anyone. Meet me at the usual place? Eight o'clock?'

'Yes. Thank you, again, Mr Haxall,' she added loudly, extending a hand.

'You're very welcome,' he said. And winked.

He followed them in the van for a mile or so, before swinging off towards his house, the one he lived in, as opposed to the one he was building, and she wished she were going with him. When they'd first met, she'd been sitting in another stalled car – the enormous Rover – in the middle of an unexpectedly deep ford on the road to Wendover, watching a mallard with a row of ducklings paddle past the running board. Benny had waded in up to his knees in order to attach a tow-rope, and then she'd bumped into him again only hours later, outside Wendover Town Hall, where she'd been in an interminable Savings Committee meeting. He'd been delivering two crates of canine conditioning powders to the Hunt Kennels and he'd offered her a spare tin as a gift, possibly the most gauche present ever given. What a nice, cheerful man, she'd thought, and what a lovely, curly head of hair.

That had been three years ago. Had she known it, she'd already been widowed by then, but at the time it had seemed possible that Felix might still be alive, so guilt had loured over every subsequent liaison. And now that she was officially a relict, she had no idea how to proceed.

Should she and Benny pretend to click for the first time at a local event, semaphoring to each other across the social canyon that separated Vere-Thissett and Haxall? Perhaps she could begin by congratulating him on the now public news that his patent bovine throat syrup, Koffa-Kow, had been bought by a major pharmaceutical company? Might they conduct a formal courtship, as if from scratch? And if they did, how shocked would all her committee ladies be? And what would her daughters think about their father being replaced so quickly? And what (here was the nub) would Irene say?

Sometimes, during one of the fretting sessions that kept her awake almost every night, it seemed possible to Barbara – even probable – even *likely* – that her mother-in-law, if introduced to Benny as a potential substitute for Felix, might actually and deliberately die, very publicly, blaming Barbara with her last breath.

For aside from the basic facts – Baronet vs farmer's son, Cambridge University vs Leighton Buzzard Agricultural College – if you were to compare the two men along the usual lines by which men were generally compared, then Felix would always win. He had been celebratedly hand-some, objectively brave and undoubtedly charming, but then, part of the reason why she'd liked Benny right from the start was that although he was good-natured, he *wasn't* charming. By the time she'd met him she'd known that charm was easy; a naturally charming person just had to turn on the tap and there it was, a directionless gift, soaking all within range. It worked every time, but it didn't last. The charming person went away and you were left standing there, growing colder by the minute.

Snow was still pattering on the windscreen, and the wipers were making the most awful scraping sound. 'It was kind of Mr Haxall to stop, wasn't it?' she asked, experimentally.

'Who?' enquired her mother-in-law.

16

Alaric woke and saw a book on his bedside table. The day felt gloriously warm, spring light spilling round the half-open shutters and burnishing the ruby calfskin of the binding. He knew in an instant which book it was: his diligence at last rewarded, the long wait over. Joy enveloped him and melded with the morning light, so that the room seemed bathed in golden ichor, and he leaned across and opened the book-cover. And realized that it wasn't a book at all, but a cheap box, and instead of a title-page reading *Woodsman to the King: The Vere-Thissetts of Buckinghamshire*, by Alaric Vere-Thissett, there was a set of electroplated toenail clippers and a tin of moustache wax.

He closed the lid again and night fell instantly, ash dumped on a fire, and then he opened his eyes and it was his usual time of waking, half past five, the room bitterly cold, the long day stretching before him like a darkling plain. His bladder felt the size of an airship and he urinated for minutes on end into the pansy-sprigged chamber pot. He dressed, then, and took his torch and walked through the house towards the garden door. He could hear Priscilla's dogs yapping in the scullery, and the occasional groan as the house shifted its joints.

The sky was clear, the moon almost full, and he switched

off his torch. The light snowfall from two days before still lay unmelted. As he began on his usual route – a wide oval around the house, like a guardsman's patrol – he could see his own tracks from yesterday's circuits, each foot-mark quite close to the next. Every day he left the house intending to stride out, and every day he found himself, an hour or two later, plodding along with no awareness of having had a single thought in the time elapsed, mud on his boots, mud in his head, *per ardua ad ardua*. Today, the brightness of the view kept him alert for longer, his own blue shadow sliding ahead of him, Dimperley like an iced cake on a porcelain plate. Every movement leaped out against the snow; he saw a fox pause beside the statue of Minerva and sniff at the sandalled feet, he saw a brace of rabbits lolloping out of the Stumpery. He wondered whether he should have brought his gun, but he'd preferred to keep that locked up, lately. And then he saw a meteor like a glowing wire above the dark block of the woods and felt a faint answering gleam within himself; perhaps today he could resume his work in the library. Perhaps today he could walk in, and greet Mrs Baxter with a careful compliment – 'May I say how awfully well you're looking?' (because on the infrequent occasions he'd glimpsed her during the past weeks, she had indeed been looking well, the cruel touch of December's icy fingers bringing a roseate warmth to her complexion) – perhaps he could begin, in every sense, a fresh chapter. A fresh century, too: Dimperley during the Napoleonic Wars, surely a topic to whet the appetite of everyone from schoolboy to elderly scholar (*'A vivid and erudite volume'* – *The Times*), and he could almost hear the creak of the chair and feel the perfect weight in his hand of the Waterman Safety Pen that he'd received for his fifteenth birthday. And then back came the mudslide, for what was the point of the book if the house were sold and there were no more Vere-Thissetts at Dimperley Manor?

His thoughts sank into the mire again and, by the time they resurfaced, a pale sun had risen behind the Wyvern Tower, and there was a tiny warmth to the air, the snow beginning to dimple around his previous footsteps. The door at the base of the tower was half open and Alaric stopped walking and looked at the structure for a while. Commissioned, of course, by John Vere-Thissett in 1739 to commemorate the naval Battle of Porto Bello in which he'd lost his youngest son. He moved towards the entrance and took out his torch again. The architect's name had not been recorded but the glazed bricks surrounding the door had come from Northampton. There were eighty-seven steps; as he started to climb, the beam spiralled up the wall ahead of him. Of the three carved wyvern on the exterior, it was notable that two had been given the leathery wings of bats, while the third had feathers.

He paused to catch his breath. From base to finial it was sixty feet tall and from the top of it, with binoculars, you could see the spire of Addenham Church, although you would need a fine, clear day for that and Alaric saw, reaching the terrace at last, that the horizon was smudged with mist. He stood with his hands on the parapet, still panting from the climb. The impulse that had drawn him up the stairs now swayed him forward, so that he was looking directly down at the snow, and it seemed to him that there was no depth to the view, as if the featureless ground were just a yard below and he might swing his legs over the parapet and stand on it – stand on it and then walk quietly away. He felt his muscles tense; there was a moment of quivering impulse, and then a black dot bounced across his vision. Instantly, the view snapped wide, the dot was a single starling probing the snow far, far beneath him, and Alaric jerked away from the parapet, gasping with shock. He couldn't. He should have known that he couldn't; he lacked the pluck, even for this. The old feeling of self-disgust, as familiar to him as hunger before luncheon, slid back into place. Heavily, he turned towards the stairs.

He had almost reached the bottom when he became aware of a fluctuating mechanical growl that rapidly became louder, and he emerged into the half-light to see a turreted vehicle with a large gun protruding from the front of it, bucking at considerable speed down the drive and then braking, apparently at the sight of him, the enormous tyres cutting a deep groove in the sodden hardcore.

'Er . . .' Alaric took an uncertain couple of steps towards it, groping for an explanation. *The Labour Government*, he thought with sickened certainty, *those monsters – they're sending the army to evict us*. Was there time to fetch his rifle? The hatch of the armoured car angled upward and a man's head appeared. It had large features, a small moustache and was hatless. 'Good morning,' it said, in the accent of a council school. 'I'm looking for Lord Vere-Thissett.'

'There is no such person.'

'What?'

212

'There is no "Lord Vere-Thissett".'

'But he told me he lived here. This is Dimperley, isn't it?' The man hoisted himself up with his elbows, revealing that he was dressed not in uniform but in stained blue overalls. 'Strewth, the *size* of it,' he said, his head swivelling as he ran an eye over the long rear elevation of the house. 'What's that thing for?' he added, nodding towards the East Wing.

'Which "thing"?'

'That dome. Nice bit of copper on there.'

'It's not *for* anything.'

'You don't keep nothing in it? Pigeons?'

'It's a decorative element. The architect took his inspiration from Sezincote House in Gloucestershire which is entirely built in the Mughal style, although the dome there is only half the size of this.'

'Went one better, did he? Must have cost a few bob.'

'The bills for the entire East Wing amounted to six hundred and forty-two guineas.'

'What's that nowadays?'

'At least thirty thousand pounds.'

'Thirty bag?'

'I beg your pardon?'

'And what's that thing there?' The fellow pointed to the columbary just beyond the Wyvern Tower.

'Ah, now that *is* a pigeon house.'

'You're having me on.'

'I assure you I'm not. It's modelled on the Great Pyramid of Giza.' There was a pause. 'Is there a reason for your visit?' he added.

'I got an invitation from Sir Valentine. "Any time you're

passing," he said.' The fellow scrambled out of the turret and jumped down. 'So, he's not a Lord?'

'No. He's a hereditary Baronet.'

'But he does live here?'

'Yes.'

'Miller,' said the man, wiping his hand on the front of his overalls, before offering it to Alaric. 'Very pleased to meet you.'

'Vere-Thissett.'

'Oh, you're his old man?'

'His uncle.'

'You another Baronet? If you don't mind me asking.'

'No.'

'Righty-ho. We was in the army together. I bumped into him a few weeks back and he said to drop by.'

'Did he really? In a . . . a tank?'

'It's an armoured car. Daimler. Builder I know's buying up army surplus from a camp near here. He's going to take off the turret and use it for hauling; it's good over any ground. Even your drive.' He gave a snort of laughter. 'Are those dragons?' he added, nodding at the tower.

'No, they're wyvern.'

'What's the difference?'

'Dragons have four legs and wyvern have two.'

'Blimey, there's not much you don't know, is there?'

This seemed to be offered as a compliment.

'Certainly, my knowledge of the history of Dimperley Manor and its denizens might be considered to be extensive,' said Alaric.

'I'm the same with the Cobblers,' said Miller.

'The Cobblers?'

'Northampton Town Football Club. Try me. Go on – ask me anything.'

There was a pause while Alaric excavated his thoughts for a possible enquiry on a subject about which he knew nothing.

'Anything at all,' repeated Miller. 'History of the club, players, records, goals, transfers.'

'Have the . . . the *Cobblers* ever won the FA League?'

'The FA Cup, you mean? Or did you mean the League?'

'The two are different, are they?'

'Right, never mind. Horses for courses. Your nephew's got a nifty left foot, did you know that? He played outside-right against the R. A. Raiders in Qassasin.'

The whole conversation seemed to have left the realms of the English language. With mingled relief and pleasure Alaric saw salvation approaching along the drive.

'My secretary,' he said, gesturing towards Mrs Baxter, who was weaving with habitual grace between the pot-holes on her black bicycle, the child perched on a seat behind her. She dismounted when she was still yards away, and stood looking open-mouthed at the armoured car.

'This is an acquaintance of Sir Valentine,' called Alaric. 'A Mr Miller. And his vehicle.'

'I'd rather have got the bus, but I didn't have sixpence,' added Miller, grinning at her.

Zena lifted Allison down and walked over to them.

'Dusty Miller,' said Miller, thrusting out a hand.

'Zena Baxter.'

He had a big-chinned, humorous face, and the easy manner of someone who knew that women generally liked him.

'And who's this?' he asked, nodding at Allison. 'A monkey?'

'Not a monkey,' she said, sternly. 'I'm a little girl.'

'Glad to hear it.'

'Are you thinking of coming to the library today, Mr Vere-Thissett?' asked Zena.

Alaric gave Miller a quick glance; one didn't want to appear a sad sap in front of the lower classes. 'Yes, I thought I would,' he said, carefully casual. 'Now, I wonder where Sir Valentine might be.'

'I saw him in the distance when I was coming past the Lodge. He's shooting rabbits, I think.' Though, actually, when Zena had spotted him, the gun had been broken over his arm and he'd been watching a hovering speck through a pair of binoculars.

'Rabbit *again*,' muttered Alaric, and then was struck by the fact that, not an hour after contemplating his own destruction, he was able to feel a degree of pique about the composition of his evening meal. Perhaps the company of this young man had acted as a useful counterirritant to the deeper affliction.

'Don't suppose a bloke could get a cup of tea?' asked Miller. 'I haven't had nothing since last night. Hitched a lift to the camp and then slept on the floor.'

'Would that be possible, Mrs Baxter?' asked Alaric.

'Well, yes,' said Zena, rather surprised. 'I'll see what I can do.'

'Bag anything?' shouted Miller through cupped hands from the door of the Orangery, and Valentine broke into a run

216

so that they met and clapped shoulders on the Elephant Walk.

'I saw the Daimler,' said Valentine. 'I knew it must be you, but I couldn't work out where you'd got to.'

'I've been made welcome,' said Miller. 'Met your uncle. Been given a brew and a wad. Been told a few things.' He grinned. 'So, you're the official "Woodsman to the King", are you? You never informed us about that.'

'Oh God.'

He followed Miller into the Orangery, where Zena Baxter was seated composedly on one of the window benches, legs crossed neatly at the ankle. Her daughter was shunting a flower-pot containing the baby doll in a zig-zag path across the floor tiles. Miller pointed to the bench.

'This is Indian hand-carved teak. The seat lifts up. When it arrived here from . . . Mad—'

'Madhya Pradesh,' supplied Zena.

'. . . they looked inside and there was a whacking great snake curled up in it.'

'I think it's still in the house,' said Valentine. 'Some-where.'

'Yes, I know. Because your ancestor was crazy about taxidermy. The third Baronet.'

'You've had the full lecture, then?'

'I have. The snake was too long to stuff, so he cut six foot out the middle and joined the head and tail. Zena knows where it is, don't you?'

'It's curled up in the cupboard in the music room,' said Zena. 'I hope you don't mind,' she said to Valentine, 'but I told Dusty about the idea of opening the house to the public. I wanted to know whether he thought people would come here.'

'I see. OK.' They'd had quite the conversation, then. Zena and Dusty. He wasn't sure why the idea of it seemed to chafe at him. 'And what did you think?'

Miller folded his arms and considered the question. 'To be honest with you, Toff, I've never seen nothing quite like it. I mean, it's got all sorts, hasn't it? What you might call novelty value – bit of castle, bit of Brighton Pavilion, bit of Gawd knows what, tunnels, fruity statues, snakes. You'd have to do something about that road, though; people won't want to fritz their suspension and you won't get a charabanc down it. At the very least, you need to patch it.'

'There's supposed to be gravel under the lake here.'

'How deep's the water?'

'There's no water. It's been silted up for years.'

'Well, that would probably do you. I could get you a deal on a digger.'

'Could you? Well, that would be . . .'

'I've found it!' announced Alaric, from the far end of the Orangery. He approached them carrying a box the size of a picnic hamper, pilled with dust.

'Need some help?' asked Miller.

'No, no, it's not heavy. I found it in the East Attic – do you remember, Mrs Baxter, I was looking for it during our inventory? It didn't occur to me to search behind the Vycott Legacy – that's a dismantled bed given as a marital gift to Alys Vere-Thissett in 1742 by the Vycott family, who were a cadet branch of the' – he looked around for somewhere to put it, and Zena rose and patted the bench where she'd been sitting – 'anyway, there it was.' He placed the box on the seat and lifted the lid, and a violent smell of mothballs sprang from the folded cloth within. 'Originally, I believe, the costume was packed in dried lavender and cloves,' said Alaric, his eyes beginning to water. 'Of course, the last time it was actually repaired and worn was at William the Fourth's coronation, but one lives in hope that the practice might one day be revived by a monarch who embraces tradition.' He was lifting out a garment as he spoke, turning it doubtfully, the cloth a rusty green, darker along the folds.

'Shouldn't it be the other way up?' asked Zena.

'Yes, it needs a feminine eye,' said Alaric, handing it to her and delving into the box again.

'What is it?' asked Miller, inspecting the shapeless tunic, the preposterously puffed sleeves, the crushed and tarnished rosettes stitched in rows across the chest.

'The official uniform for the King's Woodsman,' said Alaric. 'Ah, now these are the breeches.'

More rosettes, noted Valentine, taking an involuntary step back, but Miller had already swung round to look at him.

'I've got to tell you,' he said, 'I'd give the whole of my back pay to see you walking through Westminster Abbey dressed in this. Wasn't you supposed to be carrying something as well? A log, wasn't it?'

'And some bundles of brushwood, yes.'

'And a bushel of hazel-nuts,' added Alaric.

'Nuts!' said Miller, delighted.

'Ah,' said Alaric. 'Now here's the hat.'

Miller almost folded in half when he saw it, and Zena had to walk quickly away towards where Allison was trying

to unscrew one of the window latches, but couldn't pre-
vent herself from making a sort of keening sound.

'Ha ha *haaa*!' contributed Allison, unhelpfully.

'Try it on?' suggested Miller.

'No.' Valentine tried to keep his tone light, but there was
only so much humiliation a man could take. 'Would you
come and have a look at the lake – see what you think?'

'Okeydoke. And then I suppose I'd better get going.
Honour and a pleasure to meet you, Mr Vere-Thissett.'

'Yes indeed,' said Alaric, still inspecting the hat, apparently mystified that something that looked like a gilt-
encrusted cow-pat could cause such hilarity.

'Ta very much for the hospitality, Mrs Baxter,' said
Miller, nodding at her. 'Monkey,' he added.

'I'm not a monkey.'

Outside it was all drip and puddles, a rapid thaw setting in.

'How's the roof?' asked Miller, shrewdly, as they walked
towards his vehicle.

'I need to go up and take a proper look. The guttering's
all to pot.'

'I could give you a hand if you like. Not today, but if I
come back with the digger. First or second week of January, maybe.'

'What about your job?'

'It's casual. And anyway, I've got – what's that thing the
Yanks say? Ants in my pants, that's it. Feel like I've got my
head in a vice. No room to breathe, not like here ...' He
looked back at the house and Valentine turned to look too.
Zena was walking along the Orangery path, the child running

ahead of her. '*She's* a bit of all right, isn't she?' said Miller. 'Smashing figure. Sharp as all get-out. Where's her husband?'

'Malta. RAMC.'

'So once he comes and fetches her, who's going to be running this show? Can't see your uncle tearing the tickets.'

'No. Well, I suppose I . . .' Christ, why hadn't he thought about that? Zena hadn't mentioned it and he hadn't asked, he'd just assumed that she'd stay and organize everything; he'd be sunk if she left.

''Course,' said Miller, 'it all depends on when he went in – could still be the guts of a year away. You got yourself a bird yet, Toff, or are you still too busy watching them?' He curled his hands to his eyes and scanned the horizon.

'Ha. No. Well, yes, in a way.'

'What way?'

'Someone's been . . . lined up for me, in a manner of speaking.'

'You don't sound too happy about it. She a good-looker?'

'She's very pretty.'

'Young?'

'Yes.'

'Rich?'

'Oh yes. That's the whole point.'

Miller pantomimed bafflement. 'What's the problem, then? She learning the trombone? Got an extra leg?'

'The problem is that I barely know her and she wants to be a nun.'

'What's that noise?' asked Allison.

'Mr Miller's laughing, I think,' said Zena.

'WHY ARE YOU LAUGHING?' shouted her daughter, and the men turned to look. First Miller and then Valentine raised an arm.

'Wave,' said Zena.

'They're waving at *you*,' said Allison.

After a moment, Zena waved back.

17

Bucks Herald, 28th December 1945:

AUNTIE KAY'S KLUB KORNER

Hello, Klubbers – Auntie Kay here! I hope that you had a splendid Christmas! Sweets and chocolate might have been in short supply, but I'm sure that you all enjoyed lots of games and festive jollity, especially those lucky youngsters whose brave soldier Daddies are back home again.

For our final Klub Kompetition of the year I asked you to write a poem on the theme of Your Hopes for 1946. I was a little bit disappointed not to receive more entries, and those that I did receive were, I'm afraid, of quite a low standard. As a result, I'm withholding the ten-shilling postal order that was going to go to the winner of the first prize. Instead, I'll be sending lovely geometry sets to Angus Prince for 'Peace for All Mankind' (perhaps check your spelling next time, Angus) and to Priscilla Vere-Thissett for 'A Home for Every Puppy', which was very good, apart from the last verse. I think we all prefer to read <u>optimistic</u> poetry, don't we, Priscilla? See you in 1946, Klubbers!

The dogs usually had to sleep downstairs, all on their sad little lonely-own, because Kitty had kicked up an almighty fuss about Sinbad doing a piddle on her shoes in the middle of the night, although it had only happened once, ages ago, and the shoes were horrible anyway. But since Kitty was staying the night with a girlfriend in Aylesbury in order to perform in their Music and Drama Society Concert, Priss had decided not only to let the dogs sleep on her sister's bed, but also to throw a late-night canine New Year's Eve party, with fancy-dress, games and a cake. Sinbad was going to be a ghost, and Toto a nun. Miss Hersey had made the costumes out of an old sheet, although unfortunately she had now gone away on holiday for a few days, so last-minute adjustments would have to be made using safety pins. Priss herself was dressing as a dog-trainer, in a red jacket and top hat that she'd found in her father's wardrobe, and a pair of rolled-up jodhpurs.

Mummy was going out for the whole evening, and so was Uncle Val, which was excellent because it meant that the East corridor could be used for races, and the only slight blot on the horizon was that Uncle Alaric had been threatening to teach her halma. Priss liked board games but (as she had noted in her diary, underlining the words because it was a very good joke) Uncle Alaric made every board game into a *bored* game; even when he played draughts he took about a minute to decide on every move. She was thinking of feigning a stomach-ache to cut the evening short.

At her brother's in Deddington, Thelma Hersey was wondering whether her maroon two-piece was too smart for the little get-together at a neighbour's house to which the family had been invited. She checked her appearance in the wardrobe mirror and then leaned in to inspect her complexion. As far as she could see, she appeared just as usual; she'd always been pale, but her skin was still soft and clear (she used Pond's Cold Cream when she could get it) and she'd had no thinning of her hair, which she'd noticed that some ladies could develop after The Change. Lady Irene didn't suffer from it either. Perhaps it was something in the water at Dimperley.

And yet, Tom's first comment when she'd arrived had been 'You look dead on your feet, Thelma,' and his wife, Emmie, had gaspingly agreed – 'We'll have to build you up, I can see' – and she'd been brought cups of tea and told to put her feet up, and reminded that there was always a bed for her in Deddington – 'I'd say it was about time you started being looked after yourself instead of waiting on others,' Tom had said. They were busy enough themselves, with the little hardware shop and four children, five grand-children (another on the way) and Emmie's Aunt Dolly in the back bedroom, talking gently but persistently about her friends at school while occasionally trying to take the curtains down.

It was Emmie who seemed to need the rest, dropping off to sleep after tea and complaining of back-ache from all the stooping in the shop, and Thelma had offered to take her place at the counter one morning; her sister-in-law had agreed reluctantly ('It's your *holiday*, Thelma') but had then been flatteringly effusive about Thelma's competence. Apparently, two people had come up to Tom to compliment him on the pleasant manner of the new assistant.

Thelma had quite enjoyed it, though the shop was dark and awfully cramped.

The maroon jacket could take a brooch, she thought. She pinned on the delicate enamelled-silver rose – palest pink on white – that she kept for special occasions and which had been her fiftieth-birthday present from her ladyship. 'And how's your other family?' Tom had enquired, a bit of a tease as usual, but not said in a nasty way; Emmie, on the other hand, never asked a single thing about the Vere-Thissetts, and if Thelma ever talked about any aspect of her life at Dimperley would say 'Oh yes?', but inattentively, as if the subject could have no possible relevance or interest to her. Thelma did wonder, sometimes, if Emmie were a little bit jealous.

From the next room she could hear Aunt Dolly singing a song about a porridge pot and then the clatter of curtain rings hitting the floor.

'. . . this Miller chap was clearly uneducated, but he was hanging on to my words, terribly grateful for the opportunity to find out more about the history of the house,' Alaric was saying, 'and it goes to show that one shouldn't always make assumptions. Indeed, some of his questions were surprisingly intelligent and it has caused me to wonder, Irene, it has caused me to wonder whether perhaps Valentine might not be "on to" something, as the Americans are . . . er . . . wont to say . . . and . . . er . . .' He faltered. He'd spent several days preparing this speech in his dressing-room, transported back to his golden years in the school Debating Society ("This House believes that women lack the intellectual capacity to vote'), but the calm yet persuasive arguments he'd practised in front of the mirror sounded querulous now, mere paper darts aimed at Irene's steel carapace. She was playing Demon Patience, the cards scuffing softly across the worn baize of the table-top. Behind her, seated at the writing desk, Ceddy was arranging Christmas cards into a series of ever-changing piles.

Alaric tried to recall the thread of his speech. What came next? Something about working people, wasn't it?

'Could you pour me a sherry?' asked Irene.

Of course, that was it! 'I believe,' he continued, moving over towards the decanters, 'that there may be a real thirst amongst the lower classes to learn more about our island heritage, a heritage so recently threatened by brutal invasion, and perhaps it is a bounden duty of those whose privilege it is to steward the land, to open the eyes of its humbler citizens to the glories of the past.'

He looked around the blue drawing room and a line of imagined visitors looked back at him, visitors who were undeniably of peasant stock: stolid, unlettered – possibly even grubby, but who yet were held entranced by his words and by the beauty and significance of their surroundings. And was that the gentle tug of fate he could feel? Had his years of seclusion been merely a cocoon from which his true purpose might struggle into the sunlight and unfold its wings?

'So you propose that any passing stranger who offers twopence will be able to stroll into Dimperley,' said Irene, accepting a small glass of the amontillado which had been part of an enormously generous Christmas hamper from the Maberlys.

'No, no, far from that. Mrs Baxter suggests an entrance fee of six shillings for adults and a shilling for those under fourteen. And if refreshments are offered, then the profits on a single day might be as much as—'

'*Refreshments?*'

'Cups of tea and so forth. Rock buns.'

'In *here*?'

'No, no, in the kitchens, I expect. Or the stable block. And of course, there would have to be' – he checked himself; at this early juncture, the mention of the necessity of installing water closets for the use of the general public might be unwise – 'a certain amount of outlay.'

'But it all seems so unnecessary.' Besides three bottles of sherry and two of port, the Maberlys' hamper had contained an entire ham, several jars of pickled onions, a Christmas pudding, a packet of digestive biscuits and a box of Swiss chocolates. Yvonne's family was clearly very serious indeed about an alliance.

Mr Maberly waylaid Valentine in the entrance hall, and steered him into the study, where two enormous barrel-back leather chairs, as solid as bullocks, stood on either side of a generous fire. The house was extraordinarily warm, well maintained, *shiny*; while his host poured a whisky, Valentine found himself staring at a skirting board, the top of which was actually flush with the panelling, as opposed to the whistling gaps visible in every room at Dimperley.

'Here we go, Sir Valentine,' said Maberly, holding out a glass. 'Chin chin.'

'Cheers.'

His host seated himself. He was a florid but still hand-some man in his fifties, his expression grave but determined, as if just about to regretfully sack a large proportion of his work-force.

'How's the injury, may I ask?' Maberly nodded at Valentine's gloved right hand.

'Oh, it's not so bad. I find that I'm getting used to it – I can do most things that I could before.'

'Where did it happen?'

Valentine hesitated, and took a mouthful of whisky to stop himself smirking before providing the answer sug-gested by Miller.

'In the field.'

Maberly nodded, sombrely. 'We have you to thank for our freedom,' he said.

'Oh, er . . .' Valentine found himself giving a slight shrug, as if aware that he was entirely responsible for the Allied Victory, but too modest to actually say so.

'I was pleased you could come to the party this evening,' said Maberly. 'My wife and I were both pleased.'

'Good. I mean, I'm pleased to be here.'

'And Yvonne. Yvonne said she was pleased too.'

'Oh, well, I'm, er . . .' He tried to think of a word that wasn't 'pleased' but which meant the same thing. Was there one? No. '. . . I'm pleased too.'

'Yvonne says she likes you. So I wanted to have a few words. Man to man.'

'Right.' For a ghastly couple of seconds, Valentine was back at school, squirming as the chaplain delivered his pi-jaw on the Facts of Life: *now, some of you chaps may have noticed, between your legs* . . .

'You know, don't you, about Yvonne and this Catholic business?'

'Yes.'

'What's your view on Popery?'

'I don't really have one.'

'You know she goes to Mass every day?'

'I didn't.'

'*Every* day. The chauffeur has to drive her to Tring because that's the only church where they do it correctly, according to her. Nevertheless, she's a lovely girl, don't you think?'

'Yes. She is.'

'And I'm sure she'd stop all this nonsense once she was married.'

This exact sentence had also been used by Valentine's mother.

'Well, I . . .'

'As a matter of fact, we're considering suing the school. When I think of the fees . . .' Maberly paused, his jaw grinding; for a few seconds, he actually seemed to be staring at an internal credit and debit sheet. A thread of gramophone music wound from somewhere upstairs.

'Frankly, the last year's been a bitter pill,' said Maberly. 'As a man of business, I'd like to think I'm prepared for all eventualities, but first Yvonne catching Roman fever and then the Socialists getting in and my own returning work-force turning into a bunch of Reds . . .' He shook his head. 'Who could have predicted that?'

Only every single person who'd served in the ranks, thought Valentine, emptying his glass; it was still amazing to him that anyone had been surprised by the Labour landslide. Soldiers grumbled all the time, obviously (and for the final few months it had mainly been about the length of time demob was taking), but for the duration of his service, every conversation about 'after the war' had dwelt on rotten housing and rotten jobs and had contained the phrase 'those bastard Tories', which had later solidified into 'Churchill for war, Clem for peace'. In fact, during a month's battle-training course in Perthshire, when it had rained so much that the tents had gone mouldy and everyone was going mad with boredom and midge bites, the Recreation Officer had organized a mock-election and Crockett, a postman in civilian life, had stood as a Communist and after giving a fiery and eloquent speech had won with 80 per cent of the vote, beating Miller (Independent, on a 'Free Beer and Fags' ticket) into second place.

'So what do you say?' Maberly was leaning towards him, the bottle in his hand.

'Oh, well, yes,' said Valentine, holding out his glass. 'I'd be delighted.'

'Excellent.' Maberly beamed as he poured out the whisky. '*Excellent*. I cannot tell you how happy that makes me.'

'Some evenings, she just won't settle,' said Emmie, after she and Thelma had re-hung the curtains. Aunt Dolly sat watching them, plucking at the bed quilt.

'Shall I put the wireless on for you, Auntie?' asked Emmie. 'A bit of music?'

'I sit next to Alice, and Alice sits next to May,' said Dolly. 'Mr Darley lets us sit at the back of the class because he can trust us.' She pushed back the coverings and started to edge over to the side of the bed, her thin little legs like laths under her nightie, the ankles scaly above knitted bed-socks. 'I would like to sit on the chair next to Alice.'

'This is just the start of it,' said Emmie, flatly. 'I'll have to stay – it'll be *in* bed, *out* of bed all evening. Exactly the same happened when Tom and I went to the whist drive in November. You might think she doesn't know what's going on, but if she gets the hint she's been left alone, then it's merry hell to pay and we'll come back to havoc. I was looking forward to that little party.'

'I want to sit on the chair next to Alice.'

'I could stay instead,' said Thelma, feeling that the offer should be made.

'Thank you very much, that's very kind,' said Emmie, instantly. 'Thelma's going to stay with you, Auntie! Mind,' she added, sotto voce, 'if she asks for tea, just give her a bit in a saucer or she'll be wet as a ditch in the morning. I don't know if we'll stay to see the New Year in, but don't wait up for us.'

Thelma had brought some tatting with her, a collar for a frock she was running up for Zena's little girl, and she changed out of her two-piece, and placed the brooch back in its velvet pouch, and sat beside Auntie's bed until the old lady had settled. She could hear odd whoops and the crack of caps from children playing in the village street outside. Tom had looked a bit uncomfortable about leaving her behind, but she'd be a fool not to suspect that if she took up the couple's offer, and came to live with them in Dedding-ton, then his discomfort might fade rather quickly, and she'd end up spending many more evenings sitting with Auntie.

And then one day, perhaps, she'd find that she in her turn had become Auntie. ('Oh, is she still going on about that blessed house? Just nod and smile at her.')

She wanted to go home.

The very first person Barbara saw, when Benny helped her out of the motorcycle side-car on their arrival at RAF Grove, was Roy Epple, who'd been working with his uncle in the Dimperley gardens since the summer. She ducked down, pretending to adjust her shoe, and he didn't spot her, but since the whole point of driving all the way to Wantage was that no-one would recognize them, it had scraped the sparkle from the entire enterprise; instead of laughing off the usual side-car side-effects (deafness, wooden neck and a million creases in her blue silk dress), Barbara had felt a crackle of annoyance, which she had taken out on Benny by refusing the beer he'd bought her from the bar while she was in the Ladies, and asking for the fruit cup instead, so that he'd had to plunge again into the scrummage of broad backs and elbows.

She'd felt self-conscious, then, waiting alone, and had edged into the crowd that lined the walls of the hangar; a few tables and chairs (all taken) were clustered at the end opposite the stage, but most of the space was dance-floor, and it was already absolutely full, a throng of near-stationary couples, jigging on the spot to 'Pennsylvania 6-5000' under a pall of cigarette smoke. Amongst the dancers, there were as many men in civvies as in uniform, but the band members were all American airmen, the music a flare of brass.

'They were all out of fruit cup,' said Benny. 'I got you a lemonade.'

'Thank you,' she said. 'Sorry I was snappy.' He squeezed her arm, and they turned to watch the floor, Barbara concentrating on the faces, Benny unconsciously tapping a foot and adding the odd finger-click. He loved dancing.

'Pennsylvania 6-5000' came to an end, and the singer made an unintelligible announcement over the applause. There was a tidal movement as some couples left the floor and others surged on.

'Come on, Babs,' said Benny, draining his glass, 'no-one's looking at us,' and she let him steer her onward, snaking towards the centre of the crowd, and it was true, no-one was looking, and as the music started again, first a squeal of trumpets and then a cool female voice, he took her in his arms and somehow found a passage between the clashing bodies so they could glide along to the lazily suggestive lyrics – *I've wrapped you a Christmas present, but don't look under the tree. Just come over here my darling, because your Christmas present is me.* Barbara leaned her head against his chest and let the glimpses of other couples slide past until a sudden blink of brilliance made her look up; a spotlight was passing over the couple next to her, briefly illuminating the man's bald patch before moving on. 'Oh, it's a spot prize dance,' she said to Benny. 'I don't want us to win that!'

'I'll make it my job to avoid it,' he said. 'Don't worry.' He executed a neat turn and then seemed to flinch, checking the movement so suddenly that she stood on his foot.

'What's the matter?'

'No, nothing.' He was now trying to manoeuvre her the other way, but the rhythm of the dance had been lost, so that they were jogging uneasily in a thicket of elbows. Barbara looked up at him; his neck had gone red.

'What *is* it?'

She saw his gaze flick inadvertently towards the stage, and she craned in the same direction. Above the shifting heads she could see only bits and pieces, a stubble-headed bassist, the swaying cymbal on the drum kit, the microphone that partially blocked the view of the singer . . . *so untie the ribbons, darling, snip all the strings away. When you unwrap this Christmas present, oh baby, you'll want* . . . the singer stepped back slightly, lifting her arms for the final words . . . *to play!* It was Kitty. Kitty wearing a strapless yellow dress slit up to the thigh and a silk rose in her hair.

'Oh my *God*!' exclaimed Barbara.

Benny was still trying to steer her away, but she pulled against him so that they swayed to a halt again just as the song ended on a twiddling saxophone phrase and scattered applause. A blinding light was suddenly shining in Barbara's eyes.

'And congratulations to our "On the Spot" winners!' called the announcer. 'If you come to the stage you can take your pick of prizes. Nylons for the pretty lady in blue, perhaps?'

The applause intensified and people all around them were turning to stare.

235

'Isn't that Lady Vere-Thissett?' remarked someone just behind Barbara.

'You know that's her daughter on the stage,' said someone else.

For a second, Barbara thought she might run away, burrowing through the crowd to the exit, fleeing cross-country in her stockinged feet, but Benny was still holding her – well, actually, he wasn't merely holding her, he was stooping over and planting a firm kiss, right on her lips. And, honestly, there really didn't seem to be, by this juncture, any reason not to kiss him back.

At half past seven, which was when the quiz was supposed to start, Zena was mopping sick from the bedroom floor. Allison's post-Christmas cold had developed into a rattling cough and she was watching her mother apathetically from the cot, her cheeks an unhealthy red and a thick sheen of mucus on her upper lip.

'When I've done this shall I read you a story?'

'No. I want milk.'

'I think it was the milk that made you sick. I'll fetch you some rosehip syrup.'

'No! *No!*' Allison keeled over despairingly, all hope lost.

'Mrs Procter brought a jelly across from the party. Would you like a bit of jelly?'

'No.'

'It's strawberry.'

'No, I don't want it!'

'What would you like, then?'

Allison rested her face on her doll's stomach and made a thin little sound of pure misery.

From the window of the kitchen area, Zena could see the lights of the Parish Hall. She'd been looking forward to the quiz; she'd thought it quite possible that she might win, and would therefore have her pick of the advertised prizes, most of which she wouldn't have been able to use (half-ton of firewood, turkey, box of cigars) but which she could have given to her landlady as a thank-you present for her discretion and kindness over the years.

Mrs Procter had been very apologetic, but there was now a steady stream of young men coming home, and wanting to marry their sweetheart, or to move their bride out of their parents' house, and though, supposedly, there was going to be a big new council estate built on the edge of Addenham, goodness knows when that would be ready, and in the meantime, she really had to offer the flat to a young couple. She hoped Zena would understand. 'And surely,' she'd said, 'they could find a room for you at Dimperley?'

If she'd suggested this even a few months ago, Zena would have had to suppress a snort, but it was a marker of how much had altered that when she had diffidently mentioned the idea to Sir Valentine, he'd said, 'Help yourself to the East Wing,' which had made her laugh, and Thelma's face had lighted with pleasure and she'd immediately offered to 'make all the necessary arrangements', which presumably meant choosing a room that would ensure Lady Basilisk would never be troubled by the sound of

Allison shouting, 'IT'S MORNING TIME!' just after dawn. Not that Zena had ever discussed her ladyship with Thelma; their friendship was still too new to test the obvious disjunction between their views.

Zena drew up a chair by the cot and gently rubbed her daughter's back. 'Story,' said Allison, into the doll's stomach.

'Which do you want?'

'"Three Little Pigs".'

'Once upon a time there were three little pigs who were sent out into the world by their mother to seek their fortune . . .'

'*No.*'

'What's the matter?'

'You're saying it all *wrong*.' Allison rolled on to her back, immediately started coughing and was sick again.

By midnight, she was still awake, sitting heavy on Zena's hip, her hot, damp head resting on Zena's shoulder.

'It's 1946, little girl,' said Zena, tidying up the kitchen with one hand.

'What's that mean?'

'It means it's January. And it means that you'll quite soon be four.'

'What else?'

'I don't know what else.' Zena took a mouthful of lukewarm tea and then, on impulse, swirled the remainder and poured it down the sink before tilting the cup towards the light. One of her foster mothers had been keen on reading the tea-leaves.

'What you doing?'

'Seeing if there's a tiny picture in here.' There wasn't. 'Can you spot anything?'

'Lickle dots.'

'Yes, that's what I can see too.' A swirl of dust? A flock of birds, a scattering of rice?

The faint strains of 'Auld Lang Syne' were audible from a house across the village green. Allison yawned, and then didn't cough afterwards.

'Come on,' said Zena. 'Let's get you to bed.'

18

The Times, Friday, 12th January 1946

SIR VALENTINE VERE-THISSETT BT AND MISS Y. J. MABERLY

The engagement is announced between Sir Valentine Eglamore Philip de Clancy Talbot Vere-Thissett, Bart, third son of the late Sir Arthur and Lady Irene Vere-Thissett of Dimperley Manor, Addenham, Buckinghamshire, and Miss Yvonne Jane Maberly, only daughter of Mr and Mrs Robert K. Maberly of Maberly Hall, Flixton, Oxfordshire.

The Maberlys' butler answered the telephone, and during the minute or so that passed while he waited to speak to Yvonne, Valentine could hear a succession of odd clicks, which might have been attributable to faulty wires but which might, on the other hand, have been the local telephonist settling in for a good old listen.

'Hello, Valentine.' There was less of the usual fizz in her voice. 'I was wondering when you'd call. I've seen the newspaper.'

'I had no idea about this,' said Valentine, hurriedly. 'I didn't know anything about the engagement until my uncle showed me this morning's *Times*.'

'Really?'

'Really. Not the foggiest.'

'But Daddy said – could you wait just a moment?' There was a clunk, followed by footsteps and then a door shutting before the receiver was lifted again.

'Daddy said that he'd spoken to you before the party, and that you were very, very keen. As keen as mustard, he said.'

'No. No, I wasn't. I mean . . . sorry, that doesn't sound very gallant, but we were talking about the war, and the government. And whisky. The question of getting engaged didn't even arise.' Though he kept having uneasy flashbacks to the disproportionate delight with which Mr Maberly had refilled his glass; had he missed something – some crucial exchange? The party had been a jolly blur; there'd been games and dancing and many more drinks and more games and several passing glimpses of a beaming Mr and Mrs Maberly. Yvonne had looked very pretty and they had danced together several times, but nothing that could be classed as conversation had passed between them. He had not seen her since.

'So you didn't tell Daddy that you wanted to marry me?'

'No. I mean – I would definitely have asked you first.'

'Would you? They're both terribly happy about it. My parents.'

'Are they?'

'Oh yes, absolutely thrilled. What about your mother? Is she absolutely thrilled?'

While 'thrilled' was emphatically the wrong word, the expression on his mother's face that morning had been one that he'd never seen aimed in his direction before, and it had taken a few moments for him to recognize its import. It was not merely that she was *pleased*, but that she was pleased *with him*.

'Yes, she's very glad indeed.'

There was a click-filled silence.

'I'll come over this morning and talk to your father,' said Valentine. 'And explain that he's mistaken.'

'No, don't do that!'

'No?'

'You do like me, don't you, Valentine?'

'Yes, of course I do – I like you very much indeed.'

'Good. Because the thing is that I . . .'

In the second before she spoke again, he had an astonishing thought: she hadn't *fallen* for him, had she?

'. . . I need to ask you something – a sort of favour. Do you remember when I told you what I was hoping for?'

'You were hoping to become a nun?'

'Yes. And do you remember that Mother told me – that's the Mother Superior, not *my* mother – that if God really wants me to become a nun, then He'll send me a clear sign?'

'Yes. Has he, then?'

'Not yet. And of course, that might mean that He thinks the best way I can serve Him is by marrying a very nice man and being a good wife and a happy mother, which is why He's arranged this engagement.'

'I see.'

'And that would be lovely in its own way, of course.'

'Right.' No, she definitely hadn't fallen for him.

'But the thing is, there are heaps of nuns who didn't find

their vocation immediately, for instance St Birgitta of Sweden didn't enter a convent until she'd been married for twenty-eight years and had had eight children. Obviously, that's not a' – she started to giggle – 'not a very helpful example, but it might be that God is testing my persever-ance and fortitude. And if I were able to have a bit more time *before* we got married, then it could well be that the sign *will* appear.'

'A bit more time?'

'Yes.'

'You mean, you want us to stay engaged but you want it to be a long engagement?'

'Yes!' She sounded delighted that he'd grasped her mean-ing. 'I'd be terrifically grateful, Valentine, and it would ensure that my parents stopped worrying and didn't keep telling me that I'm intending to throw my life away. And then, eventually, of course, if the sign doesn't appear – well, we'd know that God had made His decision and that I should get married to you after all. Which of course would be . . .'

A very poor second to Jesus.

'. . . absolutely *super*,' said Yvonne, firmly.

The splutter of Miller's digger was audible from the back of the house, twin stripes of mud across the greensward showing where the caterpillar tracks had churned the turf on the way to the lake. In the far distance, Valentine could see the long arm dipping and swivelling.

'So, Mother, the thing is . . .' he practised, setting out towards it, '. . . that Yvonne is still very young, so we thought that . . . we thought that we should wait at least a year, because Yvonne doesn't feel she's quite ready yet, we should wait at least eighteen months, we should wait for a while . . . for quite a long while . . . until she . . . and what it means, of course, is that there's no question of . . . the money won't be . . . what it means is that we shall have to continue with the plan of opening the house to the . . . the . . .' His mother's imaginary face was no longer looking in the tiniest bit pleased.

The tracks skirted the green-tinged stucco of the Temple of Jupiter, but Valentine walked through the central arch and towards the ridge of gravel that was already forming a bulwark along the southern shore of the silted lake. He'd nearly reached it when a small head in a mauve tam-o'-shanter appeared from the other side of the heap, shouted 'I'm a King of a Castle!', coughed a couple of times and then abruptly disappeared again.

'And now you're filthy,' said Zena, emerging with her daughter's mittened hand gripped firmly in hers. 'Hello!' she said, seeing Valentine. She was wearing a natty little fawn hat with a jay's feather that caught the light. 'We've just come to watch the digger, again.'

Automatically, they all turned to look at the vehicle as it swung and wallowed, Miller silhouetted in the lurching cab, outstretched arms manfully gripping the controls, like Perseus wrestling the Titan.

'It's a digger,' said Allison, pointing.

'Yes.'

'The man let me sit on it.'

'Yes, it was very kind of Mr Miller, wasn't it?' said Zena. 'It was *very* kind,' agreed Allison. She looked at

Valentine expectantly, apparently waiting for him to join in the chorus of praise.

'Isn't someone from the *Bucks Herald* coming to talk about the opening?' he asked.

'Yes, this afternoon,' said Zena. 'Oh, and your uncle showed me the newspaper. Congratulations to you and Miss Maberly.'

'Thank you.' Valentine could hear the flabbiness of his tone – it was the sort of thanks that one would give for the return of a dropped handkerchief; he'd clearly have to practise, especially when speaking to someone as astute as Zena, who was already looking quizzical.

'So is it going to be a double wedding?' she asked.

'What? Oh, you mean Barbara? No, I think they're already reading the banns, whereas we – er, Miss Maberly and I – we've decided to . . . er . . .' There was a longish pause. Zena's expression softened from quizzical to something dangerously close to concern. 'So anyway,' he said, switching his gaze to the porridge-grey mud of the lake, 'are you going to move into the East Wing, or did you decide on a room with a ceiling?'

'We're going to be at the end of the Bishop's corridor and we have an intact ceiling, we have a very nice rug, we have a wardrobe that's about the size of our current living room and—'

'A reindeer,' said Allison.

'Yes, we have a moose's head, and also a glass dome containing three stuffed toads scaling a pyramid of plaster citrus fruits, which I'm keen to put somewhere else, partly because it's so fragile and partly because it's—'

245

'Hideous.'

'Yes.'

'One of the toads has a little pick-axe and a coil of rope, hasn't he?'

'And tiny crampons, yes. It's fascinating as well as hideous.'

'I loved it when I was a child.'

'Allison loves it too – in fact, I had a thought. You know the very large oval table in the Duke of Rutland room? I wondered if we could get some of the best stuffed items – the most fascinating ones – and put them together on it, and then it would give children, and visitors who are *less* interested in the Duke of Rutland, something extra to look at. What do you think?'

'I think it's a very clever idea.'

'Good, so do I.'

'I like your feather,' he said.

'Oh . . .' Smiling, she touched her hat. 'Could you tell me what bird it belongs to?'

'A jay. It's from the edge of one of its wings.'

'I knew you'd know. We found it in the woods, on a thorn bush; it was like a scene from a fairy tale – there was a shaft of sunlight and – no, don't kick that. Stop it, Allison.'

'I want to throw the stones.'

'They're too muddy.'

'But I want to *throw the stones*.'

'Mr Miller's spent all day picking them up and now you want to throw them away again?'

'Yes, I *want* to. Yes.'

'I think you're still a bit out of sorts, aren't you? I'll tell you what, why don't we go and play a game of hide-and-seek over in the little white house – would you like that?'

After a grudging pause, Allison nodded.

'And there's an apple and a square of chocolate in my pocket. Excuse us a moment.'

They walked away towards the Temple of Jupiter and Valentine realized that he hadn't thought about the dragging implications of his bogus engagement for at least three minutes and that his conversations with Mrs Baxter often seemed to have this effect, temporarily muting the drearier parts of life. He watched the two figures until they disappeared through the arch.

'Valentine!'

He turned to see his uncle approaching from the other direction, labouring up the shallow incline from the Hermit's Hollow, accompanied by a tall, slightly built figure wearing a long mackintosh.

'This young chap's from the local press,' called Alaric, breathlessly, when he was near enough. 'Turned up early.'

'Yes, I'm sorry, I must have been given the wrong time.' The *Bucks Herald* had clearly sent its most junior reporter, a pink-cheeked boy of about sixteen, built like a ruler, his feet the widest part of him.

'I've given him a tour. Gave you a tour, didn't I?'

'Yes, sir.'

'Took him from the attics to the cellars. He's going to write an article all about Dimperley.'

'It'll be more of a . . . a diary piece,' said the boy, with the intonation of someone who had (fruitlessly) said the same thing several times before. 'I don't do articles yet. I only . . .' He mumbled a phrase which sounded rather like 'started last week'.

'I thought Sir Valentine could show you around the grounds,' said Alaric.

'Do you have time for that?' asked Valentine.

The boy checked his wristwatch. 'I'm not sure,' he said. 'I have to be at the Addenham Women's Institute fancy goods sale by one o'clock.'

Abruptly, the digger engine cut out. In the sudden throb of silence Valentine heard Zena calling, 'Coming, ready or not!' and then there was a shout from Miller. From where he stood, Valentine could see only the back of the vehicle, and the upward slope of the raised mechanical arm.

Miller was scrambling out of the cab, lowering himself with odd delicacy on to the caterpillar track before jumping into the lake. He fell forward, picked himself up and started plunging through the knee-high mud towards the shore.

'What's wrong?'

'Run!'

'What?'

'Get out of here, I just picked up a fucking UXB!'

'*What?*' Valentine skittered back, and sideways. He could see the jaws of the digger now, and the unmistakable bloated cigar of a high-explosive bomb protruding from them at an angle, a fin barely caught in the serrated teeth, and, even as he stared, the angle of the cigar shifted slightly.

Everyone around him seemed to be shouting now – *get down, get away, run* – though a single voice, further away, was calling, 'Allison, *Allison!*'

Zena couldn't see her daughter. Everything had been normal, it had been a normal game, and she'd looked inside the temple, and then in the little alcove at the front that was Allison's usual spot to hide, and then she'd come back to her starting point and into a scene that had taken her splintered seconds to assimilate and now she was a single thread of fear, screaming from the reel – was Allison in the tump of trees beside the folly? Had she run back towards the house? Her own voice was unrecognizable, the wavering shriek and crackle of an untuned wireless. '*Allison! Where are you? Come out, Mummy's not cross!*'

She saw Valentine charge towards the gravel ramparts on the edge of the lake, she saw Alaric and Miller and an unknown man running down the hill, she saw the object caught by the digger, and it was shifting, swinging, and then she saw the mauve of Allison's hat, the roaring red of her face under Valentine's arm as he ran across the field. And the air gave a great shove, and Zena was lying on her back as a fountain of dirt rose and separated and hung like a flock of starlings before dropping into the dense smoke that bloomed across the lake – dropping with a noise that she knew and that she'd thought she would never hear again.

In the muffled silence that followed, Zena rolled over and hauled herself up and stumbled towards where she'd last seen her daughter, through lingering smoke, across grass peppered with gravel. She found the tam-o'-shanter on the ground and snatched it up and then dropped it as Allison came suddenly into view, not dead, *not dead*, but standing up and trying to hit Valentine, who was on his knees, fending her off with one hand.

And then Zena was on her knees too and her daughter
was on her lap and the warmth and weight of her was all
she could ever want, the vinegary smell of her hair, the
little loud, outraged voice in her ear – 'He *squash*-ed me, he
SQUASH-ED me! He hurted my NOSE!'

'I fell on top of her. Sorry,' said Valentine.

'No,' said Zena. 'Don't.' She was trembling so hard that
her voice was shaking.

'I don't like that man, he hurted my nose! My nose is
BLOOD.'

'Let's have a look.'

It wasn't. 'Just runny,' said Zena, fumbling in her pocket
for a handkerchief and not finding one, and wiping her
daughter's nose and muddy face with her cuff, and then
using another bit of it to wipe her own eyes. She wrapped
her arms around Allison again and rocked her.

'I couldn't find you,' she said.

'He squash-ed me.'

'She was hiding behind the gravel pile,' said Valentine. 'I
saw her hat bob up when you called.'

The smoke was clearing now, and Zena could see over
Allison's shoulder that there was no longer a gravel pile,
only a low, muddy lip along the lake edge. The digger had
mostly gone.

Valentine was twisting round, inspecting the side of his
leg.

'Are you hurt?' asked Zena.

'I've been nicked by something. Same place as before.
I'm going to check on the others.'

When he stood, a triangle of cloth flapped from the side

of his trousers, exposing a patch of thigh furrowed by a V-shaped purple scar, one end of it intersected by a thin line of blood.

'Let me go instead,' said Zena, getting to her feet. Shifting Allison on to her hip, she saw something on the ground; exactly where her daughter had been standing was a twisted flake of silvery metal, as long as a hand, one dreadful curved edge streaked with red. The grass tilted like the deck of a ship, and she set Allison down again, carefully, and then bent over with her hands on her knees.

'Stay here, sit down,' said Valentine. 'Please.'

His name was being called and he could see Miller in the distance, up by the lake shore, beckoning. He set off at a fast limp.

Dear Mum,

I know you won't be expecting another letter quite so soon after the last, but your favourite son has been having quite the adventure — see the enclosed cutting, credited to yours truly. I bet you never imagined I'd be IN the paper as well as writing it! The whole article was a lot longer and about FIFTY times more exciting before it was 'edited' (or 'butchered') by Mr Paget (Features), who's a right old stick, but, in any case, it's definitely a big step up from the 'Daily Diary' (or 'silly snippets', as Mr Paget calls them). There's nothing like being 'on the spot' at a story!

Before you start worrying, I wasn't in any danger, as the Baronet's uncle led us down the hill to a peculiar little ruin and we ducked behind the wall there just before the bomb

251

exploded. The only person to panic was the Baronet himself, who's not all that much older than me and who seemed to lose his head and went running off in another direction altogether and ended up getting slightly hurt by a piece of shrapnel. He's only just left the army, as well!

The uncle asked if I would come back to report on the first day of the public opening just after Easter (which is why I was sent there in the first place) and he gave me a bent fork (silver-plated) as a souvenir of the event, though even without that, I'm sure I'll never 'fork-et' it.

Your best pal and loving son,
Nick

Bucks Herald

UNEXPECTED EXPLOSION

A German bomb exploded last Wednesday in the grounds of Dimperley Manor, Addenham, after being unearthed by an excavator engaged in clearing a silted lake. There were no major injuries.

The device (believed to be an SC 500 — commonly known as a 'half-tonner') was discovered no more than a quarter of a mile from the crater left in farmland by a bomb in 1941, and it is surmised that it was dropped at the same time as the first, but failed to explode until it was disturbed by the digging machine.

The driver of the excavator, Mr R. Miller, and a visiting reporter from the Bucks Herald, *Mr Nicholas Wills, were* directed to safety by Mr Alaric Vere-Thissett, of Dimperley, whose quick thinking prevented any serious casualties.

Investigating the damage afterwards, Mr Vere-Thissett found the scattered remains of several items of Georgian cutlery, distorted from the blast. He is hoping that his researches may reveal the reason why the cutlery had been dropped into the lake. Mr Vere-Thissett, a noted historian, described the discovery as 'most exciting'.

19

'I've brought you tea,' said Zena, edging round a palisade of chimney stacks towards the spot where Miller was kneeling on the leads. It was very bright up here, a sharp wind ruffling the puddles, cloud shadows sliding, one after another, over the haphazard peaks and valleys of the rooftops.

'Oi, sir, tea's up,' said Miller.

Valentine was lying face-down with one arm extended over the edge.

'I think it's a jackdaw nest,' he said, rolling over, 'but I can only just touch the top of it. We need a sort of hook. Oh hello, that's a welcome sight,' he said, in Zena's direction.

She gave him a brief half-smile, her attention on the tea.

'I can make us a hook,' said Miller. He reached out for one of the mugs and Zena jerked it away, spilling a few drops, and offered him the other one, before apparently changing her mind mid-gesture and giving him the first instead, reddening as she did so.

'Thank you,' said Miller, drily.

Her expression snapped shut. 'The coach company sent their list of rates,' she said, setting the other mug down beside Valentine. 'If we could guarantee enough visitors, they'd bring them from Aylesbury Station at a shilling a head.'

'Well, that's good,' said Valentine. 'Isn't it?'

'I'm still hoping to get them down to ninepence. And the scrapyard's agreed a good price on the army bedframes, and they'll collect them next Wednesday. Oh, and Watford Council confirmed the boat purchase.' She was already turning to leave.

'Shall I come to the library when we've finished up here?' he asked.

She nodded and was gone.

Miller watched her as she disappeared again behind the chimneys.

'If I was her husband, I'd hurry up and come home,' he said.

'What?'

'Nothing.'

In the East Attic corridor, Zena stood and gripped her elbows as if she might fall like a bunch of spillikins if she let go.

She'd seen the long, amused, sardonic look that Miller had given her. *He's guessed*, she thought, furious with herself; she supposed he'd seen enough women being silly, about him, to recognize all the usual signs. That business with the mugs. Carrying them up the stairs, she'd noticed that one of them was chipped, and, once on the rooftop, she'd found herself ruminating over which man should receive which mug. Would offering the undamaged one be a dangerously obvious indication of her preference? Should she therefore go for the reverse option? And although she knew that the whole chain of 'reasoning' was ludicrous, as unlike her usual deliberations as a carnival costume stuffed amongst the neatly folded blouses in her wardrobe, she also knew that she was not currently fully in charge of her thoughts, not entirely recognizable as the Zena who had once been described in a gratifying memorandum from the Head of Ordering to the Managing Director as 'commendably composed in trying circumstances' and 'unflustered by sudden change'.

That composure had been acquired very early in life; she'd discovered that if she thought ahead, and worked out all the possible implications of every switch of teacher, school, house and foster mother, then she wouldn't be caught by surprise. The worst aspects of each would end up stinging less if she'd already anticipated them.

When Raymond had been taken into Hackney Children's Ward, she'd informed herself that she might never see her little brother again, since people in books who were admitted to hospital usually died, and she'd been right. And as, by then, she'd secretly wept herself to a husk beneath the bedclothes every night, she'd reacted to the news in silence, earning the epithet 'hard as a box of nails' from her fosterer Mrs Davidson, who'd been deeply affected by the death.

But all those had been changes that Zena could anticipate; this one had dropped on her like a water-balloon from an upstairs window.

For several days after the explosion, she had only wanted to stay close to her daughter, doing small things quietly, swaddled from the world, but then she had gone to find Valentine, to thank him properly, and had spotted him pushing a garden roller across a filled pothole in the drive; he'd paused and smiled, and her view of him had seemed to slide towards her like a pulled rug so that although she was still yards away, he completely filled her vision. She'd taken an involuntary step back. That object in the cabinet – that interesting, uncommon object – was no longer behind glass, no longer distanced, pinned and labelled.

She could scarcely remember what she'd said to him; you couldn't stand and talk to someone normally when you were feeling like that, and she'd been in such a hurry to leave again that she must have sounded abrupt. But that same feeling had walked away with her, and now, weeks later, it infused every thought, and though she'd tried hard to convince herself that it was nothing more than a case of intense gratitude, she also knew with certainty that if it had been Alaric who'd snatched Allison from danger, taking an eighteenth-century fish slice to the leg in the bargain, then she would have been forever beholden, but she wouldn't have felt like this: pricked, strung, as sensitive to his presence as a cat to a draught.

And the trouble was that there was no point to all this *feeling*, and therefore no joy in it: she was Mrs Zena Baxter, with a husband in Malta; he was a Vere-Thissett, recently engaged to be married, and all that she, Zena, could do was to keep trudging forward, like someone with an exquisitely painful blister who was trying not to limp, hoping that when it burst she'd be back to her normal gait.

What it did mean, though, was that all the old, easy,

ordinary conversations were now difficult, and that instead of relishing his company as they planned the details of the public opening, she found she was constantly checking herself, like a driver watching the instruments instead of the road. It was simpler to keep their encounters business-like, and to hurry back to the library, where Alaric had pushed *Woodsman to the King* aside while he investigated the Great Georgian Cutlery Crime. Zena had scored a recent triumph by finding a 1787 steward's note referring to the purchase of three new fiddle-pattern, crested basting-spoons '*to replace thofe that are miffing*'.

'What's that whistle?' asked Miller, peering over the para-pet. A small figure was marching across the Great Lawn, followed by two servile blobs.

'My niece doing her dog training,' said Valentine. A fur-ther series of whistles saw the blobs running, lying and rolling over in unison.

'And what's that?' asked Miller, pointing to something moving from the fringe of trees beyond the Chinese Pavil-ion: a white-and-brown shape that flowed and separated and became a running pack of dogs, with a horse behind them bearing a red-jacketed rider. 'Oh, it's a hunt!'

'That'll be the Vale of Aylesbury,' said Valentine. More horses poured out of the woods. 'I heard they'd started up again. I used to have to turn out for them sometimes. Thank heavens that Smokey Minor's not a jumper.'

'Isn't it all a bit of a laugh, though?' asked Miller. 'Stir-rup cup first and more booze afterwards?'

'Being catapulted into a ditch. Half a ton of horse

stepping on your foot. A retired colonel screaming in front of the whole field that you ride like a pregnant woman.' The hounds were doubling back now, milling around, nosing aimlessly across the damp sward. 'They've lost the scent,' he said. 'I bet Ceddy would like to see it, though. I should go and find him.' His brother had been with Miss Hersey earlier, sitting next to Allison on the floor of the sewing room, arranging cotton reels into a long chain.

'Hang on,' said Miller, 'what's happening now?' A hysterical baying had begun and the hounds were surging in the direction of the house.

'Fox!' said Valentine, pointing. A russet streak zipped past the Wyvern Tower. A horn squealed. Someone shouted, 'Tally ho!' A stout man rose in his stirrups and pointed his hat towards the Great Lawn.

'It's like something off a biscuit tin,' said Miller, entranced. 'That fat one on the bay's wearing a fucking topper!'

'He's the one who said I rode like a pregnant woman.'

'And what's that old girl doing?'

A grey-haired woman in trousers had reined in her horse and was leaning over its withers, aiming a short whip at one of the hounds, whose head was down a rabbit-hole.

'*Priss, don't!*' shouted Valentine, suddenly. '*Don't interfere! Priss!*'

With a dog under each arm, she was wading thigh-high through the hounds towards the woman rider.

'What's she doing?'

'*Priss!*' shouted Valentine again, the wind snatching his voice away before it could cross the parapet. The woman aimed another blow at the hound, and then straightened in obvious incredulity as Priss arrived at her side and attempted to grab the whip. Toto – or possibly Sinbad – took advantage of Priss's loosened hold, and lunged towards the horse's head. It reared and bucked and the rider fell off.

'Oh Christ,' said Valentine.

'I am not going to apologize,' said Priss. 'She was *hitting* a *dog*.'

'You are being extremely rude to Countess Munthorpe and you must go to your room at once,' said Irene.

'Good. I'd much rather go to my room than stay in the presence of a *dog hitter*.'

'It was a hound, not a dog,' corrected Countess Munthorpe, speaking as if to a deaf relative in the next room. 'And it would've choked its silly self to death on a bunny if I hadn't tried to stop it.'

'I don't believe it would have done any such thing. And there is no need to *shout*,' said Priss, stalking off.

'I'm afraid she spent much of the last five years in the United States of America,' said Irene, as the door closed. 'Consequently, her manners are appalling.'

'Little Spitfire,' announced the Countess, without apparent rancour. She had been carried to the Morning Room by three of the other riders and was now lying on a chaise-longue, one ankle swathed in a wet towel and resting on a folded oilcloth. 'Does she hunt?'

'No.'

'Pity. Frankly, I'm disgusted with myself for taking such a silly tumble.' She lunged forward and lifted the towel. 'Just a sprain, I should think. Such a crashing bore, though – I'm only at Peggy's for the month and I was hoping for a good few runs; the hunting here's so much better than at home. East Hampshire, you know. I imagine you've met my daughter Peggy? Mrs Grocott at Wendover Grange.'

'Yes, of course.' Irene had at one time wondered if the Honourable Peggy Munthorpe – a good-looking if rather fleshy girl, who'd often come to stay with her cousins near Aylesbury – might do for Felix. Reportedly, Peggy had been devastated when he'd married Barbara and she'd quickly become engaged to another of their set, a hearty buck-toothed businessman who spent half his time in Hong Kong. Irene seemed to recall that Felix had remained friends with the Grocotts. 'Was your daughter riding today?'

'No, she's about to pop – her sixth, would you believe? Shells them like peas. Hoping for a girl this time, she says. Now, you mentioned that we've met before?'

'Yes, in the spring of 1930. At the Fazackerly wedding in Temple Weedenshaw.'

'Temple Weedenshaw . . .' The Countess tapped her lip, thoughtfully, with a large, chapped finger. 'Was Munthorpe there too?'

'Yes, the Earl spoke to my late husband for some min-utes.' It had been shortly before Arthur's declining health had precluded any more journeys from home.

'Let me see if I can remember . . .' The Countess half closed her eyes, like a medium trying to summon a nebulous spirit. An insultingly large number of seconds ticked by.

'No,' she announced at last, 'no recollection whatsoever, but then I never did have a very good memory for anything except horses. And of course, none of us are getting any younger – I expect we've both changed a great deal.'

As Hersey entered the room, Irene briefly checked her own appearance in the mantel mirror and was reassured. The Countess might have eschewed stays, hand-cream, manners and a hat over the intervening years, but she herself had maintained her standards.

'Excuse me, Lady Munthorpe, but I've found the arnica,' said Hersey, 'and I've spoken on the telephone to Mrs Grocott's housekeeper and she says that they'll send the car immediately.'

'Splendid work,' said the Countess, whisking the towel away again. 'Could you?'

'Of course, my Lady.' Hersey drew up a footstool and started to apply the pink cream.

'How are you managing for staff?' asked the Countess, over her shoulder.

'It has not been easy,' said Irene, rather stiffly; she had always considered it bad form to talk about the servants *in front of* the servants. The Countess rattled on.

'We only have six living in these days, and Munthorpe says the place looks like a pigsty. Mind, he spent most of the war at the Admiralty, so he didn't see it when it really *was* a pigsty – we had twenty-four Gloucester Old Spots in the tennis courts. Not to mention a hundred and fifty girls on the first floor. Munthorpe was very clever, you see – he knew with the size of the place we were bound to be requisitioned, so early on he suggested to Peggy's old school they come to us and instead of hordes of infantry we had hordes of young ladies. Of course, the gardens are still in a frightful state, and we've been trying for *months* to find a second under-gardener . . .'

By the time that Hersey had brought them a tray of tea, Irene had heard far more than she wanted to about the exigencies of the Munthorpe estate. The stables there might need a new roof, but at least they were in no danger of being converted into public lavatories.

Munthorpe Water might have been emptied of fish by delinquent evacuees, but it would be escaping the fate of the lake at Dimperley, currently slowly re-filling in anticipation of the arrival of a flotilla of municipal rowing boats, purchased 'for a song' (Valentine's phrase) from Watford Council.

'. . . and land prices being what they are, he says we may only have to sell the one farm,' continued Countess Munthorpe. 'Which would be an awful shame, obviously, but – oh, the Spitfire's back!'

Priss had silently re-entered and was standing beside the case of squirrels with a large book in her hand.

'I thought I had asked you to go to your room,' said Irene.

'I know, Grannie, but this is terribly important.' She turned to address the Countess. 'I've looked it up in *Edgell's Complete Encyclopaedia of Canine Health* and there is no mention at all of choking on rabbits as a cause of death. Which means there was *no* reason whatsoever for you to hit your dog, and I'm glad you fell off your horse. That is all.'

She left the room again and the Countess stared after her, open-mouthed, before unexpectedly emitting a bark of laughter. 'Good Lord.'

'Again, my apologies,' said Irene.

'No, she's rather splendid – touch of the tiger cub. Who does she take after?'

'Who ...' Irene found herself looking at the door through which Priss had just exited. She had never before dwelt on the pedigree of this peculiar child; she was certainly nothing like her mother.

The door opened yet again. 'Some young gentlemen have come to collect Lady Munthorpe,' said Hersey, looking oddly perturbed.

'Yes, we've come to carry you off, Grandma,' announced a tall, sandy-haired boy, entering first, the others clumping rapidly after him, the room suddenly vital with loud voices and school-boy exclamations, the largest of the five tripping over the base of a lamp-stand, the smallest veering off to stare at the stuffed squirrels – 'Crikey, one of them's dressed as *Napoleon*!' – before the Countess was plucked from the couch and borne away amidst thanks and laughter. The room seemed to contract.

Hersey turned away to collect the tea things. She knocked over a cup and then dropped a spoon, and as she stooped to pick up the latter, her gaze met Irene's. They had both seen it, both heard it. The Grocott boys were a mismatched set: some brown-haired, some fair, some beefy, some spindly, at least two of them had the splayed teeth of their father, but only one had a smile that had caught Irene like a hook to the throat. And when his brother had fallen over the lamp, this boy had laughed, and she'd known that laugh; that laugh had left not the smallest speck of doubt. Felix had indeed remained a friend of Peggy Grocott.

The door to the girls' room was at the end of the yellow corridor, and it opened as Irene approached.

'The dogs always know when someone's outside,' said Priss. 'Have you come to ask me to apologize? I've just remembered that Mummy told me to behave extra well while they're away and now I haven't, so I can definitely say I'm sorry about *that*. Does that count?'

It had been Ceddy's room, once. He had had a clockwork railway, with a track that ran all the way round the perimeter and under the bed and out on the other side. Irene stood by the fireplace, and Sinbad sniffed delicately at her shoes; she was not altogether sure why she had come here.

'Where is Kitty?'

'At her singing lesson. Mummy's said she can only sing with the band if she auditions for the Royal College of Music, so now she's stopped practising the rude songs and everything's "Oh, the merry, merry blossom in the *spreeeeeeeeeengtime*". I'm teaching Toto to howl whenever she hits top C. Did I tell you that we got a postcard from Mummy? It's just behind you.'

The card on the mantelpiece showed an unseasonal floral clock and a bandstand in brilliant sunshine, with the caption 'Greetings from Broadstairs'. She turned it over and glanced at the final lines: . . . *jolly glad I brought my fur coat! Back on Wednesday, can't wait to see you both, lots of love from Mummy and Benny.*

Irene hadn't attended the wedding; her headache had been genuine and severe.

'I've come to tell you,' she said, replacing the postcard, 'that Countess Munthorpe was not angry with you. In fact, she said that she admired your pluck.'

'Did she? Well, I don't admire *hers*.'

'She asked me who you take after.'

Priss waited, moving her jaw uncertainly, which had the effect of making her look even plainer than usual. 'What did you say to her?' she asked, eventually.

Irene hesitated a second or two longer. 'You know that your father was an exceptionally brave man,' she said.

'Yes, because he – *oh*.' Priss went pink. 'You mean that I'm brave like him?' She gave one of her small, tight smiles and performed a sudden, celebratory bounce. 'Wait till I tell Kitty, *won't* she be jealous?'

'Do you like Mr Haxall?' asked Irene, the question emerging before she even knew that she was asking it.

'Yes. I mean, I don't *not* like him. He's building two kennels that are smaller versions of the new house, with the dogs' names in poker-work over the doors,' said Priss. 'He says they'll be ready for when we move in.'

'And when will that be?'

'The beginning of April. But can I come back and stay here sometimes?'

'Yes.'

'Good. And do I have to go and say sorry to that awful lady?'

'No.'

'Hoorah!' This time they both smiled; small, tight, identical smiles.

20

DIMPERLEY MANOR GRAND PUBLIC OPENING
Saturday, 6th APRIL, 10.30 a.m. to 4 p.m.
'Architectural harmony . . . pleasing to the eye. Extensive
grounds' (from Prosser's Companion to Buckinghamshire).
11 a.m. Speech of welcome by Mr A. Vere-Thissett
2 p.m. Concert in the Rose Garden by Aylesbury
Madrigal Society
(weather permitting)
2.30 p.m. Canine obedience display
3 p.m. Valedictory address by Mr A. Vere-Thissett
Entrance fee to house and grounds: 6s adults, 1s for children aged
13 and under, babes-in-arms admitted free of charge.
Dimperley – A History (introductory guidebook by Mr
A. Vere-Thissett) 6d
Refreshments available for purchase.

'I've put a padlock on the door to the kitchen garden,' said Mr Epple, as he helped Zena with the trestle table, 'to stop any trippers getting in there, and there's a padlock on the tool shed and one on the stable, and Miss Priscilla drew me up a nice sign for the greenhouses that says "Strictly No Entry to Visitors".'

'Right,' said Zena. 'Down here, please, under the arch.'

'But just in case, I've put a line of rakes on the floor so anyone that goes in will get a nasty old shock, won't they?' He shifted his pipe, apparently in order to emit a single, sharp 'Heh!'

'Do you think it's going to stay dry?' asked Zena, making a mental note to remove the rakes, *First-day Visitor to Dimperley Manor Dies of Tetanus* being a headline that she was keen to avoid.

'I'd bet an orchard on it,' said Epple. 'Beautiful spring day.'

'Now, what's this?' asked Alaric.

'It's from my mother.' The young reporter from the *Bucks Herald* had arrived at the Orangery pleasingly early and, looking slightly embarrassed, had handed over a small package.

'From your *mother*? But I don't . . .' Perplexed, Alaric unfolded the brown paper. Inside was a pale blue knitted object, and a note, signed 'Mrs D. Wills', thanking him in the most effusive terms for saving her son's life. *'If it hadn't been for your calmness and initiative, Mr Vere-Thissett, I might have lost my only boy.'*

'My goodness.' The object was a muffler, embroidered with his initials. 'Well, how very kind. Really, most kind. All I did, after all, was to . . .' He read the note again. *Calmness and initiative.* A phrase that he'd typed out himself a few times, back in his army days. Always about others. Carefully, he placed it in the drawer of the desk.

'Do you know where Zena is, Uncle Alaric?' asked

Kitty, opening the library door, dressed, he thought, rather unsuitably for the time of day. 'Oh, hello, who are you?'

'Nicholas,' said the reporter, swallowing. 'I mean Nick. Nick Wills. Nick. Mr Nicholas Wills.'

'That's a lot of names.'

'Kitty, I last saw Mrs Baxter in the Chamberlain's Parlour, instructing the day ladies.'

'Is that the room with the walrus in it?'

'No, no, no. The Chamberlain's Parlour is at the end of the King's corridor and has the Vere-Thissett coat of arms on the escutcheon above the door.'

Kitty looked blank. 'What colour are the curtains?'

'I believe they're red and yellow.'

She disappeared again.

'Now,' said Alaric, 'I expect you'd like to transcribe my speech of welcome.'

'Ah,' said the boy, unpeeling his gaze from the closing door. 'Yes.'

Valentine turned at the sound of brisk footsteps and saw Zena crossing the stable-yard. 'Oh, there you are,' he said. 'I was looking for you.'

She flicked a glance at the binoculars he'd been gazing through just a couple of seconds before.

'There was a hen harrier above the Wyvern Tower,' he admitted. 'But I honestly was looking for you. Is there anything you'd like me to do?'

'Yes, please, could you go to the greenhouses and remove any rakes you see on the floor?'

He hesitated. 'That sounds very much like "Go to the ironmonger's and ask for a tin of elbow grease".'

'No, truly. It's Mr Epple's attempt at a booby trap. But after that, I think we're ready. I've just checked that all the signs and arrows are up and your map of the grounds is on the easel and Mrs Parnaby is very happy to sit in a corner of the Duke of Rutland's room and warn people not to touch any of the glass cases. And the tea-urn is full, there are seventy-eight rock cakes, nineteen loaves for slicing, we have three pounds in the ticket float and your oldest niece is looking . . .'

'Like Hedy Lamarr. Yes, I saw her.'

'Well, I was going to say "for a music stand", but yes, she does a bit.'

'Did she find one?'

'No, but she seems to have found a young man who's willing to hold the score for her. So. There we go. We're all ready for the visitors.'

She could hear the willed, habitual confidence in her own voice; she didn't add – hardly dared think – the words '*if* they come'.

'Synchronize watches,' said Valentine, checking his own. 'Fifteen minutes to zero hour.'

'Is that the—' Zena pointed over his shoulder. 'What did you call it? Harrier?'

'Hen harrier,' he said, turning to see the pale shape sliding down the air above the hillside. 'Yes, that's it. A male. Would you like a go with the binocs?'

She took them hesitantly. 'I've never tried these before.' Raising them to her eyes, she could see only brilliant blurs. She lowered them again.

'Point them at something static first, and then turn the little wheel to get the focus right,' he said.

She aimed at the Wyvern Tower. 'Where's the wheel?'

'Here.' His hand was over hers. 'Now try.'

She could see nothing but a scoop of brightness, her heart scuttling in her chest. 'I think it's easier just to watch it,' she said, handing them back. 'Thank you.'

'Actually,' he said, 'I wanted to thank *you*. You know that all this would never have happened without you. You know that I wouldn't have had the foggiest notion where to start.'

'I've enjoyed it,' she said, and it was true.

'Even so.'

He was looking at her with such earnestness that she couldn't bear it, couldn't bear the nearness of this face that she could no longer judge by the usual parameters of plain and handsome, and she walked across to the ticket table and pretended to look in the accounts book for which she'd paid Mrs Procter sixpence this morning, after handing Allison over to her for the day, and which was, so far, completely blank.

'Um . . .' Valentine had followed her. 'My, er – Miss Maberly – Yvonne – is coming later and she says she'd very much like to help out. What would you suggest?'

The parp of a horn intervened before Zena had to answer, and a yellow-and-green motor-coach edged into view, herding a couple of startled sheep ahead of it along the newly gravelled back drive. The sun emerged from behind a cloud, and Zena felt all her bottled nervousness suddenly evaporate. Valentine clapped his hands together, gloved and ungloved. 'And here they come,' he said. 'The invasion begins. All volunteers for rake removal take one step forward . . .'

Lady Irene had chosen to sit with Ceddy in the Yellow Parlour, a room on the upper storey of the Dower Wing, its single window giving a partial view of the clock tower; there was no chance, therefore, of either occupant being disturbed by the sight of trippers roaming the grounds. Even when Irene opened the casement and leaned out slightly, she could see no more than a strip of rooftop and the wedge of woodland that separated the Chinese Pavilion from the Pavilion of the Four Winds. No unwanted visitors were currently visible, though she could hear an indistinct and ugly noise, as if a flock of geese were squabbling on the moat.

She rang the bell again and returned to her task of copying the entries in her old address book into the one that she had received as a Christmas gift from Valentine. Ceddy was making faint popping noises as he pushed his own present – a tin racing-car – along a cardboard track.

'Sorry, my Lady,' said Hersey, re-entering. 'I meant to be back sooner but one or two things . . . arose.' She set down a tray of tea, started to say something else and then checked herself and glanced at Lady Irene, who was studiously carrying on with her transcription. 'We shall proceed as if it were a completely normal day' had been her instructions, this morning. Hersey handed a glass of milk to Ceddy, picked up her mending and sat down. For a minute or two, all was quiet industry.

'While you were out of the room,' said Lady Irene,

'there was a noise, rather like a gunshot, which seemed to proceed from the front of the house. And then a scream.'

'It was Mr Haxall's motorbike backfiring. It startled one of the visitors – Mrs Saxton. The verger's mother from St Aelfric's.'

'Mrs Saxton. Is she a large person?'

'Yes, and she always wears a green hat to church, with a little bunch of artificial lily-of-the-valley pinned to the band.'

'Ah, yes.'

Hersey poured the tea and picked up Ceddy's empty glass. 'Good boy.'

Irene turned a page. 'So, are many of the visitors from the village?'

'Quite a few. I overheard Mrs Stack – from the haberdashery – hoping that she might catch a glimpse of the family.'

'I see.'

'And her sister-in-law was with her, and she said that she hoped so too, and that the house was much prettier than Benchley Court, that she'd been to before the war. She said that Benchley was very disappointing. Do you remember, my Lady, we stayed there in 1929? There was a house party. The Radlett-Arnolds.'

'The butler wore a coloured tie.'

'*Yes!* And they rang an electric bell for dinner. It was terribly loud.'

'Arthur remarked that one would think that a fire engine were driving through the entrance hall.' She took a sip of tea. 'You said that something arose to delay you?'

'Oh, only that I had a quick word with Lady Ba— Mrs Haxall, I mean.' The quick word had involved finding a seat and a glass of water for Barbara, who was looking slightly fuller in the face than usual and had been feeling rather faint and nauseous due to the length of Mr Alaric's opening speech, and Hersey thought it best not to mention any of these things. 'And I needed to find a hair-ribbon for Miss Priscilla. One that matches the dogs' collars. She's very excited about the display. She's worked ever so hard for it.'

'And what time does that take place?'

'At two thirty.'

Lady Vere-Thissett took a moment to examine the nib of her pen.

'Perhaps one could spare a few minutes,' she said.

Hersey had to pretend she'd dropped a needle, in order to hide her smile.

Zena had spent much of the morning eavesdropping, and compiling a list of mental notes for future use: the area where coaches and motor-cars were parked was already muddy, and would ideally need to be gravelled; no-one had complained about the ticket prices and, in fact, several people had used the phrase 'Is that all?' when informed of the charge for children, which made her think she should put it up by at least sixpence; those visitors who had bought Alaric's 'guidebook' had immediately leafed through it in a vain search for illustrations or a map; almost everyone crossing the drawbridge had peered into the moat, hoping for goldfish and seeing, instead, green scum; almost everyone had remarked that the clock on the clock tower was not working; the arrows clearly marking the route inside the house didn't stop visitors from trying the handle of every single door along the way; the stuffed walrus needed a 'DO NOT TOUCH' sign; the family portraits were lingered over to a surprising extent, by people intent on following a 'family resemblance' through the centuries (the jutting ears of the eighteenth-century Vere-Thissetts being much remarked upon); Alaric's habit of looming up behind people and delivering gobbets of history was a useful way of hurrying visitors onward in the more congested areas; the rock cakes were no more than adequate; the Wyvern Tower was so popular that it might be worth charging people to climb it; the Shell Grotto was also popular, but Mr Epple had reported that he'd already caught a child attempting to prise a scallop off the wall; of the day ladies, Mrs Parnaby couldn't be trusted on tickets as she was unable to distinguish a florin from a half-crown, while Mrs Skates's tendency to stare very hard at people in a way that looked slightly deranged was a useful deterrent to any unwanted behaviour in the Duke of Rutland's room, where most of the taxidermy was displayed.

What was most noticeable was the enthusiasm; when Dimperley had been a maternity home there had always been plenty of comments about the house, but the undertone had been one of dissatisfaction, a yearning to be somewhere warm, somewhere modern, somewhere *else*. Now the visitors were here by choice, and the chatter was cheerfully opinionated. *Nice fireplace, but you wouldn't want to sit in here with that big old thing staring at you, would you, Mum?*

Your Auntie Bel used to have to dust that when she was a tweeny here; she said she was always afraid it would bite her. This corridor could do with a carpet. Look at the face on the one with the ruff; I thought portraits were supposed to be flattering. Like the milkman? Yes, he does a bit. No, don't touch that, Roy.

Which aspects of the visit would they remember most, she wondered? What would they tell their friends about? And all the while, the sun continued to shine and children hared across the grounds, and people complained that the tea was weak but they still drank gallons of it.

It was after half past one before Zena took a cup herself. She stood to drink it, casting an eye across the Great Hall, a room unused and dust-sheeted for a decade and now once again the site of carousing, a line of trestle tables and benches down the centre, rock cakes sold out, the marmalade finished so that bread-and-jam was now superseded by bread-and-Bovril, Mrs Parnaby's great-nieces proving an asset behind the counter. The bare floorboards boomed as a child ran across the room and a little dust sifted down from the roof beams.

'I'll have to get a ladder up at some point,' said Valentine, back from filling the tea-urn. 'Probably hasn't been cleaned since the 1500s. I might find a priest or two hiding there. Oh yes, hello!' he said, shaking hands with someone whose name he couldn't remember. 'I'm very glad that you're enjoying it. Did you, um . . .' He turned to Zena again. '. . . did you manage to find a job for Yvonne?'

'Yes, she's on the ticket table. I was just about to go back and see how she's getting on.'

'I'll come with you, shall I?'

He was looking, she thought, remarkably chipper.

'Does it bother you?' she asked, as they walked back against the tide of visitors. 'Seeing all these strangers wandering through your house?'

'I think I like a bit of bustle,' he said. 'And it was meant to be full of people, wasn't it? It wasn't built to be a . . . a . . .'

Mausoleum, she thought.

'Mausoleum,' said Valentine, startling her.

Outside it was as warm as May and a thin stream of 'fa-la-la's was meandering from the direction of the rose garden. Visitors were still arriving, and there was a small queue under the stable arch. Yvonne was frowning into the cash-box.

'Would you like me to take a turn?' asked Zena.

'No, no,' said Yvonne. 'It's terrifically fun, I've never done anything like this before. So . . . three adults and two children. Three adults, so that's three sixes . . .'

'It's a pound,' muttered one of the children.

'Twelve plus six, and then . . .'

'It's a pound,' said the child, louder this time.

'He's very good at arithmetic,' said the mother, apologetically.

'Oh, I forgot,' said Yvonne, breaking off mid-calculation. 'A lady was looking for you, Mrs Baxter. I wasn't sure where to send her, so I suggested that she ask in the house. Did she find you?'

'No. Did she give a name?'

'I'm afraid not. Shall I see if . . . oh, she's over there.'

Yvonne pointed towards the statue of Zeus and the Cow, twenty yards away. Beside it stood a woman in a royal-blue coat and a white hairband. She was clearly watching them, because she started to walk towards Zena as soon as Yvonne lowered her hand; Zena stepped away from the table and waited for her.

'Mrs Baxter?' She was young, with an oval face and olive skin, her dark hair parted in the middle.

'Yes, how can I help you?'

The woman kept her hands clasped very tightly in front of her.

'Mrs *Zena* Baxter?' Her accent was foreign, her voice quiet but clear, her expression rigid.

'Yes.'

'I would like my rings.'

'What?'

'My wedding ring and my engagement ring. May I have them, please?'

The world juddered, blurred and returned to a focus of dreadful clarity.

'Not here,' Zena managed to say. 'Please come with me.' People were already beginning to watch; there was a stillness around the ticket table. Zena took a step or two from the stable arch, her arm extended in invitation, but the woman stayed put; she seemed held in place by a terrible tension, like a clockwork engine, slowly and deliberately wound and now waiting to race along the track.

'I want my rings,' she said. 'You are wearing them.'

She's not going to stop, thought Zena, and felt a tiny sting of respect for the guts it had taken to come here, alone.

'Not here, please, let's discuss this in pri—'

The woman's voice sliced across her own. 'My name is Mary Baxter. *Mrs* Mary Baxter. I was legally married in Valletta Town Hall and in the Collegiate Church of St Benedict in Cospicua to Mr Christopher Baxter. And *you* were *not*.'

'*Ooh!*' said someone behind Zena, as if it were a pantomime.

'The rings you are wearing belonged to my husband's mother and if you had given them back when he asked you to, I wouldn't have needed to come all the way here. My rings, please. Since you are not married, you do not need them.' Someone gasped. Mary held out her left hand, empty palm uppermost.

Zena could sense, rather than see, the riveted attention of the audience, could hear the sizzle of whispers. *Well, who'd have thought it, her with a child as well . . .* And oh! The irony – that just minutes ago she'd been wondering what it was that visitors would remember about Dimperley, and what they would tell their friends; she might as well have hired a sky-writer to inscribe the only bit of news that anyone would ever, ever want to talk about. She could do nothing, now, except end it quickly.

The rings came off more easily than she might have expected and she dropped them into the waiting hand.

'Thank you,' said Mary, crisply, turning to leave, and Zena looked round and saw that Yvonne Maberly had risen to her feet, her face all astonishment; next to her stood Valentine, his mouth open; next to him was Alaric and next to *him* was Mrs Fay from Wendover Haberdashery, who was nudging her friend, Mrs Laidlaw, who was the chairwoman of Addenham WI. And just beside the latter were Priscilla and Lady Vere-Thissett.

Everyone was staring. Even the dogs.

No direction, except one, offered anything other than further humiliation.

Before she took it, Zena glanced up at the lovely, jumbled rooftops of Dimperley – at the stopped clock, the barley-sugar chimneys, the enchanted view that had caught and held her there – and then she walked away.

21

It was raining when Valentine arrived in Northampton. From the station exit, he could see three pubs, and he chose The Eagle purely on the basis of its sign, which had been painted with a creditable stab at ornithological accuracy. The public bar was almost empty, and when he enquired of the landlady if she knew a Dusty Miller, she shook her head and asked for his order. He bought a bottle of pale ale, not to appear churlish, and drank it quickly before burping his way to The Engineer.

'Miller?' said the chap at the bar, a man in his thirties with a starburst of a scar on one cheek. 'You mean Bob Miller?'

Valentine had forgotten, or had never known, that the name 'Dusty' had been acquired in the army. 'Big chin. Moustache. He can drive just about anything.'

'That's Bob Miller, yes.'

'You wouldn't know where he lives, would you?'

'I don't, as it happens.' The barman gave his attention to the glass he was polishing. 'What do you want with him?'

'I'm an old friend. Army.'

'Oh yes?'

'Yes.'

'Got this in Arnhem,' said the barman, jerking a thumb at his own cheek. 'Corporal in the South Staffs.'

'Corporal in the Gloucesters,' said Valentine, tapping himself on the chest.

'Go on, with your accent?'

'Honestly.' He took off his glove and lifted his right hand to show the blunted fingertips. 'I got this in Knutsford.'

'Take a pint?'

'No, it's on me. What'll you have?' asked Valentine, digging into his own pocket.

'Nah. Buckshee.' The landlord raised his voice. 'Anyone here seen Bob Miller? This bloke's looking for Bob Miller. He sounds like a pongo but he's the full screw.'

Some time later, after Valentine had stood a round or three, or possibly four, an incomer named (apparently) Fatty Friday said he'd seen Miller in The Admiral Rodney and, armed with a set of directions that he immediately forgot, Valentine wandered through the twilit streets, all of which seemed to lead uphill. It started raining again as he crossed the Market Square and he ducked into The Freemason's Arms and immediately saw Miller. He was too drunk to experience any surprise.

'Toff! What the hell are you doing here?' Miller's right arm had been round the waist of a woman in a spotted dress, but now it was slapping Valentine's shoulders and in what felt like seconds he found himself in the corner of a snug with yet another pint of mild in front of him.

'Drink up,' said Miller.

'I won't. I've had a skinful trying to find you.'

'Pity to waste it,' said Miller, moving it next to his own glass. 'What's the emergency, then? Dome fallen off? Found a grenade in the Hermit's Hollow?'

'No, it's, er . . .' What was it he'd travelled forty miles to talk about? He tried to think his way back to the topic, but it was like pawing through a cupboard full of wet coats. 'We need . . . er . . . there was a coach that got stuck in the mud last week.'

'I'll be back with a digger, end of May, get a bit more gravel down. Got a tight little job on till then. I told you that, didn't I?'

'Yes.'

Miller peered at him. 'You all right? How's it going with the visitors?'

'Busy. Yes, very busy.'

'That's good, isn't it?'

'Yes. Something happened on the first day, actually.'

'Did it? What?'

Perhaps he did want that drink, after all. He took a long pull at the glass. This wasn't what he'd come to talk about, obviously, but now he was here . . .

'Mrs Baxter. Zena Baxter.'

'What about her?'

'She went away. She left with her child.'

'Why?'

'Because, er, a woman came to the house. Who was Mrs Baxter. As well. Except that Zena isn't. Wasn't. Wasn't really. Apparently.'

'I'm not following you.'

283

It took a minute or two to make the story fully comprehensible.

Miller lit a fag while he thought about it.

'As a matter of interest, who's been running the show since she went?'

'My uncle.'

Miller coughed a mouthful of smoke.

'And my sister-in-law, and Miss Hersey and various ladies taking it in turns from the village. And me, I suppose. We're not managing terribly well, to be honest – I hadn't realized quite how much there was to organize.'

'You've lost your Sergeant-Major.'

Valentine pictured Zena in the stable-yard as she'd stood waiting for the first visitors.

'Field Marshal,' he corrected. 'I ... um ...' He had another drink.

'You're not missing her, are you, Toff?' asked Miller, raising an eyebrow. 'Even though you've got that lovely girl of your own?'

'Oh,' said Valentine. 'I haven't told you that bit yet.'

In the fizz of sensation and babble that had followed Zena's exit, Yvonne had not said a word – in fact, she had turned deadly pale, and had sat down at the ticket table, staring at nothing, her eyes huge; eventually someone had telephoned her parents, who had sent the chauffeur to pick her up from Dimperley. And then, the next day, the chauffeur had returned with a letter from her to Valentine, breaking their engagement. The rounded, school-girl hand-writing had been quite easy for him to read.

284

'She'd been waiting for a sign of some kind, you see, to prove that she has a vocation. Waiting and waiting. And then, suddenly, there it was.'

'What was?'

'A woman called Mary appearing directly in front of her. Dressed in blue and white. Demanding a wedding ring. And saying she'd been married in a church called St Benedict's.'

'How's that last bit signify?'

'Because Yvonne wants to enter a Benedictine convent.'

'Ah. Righty-ho.'

'And then on the way home in the motor, she said, she saw a raven, which is the saint's symbol. And it was carrying a cross in its beak. Well, crossed twigs.' Probably a carrion crow with nesting material, now that he thought about it. 'And then she knew.'

Miller nodded, judiciously. 'Well, I can see how the evidence stacked up.'

'But *Yvonne* believes it,' said Valentine. 'She really does believe it. She believes it so much that *I* almost believe it.' Her letter had been suffused with happiness, the apology lightly tacked on. He hadn't felt hurt; he hadn't felt anything, really. Well, that wasn't true. He'd felt as if someone had kicked a door open to reveal a view that he'd never seen or even thought of before, but you couldn't say that, of course.

'So you're not engaged no more?'

'No.'

'How did that go down with the family?'

'I believe they're quite upset, especially her father.'

'I mean yours.'

'Er . . . unsurprised.' He'd let them down again. His mother's expression had been seven-eighths tightly controlled disappointment with just a soupçon of exasperation.

'So what are you going to do now?'

The bell rang for last orders; Valentine reached for his drink and found he'd finished it. He felt strangely sober, poised in the eye of the drunken storm. 'My round,' he said. He came back from the bar with two pints and two whiskies.

'Whisky? Where did that come from?'

'He said he had a bottle in the back.'

'Heard your accent and smelled your wallet.'

'God knows, there's not much in it.'

'Doesn't make no difference, Toff. If you talk the right way, then it's just people lining up to lob you stuff. Want a whisky? Want a loan? Want a job, old chap? Way of the world. Cheers!' Miller tipped the spirits neatly down his throat and set the glass back on the table. 'You know she's nuts about you?'

There was no doubt who he was talking about; the fixity of his gaze made that clear. Valentine felt suddenly drunk again.

'What? No.'

'She is, yeah.'

'She didn't tell you that, did she?'

'*No*. I know women, that's all.'

Valentine turned the thought around in his head. Zena was *nuts* about him? But if you were nuts about someone, would you confine most of your conversations with that

person – the person that you were supposedly nuts about –
to questions of sandwich logistics and the necessity for
lavatory signage? He drank some of the whisky.

At the next table, a discussion about petrol coupons was
becoming acrimonious.

'What should I do, then?'

'Do you know where she is?'

'No.'

'Well, that'd be step one.'

'Right. Find her. And . . .'

'Find her and tell her you can't manage the place without
her. Tell her she's needed – women like it when you say that.'

'Tell her she's needed,' said Valentine, as if dictating
notes to a secretary. 'And then what?'

'Yeah, that's the question,' said Miller, folding his
arms. He was looking serious, now, rather than roguish. 'I
know she's a smasher, but she's not one of your lot, is she?
Not exactly out the top drawer. Not even out the middle
drawer. No money. Kid but no husband.'

Neither spoke for a minute, and then there was a shout
from the next table and a chair smacked on to the floor; the
discussion had sprouted fists.

'Come on,' said Miller, hastily, steering Valentine out of
the snug and through the bar-room. Outside it was still
drizzling, the lamplight picking out the wet gilding of the
shield on the pub sign: a chevron, three little towers, a
selection of badly drawn heraldic beasts standing on their
hind-legs.

'If you want to come back to my mum's, you can have
the sofa.'

'I think there's a train,' said Valentine, tilting his wrist-watch and squinting at the wavering hands. 'I'm supposed to be at the Bishop Wyfield sports-day tomorrow, handing out the Vere-Thissett challenge trophy for the best all-rounder.'

For some reason, Miller laughed.

'I'll see you in a couple of weeks, then,' he said. 'Mind, that might be my last visit for a while.'

'Why?'

'Decided it's time to scratch the itch. Thought of Australia, but it's too hot – might try Canada; I've heard there's plenty of work and the women are desperate for handsome blokes like me because it's full of Scotsmen. Mind how you go,' he added, as Valentine narrowly avoided a post-box.

'How long will you be away for?'

'I dunno exactly.'

'Right.'

Dimperley without Miller. Dimperley without *Zena*. The house seemed to have expanded since she'd left, the corridors lengthening like telescopes as he trudged from one fresh difficulty to the next. He had lost her angle of view, the one from which she laughed at the absurdities of the place, and yet also regarded it with delight. It had become, once again, a house whose inhabitants might choose to go to separate wings in order to avoid a conversation, a house that was an accumulation of problems rather than a place to live, a millstone rather than a manor.

The sense of desolation stayed with him as he waited for the train and as he climbed into an empty compartment that smelled of farts and fish paste. He opened the window and let the mild, damp air blow through.

Not exactly out the top drawer. No money. Kid but no husband.

These might have been Miller's comments, but they would also, undoubtedly, be the essence of his mother's thoughts on the matter.

No money. As if that were beyond the pale, and yet if there were a single defining characteristic of Vere-Thissetts through the ages, it was that they had had no money – the difference between his family and Zena being that *they* kept being given piles of the stuff before letting it slip through their fingers: Felix was the most recent example, but there was also the Vere-Thissett who'd lost every horse in his stable over a single game of cards, or the one who'd stolen his steward's wife and had had to bribe a priest, or the one who'd sold half of Buckinghamshire to invest in a non-existent island where peaches grew to the size of armchairs; generation after generation of waste and misjudgement, bad behaviour and incompetence, forming a list that Alaric recited as reverently as a string of Biblical begats, the family's lack of any worthwhile achievement emblazoned on the coat of arms – no rampant beasts for the Vere-Thissetts, only a frog ('harmony and peace'), two squirrels and a bend sinister.

Oh. Valentine, who had been staring at the floor, sat up suddenly. A bend sinister: the diagonal stripe, 'sometimes held', as his uncle was wont to say (although not in the presence of ladies), 'as a symbol of *bastardy*'. So his own family tree had already accepted an unlicensed offshoot or two – in fact, it probably looked like the distorted, decrepit apple tree at the far end of the kitchen garden, its largest limbs held up with props, the whole spared a fate as firewood only because two or three of the grafted branches still bore edible fruit.

Valentine had sketched that tree many times in the past. His fingers twitched now, guiding an imaginary pencil.

22

Miss T. M. Hersey, costume diary, 1946

TUESDAY, 7th May
   Lady Vere-Thissett attending War Memorial ceremony in Wendover.
   Dry, but a chilly east wind.
   Grey cashmere dress, navy belt, charcoal felt with navy band, charcoal ribbed-wool 'Besswell' coat,* jet stud earrings, charcoal brogues.
   * Small split in lining fabric under right arm.

SATURDAY, 11th May
   Lady Vere-Thissett attending launching ceremony for the Dimperley boating lake.
   Weather mild, no rain.
   Eau-de-Nil crêpe dress, navy belt, navy lacquered straw with eau-de-Nil band,* pale grey duster. Moonstone clip. Glass drop earrings. Grey 'Gem' buckled shoes.
   Mr Cedric, Lovat sports jacket, navy tie, panama.
   *Band is beginning to fray, possibly replace with pale blue figured silk ribbon for summer.

WEDNESDAY, 15th May
  Lady Vere-Thissett photographed by Country Life
magazine for feature on houses opened for public viewing.
  Very warm day.
  *Lavender linen two-piece, white straw with lavender
band, moonstone clip, moonstone earrings, Grey 'Gem'
buckled shoes.*

FRIDAY, 17th May
  Sir Valentine Vere-Thissett visiting Watford.
  Weather mild.
  Cinnamon twill two-button jacket. Burgundy basket-
weave 'Alton' tie (Sir Arthur's).*
  *Breast pocket lining perished.

From her desk at the back of the typing pool at Allbright &
Nickson, conveniently situated just beside the exit, Zena
could see the clock on the wall above the duty manager's
office. During the three minutes before the lunch bell rang,
she finished off the letter she was typing (. . . *and we acknow-
ledge receipt of the following samples: AA 380, AA 384, AA 386 and
AA 390* . . .), placed the copies in the tray, slid the fragile car-
bons back into their folder, removed her cardigan from the
back of her chair and was ready to leave smoothly and un-
noticeably at the very second that the clapper hit the bell.

Seven minutes later, she was walking through the gate of
19 Vegal Crescent and taking the passage that led to the
back garden.

As usual, Allison was on the swing; as usual, her landlady,

Mrs Drew, whom Zena was paying to look after her daughter, was nowhere in sight. The two youngest Drew
grand-children were hitting each other with tin spades,
while the oldest was crouched on the cement path, staring
open-mouthed at something gelatinous.

'Mummy!' shouted Allison. 'Watch!' She waited until
the swing had almost stopped moving and then 'jumped'
the three inches to the ground.

'Very good,' said Zena, holding out a hand.

'I'm taking Allison for lunch,' she called through the open
kitchen door as they passed. A distant reply indicated that
Mrs Drew was somewhere in the house, probably reading
Tit-Bits and counting her money.

'What's in my sandwich?' asked Allison.

'Cheese and lettuce and salad cream. And there's an
orange and some sultanas for afterwards.'

'Cora found a slug and she stamped on it and Martin
stamped on it and then Roy stamped on it but I didn't.'

'What have you been doing this morning?'

'Swinging.'

'Anything else?'

'No, only swinging.'

'Did Mrs Drew give you anything to eat or drink?'

'A pink biscuit. There's dead doggie man. Hello!'

Zena stopped walking. Valentine was crossing the road
towards them. She shifted the moment around in her head,
trying to find an explanation.

'Hello!' shouted Allison again.

'Hello.' He stopped a few feet away, his expression

diffident; he was looking unusually smart. And all those weeks of pushing him from her thoughts had made not the slightest difference; she felt as if she'd swallowed a sparkler.

'You squashed me,' said Allison.

'I didn't mean to.'

'He's already said sorry to you,' said Zena, automatically. 'He gave you those crayons.'

'I had a pink biscuit,' said Allison.

There was an awkward pause.

'So, are you visiting Watford for . . .' She could think of no feasible end to that sentence.

'I came to talk to you. If that's all right.'

'I only have—' She checked her wristwatch. 'Forty-seven minutes until I need to be back at my desk. I was taking Allison to the park.'

'I had a *pink* biscuit.'

'Could I accompany you?'

'Yes, of course, if you like.'

'I had a *pink biscuit.*'

'That sounds delicious,' said Valentine.

'You must have got my address from Thelma. Miss Hersey.'

He hesitated.

'I don't mind,' she said. 'But I only sent it to her so she could forward my suitcase. I didn't expect to see . . . anyone.'

'Actually, I have something for Allison. From Miss Hersey.' He took a small object wrapped in tissue paper from his pocket.

Allison ripped off the wrapping. 'Smokey!'

It was a little grey cloth pony with a harness made from gold cord. Allison kissed it.

'That's a lovely present,' said Zena.

'My friend Cora stamped on a slug.'

'Where are you working?' asked Valentine.

'In the typing pool at a die-casting manufacturer.'

'I don't think I know what die-casting is.'

'It's a process that forces molten non-ferrous alloys into moulds at high pressure.'

'Oh. Is the job . . . interesting?'

'No, I had to take the first one I could get. But later on I'll find something better. It'll be easier when Allison starts school.'

They had reached the park gates, where her daughter usually ran ahead, but the novelty of having a guest outweighed the attractions of the shabby little playground, empty except for a large boy on one of the swings.

'Cora stamped on a slug and then Roy stamped on it. I didn't.'

'Would you like your sandwich?' asked Zena, taking it out of her handbag. She exchanged it for the horse. 'Don't take the lettuce out.'

'All right, Mummy.'

Allison started eating, glancing between the adults with a certain puzzlement. A loud, regular squeak came from the swings. For at least a minute, there was no other noise.

'We're . . . um, we're averaging two hundred and seventy visitors a day,' said Valentine. 'More on Saturdays than on Thursdays, obviously.'

'I've got new shoes.'

'So you're only opening twice a week?'

'At the moment, yes.'

'But you'll barely break even on that.'

'I know it's not ideal, but after Mrs Parnaby left—'

'Why did she leave?'

'Something about making sandwiches, I think.'

'You put her in the *kitchen*?'

'And then the coach company wanted to charge more and—'

'I've got new shoes. *Look!*' Allison stuck out a foot. The grass beside it was littered with small pieces of lettuce.

'They're very smart.'

'Would you like to go on the slide?' asked Zena.

'No, I wouldn't.'

'Please come back to Dimperley,' said Valentine.

Startled, Zena pushed Smokey into her bag, and took Allison's hand. 'Let's go on the roundabout, then. That's your favourite, isn't it?' Her voice sounded unconvincingly bright, like a jolly auntie from a wireless programme; Allison looked at her suspiciously.

'Come on!' said Zena, leading her towards the playground. She lifted her daughter on to one of the small metal seats fastened to the base.

'Mummy, you get on too.'

'No, I'll push you. Hold on tight.' She gave it a light shove.

'We can't manage without you,' said Valentine.

'How can I come back?'

'What do you mean? Why not?'

She took a moment to compose herself, to keep her voice level. 'I wasn't expecting to stay when I first came to Dimperley. I didn't plan to . . . to deceive anybody, I just needed to make myself – respectable. For the short time I was there. He was going to marry me, he gave me his mother's rings, and then he married someone else. And now everybody knows – you must have seen their faces, you must have heard all the whispers. *Everyone* knows that I'd been – lying, pretending the whole time. You can't imagine how it feels.'

'But you mustn't' – Zena gave the roundabout another push as he groped for a phrase – 'you mustn't think that that means you have to leave. You've nothing to be ashamed of.'

She straightened abruptly, then, and turned a face to him that Perseus might have seen on his shield.

'Of course I've nothing to be ashamed of. Why would I be *ashamed*?'

'I didn't mean—'

'I'm not a Victorian painting, I'm not Oliver Twist's mother. I'm not ashamed, I'm *humiliated*. I looked like a total fool, an idiot, a clown. I think about that scene and I can't . . .' Her voice cracked. She couldn't explain what it was like – to have lived a life in which all she'd ever brought to each new place was her own self: no name, no family, no money, only the wish that others might take her at her own estimation. She gestured towards Allison. 'And even if I could face it for myself, what about my daughter? I can't have people muttering behind their hands, hinting that I should be' – she gave Valentine a look – 'that word again. Ashamed.'

'I didn't mean it like that.'

'Well, other people *will* mean it like that, and I'm not, and I never was, how could I be? She's the absolute . . .' She couldn't be crying, she could not be crying, she would not allow it. She gave the rail of the roundabout a harder push than she meant to; Allison's startled face whipped past.

'So no, I'm not coming back,' she said. 'Even if Dimperley can't manage without me.'

'Want to get off!'

'*I* can't manage without you,' said Valentine.

The roundabout continued to turn.

'Wanna get *off* now!' Zena reached out a distracted hand and dragged it to a halt. 'Want to go in the sand-pit, please,' said Allison, staggering slightly as she ran to the grassy trough of pale grey dust, from which she was usually banned for reasons of hygiene.

'I can't manage without you,' said Valentine again. Zena stared at him. Her features, so taut with certainty just moments before, seemed to lose all definition. For the first time, Valentine wondered if Miller's astounding assertion might actually be true.

'I think you're marvellous,' he said. 'I think that you're the most . . .'

'No. Don't.' She sounded almost panicked. 'Don't tell me that. That doesn't help me, that doesn't lead anywhere, that's not fair. That's not *fair*.'

'What do you mean?'

'Do you want it to look as if I'm coming back to Dimperley as . . . as . . . someone who's now . . .'

'What?'

'Available. On the lookout. Back on the market.'

'No!' He was horrified. 'Of course not, no, gosh. I'm sorry, I'm sorry, I never meant you to think that.'

'Then – what?'

'I—'

Neither of them seemed able to speak for the moment and then, with a jerky, startled movement, Zena looked at her watch.

'I have to go back to work, I'll be late. Allison, we have to go!' She ran over to the sand-pit and scooped up her daughter.

'But I'm making a *rabbit-hole*.'

For a moment, Valentine watched them hurry across the balding grass, Allison gazing sternly at him over her mother's shoulder, and then he broke into a run and caught up.

'I have something else for you.' He took a folded envelope out of his breast pocket.

'I don't need anything, thank you.'

'No, it's not . . .' He dropped back a pace, and held out the envelope to Allison. She gripped it with a filthy hand.

'I'm not engaged any more,' he said, to the back of Zena's head. 'I never really was.'

She seemed to check her pace slightly, and then she gathered herself and hastened onward.

She opened the envelope that evening, when Allison was asleep, and unfolded the sheet of stiff, creamy paper it contained. It was a picture – a pencil drawing – of the view of Dimperley from the path that led to the pets' graveyard. The house was barely sketched, an airy dream in the background, less detailed than the bird hanging in the sky above it, but on the path that led down the hillside were two instantly recognizable figures: herself and Allison, hand-in-hand, feet blurred by the long summer grasses but faces raised towards the artist.

She was looking at it the next morning, when Allison woke.

'Why are you smiling?'

Zena showed her.

'It's me!'

She had never received anything comparable: she kept returning to it, each time with a shock of pleasure at the hours that must have been spent on the drawing, its gentle precision, the fact that she had been thought about so intensely in her absence. She wrote a short note of thanks, and then eyed the compressed italics of her hand-writing and typed the note instead, in capitals, and signed it with her real name, the name she was using now: 'Yours sincerely, Zena (Harris).'

It was almost twenty to five on Friday afternoon, a week later, when the request came from Mr Bifield's assistant for eight additional copies of a letter regarding the new maximum national weight limits for zinc castings; it meant that instead of being one of the first out of the door, Zena was caught in a bottleneck in the hall.

'Doing anything this weekend?' asked Janey Flett, using the question merely as a springboard to launch into an account of her own crammed schedule: '. . . and in the evening Maurice is taking me to *The Count of Monte Cristo* at the Astoria. I thought it was another war-film because they're all Monty this, Monty that, aren't they, but he says it's mainly sword fights.'

'Come *on*,' urged someone near the doors.

'And on Sunday we're going out in his Rover as far as High Wycombe . . .'

Zena could hear laughter from outside.

'. . . he let me choose the new upholstery. It's called "Lilac Cloudburst".'

The block unplugged itself and Zena passed through the double doors into the service yard of Allbright & Nickson. Most people were heading off home, but just inside the gates a small and noisy cluster had formed, staring with interest at a peculiar figure.

'Who's *that*?' asked Janey.

Zena stopped dead, and as she stopped, the figure noticed her, drew himself up, and began to walk across the yard in her direction, his pace slow and somehow formal.

He was dressed in a savagely creased knee-length tunic the colour of duck-weed, his rolled-up trousers visible just below the hem, the shoulders of the tunic too tight, the sleeves the size and shape of filled sandbags, the torso adorned with rows of what looked like scorched crumpets. There were more crumpets on the hat, as well as some loops of gold braid, one of which hung down as far as the bridge of his nose. He was carrying a small log.

The Woodsman to the King halted just in front of her, his face crimson, his expression solemn.

Zena had her hands over her mouth. A faint squeak issued from between her fingers. She tried again. 'Hazel-nuts. Aren't you supposed to have a bushel of . . .' She couldn't manage the rest of the sentence.

'It's the wrong time of year,' said Valentine. He took a deep breath. 'I've come here because—'

'Do you *know* this man?' whispered Janey Flett, incredulously.

'Yes. Yes, I do.'

'He's not dangerous, is he? Do you want me to fetch Maurice?'

'No. Thank you.'

'All right, then. If you're sure.' With a doubtful look, Janey edged away.

'He's got his dates mixed up,' said one of the idlers. 'Come back on November the fifth, mate.'

'I'm here,' said Valentine, determinedly, shifting the log into a slightly more comfortable position, 'because I want to ask you something.' He took another deep breath. 'Zena Harris—'

'Can we go somewhere else before you ask it?' said Zena, in a rush, just as he began to bend a knee. Her throat was aching; suppressed laughter, suppressed tears. 'I mean – thank you. I can't believe that you've done this for . . . But I've had quite enough of public declarations.'

'Honestly?' He hauled himself up, looking vastly relieved. 'Where shall we go?'

'Do you . . . do you have your usual clothes with you?'

'They're in the left luggage at the station.'

'You walked from Watford Station looking like that?'

302

'Yes. Well, I didn't put on the hat until I got to the entrance here.' He paused. 'Obviously I didn't want to look a complete buffoon.'

She gave a great, unladylike honk of a laugh and then she took his arm, and they walked between the phalanx of starers and out of the gates.

23

For the entire month of August, Dimperley Manor will be
open to the public on five days a week, from
Tuesday to Saturday,
10 a.m. to 5 p.m.
Coloured postcards now available at the ticket desk (3d)
Illustrated guidebook with map (9d)
Refreshments available for purchase, including bottled
pop, iced cakes and a variety of dainty sandwiches.
For a marvellous view of the entire estate, why not
climb the 87 steps of the Wyvern Tower? (3d)

What had appeared, from a distance, to be a poppy blooming bravely beside the entrance to the Shell Grotto turned out to be the crumpled wrapper of a 'Kit Kat' chocolate bar. Irene averted her eyes and continued along the path, Ceddy trailing a little behind her. What one could not change, one must needs endure.

Her initial instinct – that of withdrawing herself on the days on which the public burst through the gates and roamed Dimperley unchecked – had been replaced by a determination to carry on as if the trespassers were invisible; to behave, indeed, as if the cataclysmic events of the last few months had never occurred. Her morning walk, though differing slightly from the previous route, still began at 9 a.m., so that by the time the first visitors had begun to seep across the grounds, she and Ceddy were usually passing the Obelisk for the first time.

The photograph in *Country Life*, showing her in three-quarter profile standing beside that very monument, had (to her surprise) turned out rather well. Countess Munthorpe had seen it and had sent a laudatory note, while several county people had even taken the trouble to telephone.

It had also, as became apparent from the comments of a number of paying visitors whom Irene had happened to overhear, been reprinted in the local newspaper.

'I'm sure she's wearing the same hat as in the picture,' one of them had whispered.

Irene had passed this remark on to Hersey, who had immediately responded by steaming a trio of pleats into the hat brim and changing the pale ribbon to one of chequered silk. She had already cut out the *Country Life* photograph and article, and pasted it on to a new page of her scrap-book.

'No, don't pick that up,' said Irene, as her son stooped for the chocolate wrapper, but he continued to convey it to his pocket, where it joined a twist of silver foil that he'd found by the Chinese Pavilion and no doubt a few other scraps of rubbish that he'd spotted along the way. This new habit was a direct consequence of the public opening; the large galvanized water tank placed by Valentine in the stable-yard for the deposition of visitors' refuse (the ugly phrase used was 'litter bin') had become an object of great fascination to Ceddy. It seemed possible that he thought he was feeding it.

'Ah, Irene!'

Alaric was descending the path towards them, speaking as he came, the words tumbling over one another, so that by the time he arrived at her side she had only received a general impression of florid enthusiasm and a repetition of the word 'serpentine'. 'Imagine that!' he added, brandishing a dark splinter of wood, curved in shape and pierced by a metal eyelet.

'Yes indeed,' said Irene.

'And Lady Vere-Thissett's sure she once saw a mention of it in a steward's inventory. Possibly for 1892. What a memory she has!' He continued past Irene, still talking, and she allowed herself a tiny moment of self-congratulation for not having flinched at the gratuitous use of her new daughter-in-law's title; she herself preferred to employ the phrase 'my son's wife', when a reference was unavoidably required.

As they continued up the path and past the Hermit's Hollow, Ceddy overtook her, taking the final stretch to the lake at a lope. She heard him deliver his new phrase at some volume, and he repeated it as she approached the water.

'It's a boat!'

Eight boats, in fact, hauled up on the lake shore, each painted navy blue with a white number. Beyond them, thigh-deep in the water and holding a leaf rake, stood Valentine.

'Hello, Mother, hello, Ceddy.'

'Whatever are you doing?'

'A visitor dropped a wristwatch somewhere around here. I'm not holding out much hope.' He raked the bottom and lifted the tines to inspect them.

'And what on earth are you wearing?'

'They're my desert shorts. Zena says that if I inflated them I could attach a motor and give rides. Did you see Alaric? I dredged up part of something that might have been a Georgian cutlery container and he was very excited. Oh now, what's this?'

He bent to untangle something from the rake.

'It's a boat,' said Ceddy.

In the distance, under the arch of Jupiter, Irene could see her son's wife, and the child, and she chose not to notice them, turning instead to retrace her steps down the path.

'Come along, Ceddy.'

'Lady Irene! Do you have a moment?'

She had to wait then, for the two of them to catch up.

'I can spell "bun",' announced the child. 'Berr. Unnn. Can *you* spell "bun"?'

'A little idea has come up,' said Zena. 'I've been asked several times by visitors if Dimperley has a ghost.'

'There is no ghost at Dimperley.'

'Yes, that's exactly what I said to them, but people love the idea of a ghost. And when someone asked that last Saturday, when your younger grand-daughter was here, she overheard and she immediately suggested to me that we should open the Dower Wing tunnel to the public, and I thought that was such a good idea. She even came up with the thought that instead of an electric light we should hang up a candle lantern and she'd draw a notice that read "Not for the Faint-hearted". Isn't that brilliant?'

Lady Irene hesitated; ghastly though the whole notion was, she was unwilling to condemn Priscilla's brainchild.

'It's possibly worth trying,' she said. 'Come along, Ceddy.'

'She can't spell "bun",' said Allison, watching her go.

'I expect she can.' The conversation had actually gone rather well, by current standards. Zena had made the decision to pretend that Lady Irene was the elderly owner of Dawson's, who had visited the company three or four times a year, and who had been left, on each occasion, with the impression that everything he'd been shown was his own idea. She thought with nostalgia of the vast relief they'd always felt as he drove off through the gates . . .

There was a shout from the lake. 'Found it!' Valentine was holding a dripping object above his head.

'Does it still work? What time does it say?'

'Time to get a new one!' He began to wade towards the bank.

Zena checked her own watch. Twenty minutes until the first motor-coach arrived. 'Let's go,' she said to Allison, and waved at Valentine.

He'd reached knee-depth and, hitching up one sodden leg of the shorts, he coquettishly flashed his thigh in her direction, and then pointed to his heart.

'Why are you laughing?' asked Allison.

'Because he's being silly.'

'It used to look like a "V",' Valentine had said, when Zena had seen the full scar for the first time. 'Before the bomb, I mean. Miller used to say that I should look out for a girl called Verna.'

Zena had raised herself on one elbow; slowly, she traced a finger along the deep groove of the war wound, and the narrower purple line of the newer scratch. She studied the scar, head tilted.

'What?' he asked, seeing her smile.

'You do realize,' she said, 'that from this angle, it looks *exactly* like a "Z"?'

THE END

Acknowledgements

Alone amongst the characters in this book, B. M. Rhydderch-Jones was heavily inspired by a real person: James Lees-Milne, whose fascinating and waspish diaries chronicling his work for the National Trust were invaluable to me when researching *Small Bomb at Dimperley*.

Also invaluable to me were my dear and clever friends Kate Anthony, Gaby Chiappe, Georgia Garrett and Bill Scott-Kerr, who – as always – gave me much help, guidance and advice, and patiently supported me through the usual self-indulgent traumas of writing.

I also want to thank my husband, James, for listening patiently as I read out each day's output, and for understanding that the only editorial comment I ever want from him is a truthful answer to the question 'Did you believe that bit?'

Thanks, too, to my friend Tom Shakespeare, who provided his kitchen table for regular writing dates, and who fed me home-made soup and bread and got me hooked on jam-and-toast-flavoured Yorkshire Tea.

Finally, I want to express my massive and enduring gratitude to the ever-inspiring, ever-enthusiastic Larry Finlay, whose desire to go off and do lots of cool things in retirement I accept only grudgingly.